Also By Roy F. Wood

RESTLESS REDNECKS

Seth

Roy F. Wood

Knights
Press

Stamford, Connecticut

Designed by Graphic Arts Associates

Published by Knights Press, P.O. Box 454, Pound Ridge, NY 10576

Library of Congress Cataloging-in-Publication Data

Wood, Roy F., 1946-1986.
    Seth.

    I. Title.
PS3573.05965S4   1987   813'.54   87-12050
ISBN 0-915175-24-X

Printed in the United States of America

SWEETER FOR ME © 1976 Joan Baez. Used by permission.

RESTLESS REDNECKS © 1985 Roy F. Wood. Published by
    Grey Fox Press. Used by permission.

Cover photograph by Pascal Ferrant. Special thanks to the magazines, *Gai Pied Hebdo* of Paris and *Sortie* of Montreal for their assistance in obtaining permissions.

FOR
T.R.

Roy Wood died of complications from AIDS on April 11, 1986. In the preface to his book of short stories, *Restless Rednecks* (Grey Fox Press 1985), Wood said that when he began writing, a novel was what he had in mind: "Unhappily, I discovered it takes a very long time to complete a full-length book, particularly if one has to hold down a job and is rather lazy in the bargain! And there comes a time when people who call themselves writers, or authors, are no longer content with collecting their manuscripts in a file cabinet—before long they yearn to be published."

Hoping to be published sooner, he devoted his writing time to a series of short stories: "So, reluctantly, I put aside the book I was working on . . . " Happily, for gay readers, Wood was able to return to that full-length book—and finish it.

Seth is that book.

1

Moonlight gleamed boldly through the flimsy curtains and illuminated a pair of male bodies sprawled carelessly upon the large bed. Their flesh, in the bright moonglow, appeared marble-like. Only a slight motion from time to time gave any indication the forms on the bed were alive, and not statues sculptured by some genius from ancient Greece.

For what seemed to him to be the tenth time, Keith tried to disentangle himself from the man beside him. Every time he moved, however, his lover grabbed him, refusing to permit Keith's exit from the bed.

"Let go, Seth! It's late. I've got to get back to my place. Hell, it's nearly morning already."

Seth refused. "No," he mumbled. "I want more of you. You ain't gotta go back over there and you know it. Stop worrying so damned much. Come here!"

Rolling over onto his side, Seth pulled Keith to him, kissing lips long familiar but never fully known. Every time their bodies came together, it seemed to Seth that Keith managed to invent some new wrinkle to satisfy him. One of the countless reasons, he supposed, that their affair had continued unabated in its intensity. Once aroused, they rushed onward to the inevitable conclusion of their pleasure.

Satiated at last, Seth propped pillows behind his back, sat up, and with one arm pulled Keith close against his side.

Both men were physically strong, masculine, attractive. Seth, however, was easily the bulkier of the pair. He had been a powerful man all his life, and in spite of his present weight of two hundred plus pounds, not an ounce of superfluous flesh covered his muscular frame. Keith, thinner, had his hands full whenever they indulged in their frequent wrestling matches—not that he ever dreamed of complaining.

"You get better all the time, Keith," Seth told him. "One day soon I'm gonna stop taking no for an answer and move in with you. Then you won't have to jump out of my bed halfway through the fuckin' night. You reckon the whole damned town don't know what we're up to by now?"

Keith shrugged his shoulders, feeling the warmth of his lover's flesh. The argument was ancient history.

"I'm sure they think they do," Keith acknowledged, "but by living apart, we keep 'em guessing and save ourselves a lot of useless headaches—not to mention all the things *your* precious family would say!"

"Bullshit!"

"Please, let's not start on that tonight. Loving you is so damned good; I don't want to spoil the evening. My boss is going to pick me up at eight this morning. I've got to be waiting. It wouldn't do any harm if I were to possess some degree of alertness." He began lifting Seth's hand from his chest.

"Keith."

"What?"

"I love you."

The words weren't ones Seth used often. Keith was silent. He suspected something significant would follow. Seth always did his talking late at night—like now. Keith, impatient to be on his way, held back his irritation. He reached out a hand and caressed Seth's face, fingering the sturdy, square chin, covered as it was with a stubble of beard. "I love you, too. I always have."

"I know . . . listen . . . " The less educated of the pair, Seth always found it difficult saying anything serious unless he accompanied his words with superficial camaraderie. At the same time, they knew each other so well, words oftentimes were unnecessary. Now, shifting his thoughts carefully, like steps across a minefield, Seth continued, his hand absently stroking Keith's nipple.

" 'Member how we used to talk about what we'd do, if anything happened to one of us? You promised you'd have me cremated, toss my ashes out into the ocean, like in that Joan Baez song? Well, I got 'round to arranging it last week."

Keith tensed. Twisting around he stared at Seth. The moonlight, bright as a pale sun, showed him Seth was somber.

"God, you're morbid tonight. I promised I'd do it *if* your blasted family wasn't in the picture. Can you imagine Jeb letting me do anything like that? Besides, I'd have no legal standing. The way they feel about me, I'd be lucky being allowed to attend the funeral. Not that there's any chance I'll have too. What *is* wrong with you?"

"Nothing!" Seth was defensive. "No doubt I'll live to be a hundred and so will you. Two dirty old men, tryin' to fuck once a month." He grinned briefly. "All the same," Seth went on, "I want to be practical. You've fixed everthing so's I get your place, ain't you? Well, I made a will the other day leavin' everything to you, puttin' you in charge of gettin' me sent off." He laughed contentedly. "You don't do it right, I'll be back hauntin' you." He grew earnest, turned Keith's face towards him and said: "Seriously, I just didn't want you havin' any problems. I love you too much; you've made me too happy. I was readin' in that queer magazine you get, that families are the biggest problem guys like us have when something happens. What with the garage and everything, I didn't want you goin' through such things—just in case our luck don't hold."

"How could we be anything but lucky?" Keith questioned. "Having found you was the greatest miracle of all. Hold me, asshole. Cease your midnight ravings and do what you do best."

For the third time that night, they gave their passion full rein.

Lying together, at peace, Keith wished he could stay beside Seth—forever. He *was* tired of maintaining two addresses. He stirred, swung his legs over the side of the bed and stood up.

"I'm going," he whispered.

Seth rolled to the edge of the bed and grabbed Keith's thigh.

"What if I won't let you?"

"Come on, Seth! It's late."

"Okay, okay! But I wish you'd stay tonight. I really do."

"I'll see you tomorrow, dope. I couldn't live a day without you."

Seth grinned at Keith. "I know." He pulled the familiar face down to his own for a final kiss. "You're all I've got . . . I love you."

"Love you too, Seth. Go to sleep. You've got a busy day tomorrow."

Keith finished dressing and stood for a few breathless moments watching the moonlight illuminate his lover. Gently he reached down and tucked the sheet around Seth. The large man stirred but remained silent.

Keith let himself out of the house. He was going to be tired in the morning. Hell, it was morning! They were going to have to say to hell with orthodoxy and move in together. Half the small southern city knew about them; why not shock the other portion?

Keith, sleepy as he was, couldn't be gloomy. The night had been too beautiful, the evening too perfect. He reflected—as he had every waking moment of his life over the last ten years—how glorious living was with Seth in the world. He loved Seth. There was never a time when he had not loved the man in the house behind him. Seth always had been around when Keith needed him. He was, in order: friend, brother, lover. If there were a God, the generous Deity no doubt long ago ordained that these two men should live as one. Keith could not envision any life without Seth Rawson . . .

2

Keith Wilson's father was a man of little vision and no ambition. One of a large number of children, Leon Wilson left the South for a naval career. He suffered through the second World War, married a Yankee wife, and in 1947 retired from military service and headed south again. The Wilsons, encumbered by this time with a son, purchased a seedy little house several miles out in the country and settled down to vegetate for the rest of their lives. Leon, taking his "retirement" with a seriousness few could master, never hit another lick at anything resembling work. Keith's mother, Florrie Wilson, was a large-boned, frowsy woman. In an unsouthern, unladylike fashion, she smoked cigarettes and from time to time uttered profanities which shocked her neighbors. She was extremely discontented at finding herself stuck in the middle of nowhere and seldom let an opportunity to berate her husband slip past. It was an unhappy household. Both parents, caught up in an endless struggle with one another, ignored Keith. He became visible only when his support was needed by one parent in their indeterminable battle with each other.

Other children failed to follow Keith's birth. He played by himself—content, most of the time, in a world of his own.

Two major events shaped his early childhood: When he was six, the Rawson family moved in the house across the field; when he was eight, Keith got run over by a schoolbus.

Even though Leon was an uneducated man, he *had* lived outside the South for over twenty years: He had "suffered through" experiences which were outside the ken of his new neighbors. And Florrie separated herself from her neighbors by admitting to having attended a University for two years! Mrs. Wilson had even worked for a living before her marriage. This in particular gave Florrie a distinctly foreign attitude in the eyes of the unsophisticated farm wives who would never have dreamed of working away from home in that era. Alma Rawson expressed the neighborhood's view of Florrie Wilson by remarking, "Appears to me she's got the blue mold."

The Rawsons were everything the Wilsons were not. Jeb and Alma Rawson were typical of the Wilson's neighbors. They sharecropped some fifty acres across the road from Keith's home. The Rawsons had no education, both being barely able to write their names and read the morning devotionals—a practice Jeb Rawson followed slavishly. Jeb was what was known as a Holy Roller, a term which many years later was softened to Pentacostal. He was an extremely religious man, stern and unbending; a pale imitation of an Old Testament prophet. When he and his wife arrived across the road, they had three children: Seth was four, the two girls were three and one respectively. Over the years four more daughters joined the crowded household. Alma Rawson became a community joke, always being in "the family way."

The two families had nothing in common. The Wilsons, while poor, had a steady, ever-present income from Leon's retirement. The Rawsons lived recklessly, dependent upon the elements, their garden and the scrawny livestock they possessed.

The accident occurred in the fall of the year—in October. Keith looked upon the timing of the mishap as fortuitous. Had

it taken place in the spring, Seth would have been busy working on the farm.

Keith, eight now, had entered third grade in September
while Seth, six, was just beginning school. They attended a rural center of education which was unsophisticated and under-
staffed. In the afternoons when the yellow buses rolled into the
schoolyard, everyone raced for their particular vehicle in a
frenzy to be first on board. During the confusion of one of these
melees, Keith was shoved beneath the wheels of one of the
large monsters. Everyone attributed his rescue to a "miracle."
He lay in hospital for weeks, then was forced to spend long,
tedious hours recuperating at home. It was during these end-
lessly boring hours that his friendship with Seth flowered.

Before the accident, the pair had played together—whenever Seth had time to play. After the accident, when
Keith was at home and bedridden, Seth took to stopping by
each day for a visit. Florrie Wilson was pleased by the visits;
they gave her a respite from entertaining the whining brat her
son had become. Alma Rawson didn't care to see her small
son trudging across the field to visit his little friend, but Jeb
considered his son's example a shining beacon of inspired
Christianity, so Alma said nothing.

Had the parents been remotely aware of where the relationship would lead, the youthful meetings would have been
brought to an abrupt end. Clairvoyance, fortunately, was not a
trait of either the Wilsons or Rawsons.

The accident solidified the differences between Seth and
Keith. During his long convalescence, Keith sharpened his
reading skills with books Seth picked up for him from the
school's modest library. This dependence upon books marked
Keith's bent towards the intellectual. Seth, because of his
lack of time for schoolwork, could never keep up with Keith's
breadth of mind. Such differences, however, always comple-

mented, never acerbated, their relationship.

When, Keith wondered later, did they first become aware of sex?

He was never sure.

Even before his encounter with the schoolbus, he spent nights with Seth at the Rawson house. Seth, being the only male child in his family was given a room to himself—a fact which grated on the nerves of his many sisters. It was true the chamber was exceptionally small—more like an over-large pantry than an actual room—but it was Seth's and afforded the boys some measure of privacy. Fixed in Keith's mind was one specific evening. The night was cold. He and Seth huddled together, whispering, giggling as is the wont of young children.

Seth put his hand on Keith's crotch, which was covered only by the thin, cheap underwear both wore.

"Let me see your thing," Seth whispered.

"Why?" Keith wanted to know, adding virtuously, "It's not nice."

"Nobody's gonna know," Seth retorted, wise beyond his years. "If you don't let me see it, I'll pinch you!"

Reluctantly, Keith agreed. As the room was dark, neither boy could actually *see* anything. Such practical considerations did not deter Seth's curiosity. He pushed Keith's shorts down and cupped his hands around the small penis and balls which nestled there.

"It's as big as mine." Seth complained, forgetting as he always did, that he was two years younger than Keith.

Finding Seth's hands warm and pleasant, Keith's interest was aroused. "Let me feel yours," he asked.

Seth obliged.

Thus began an exploration which continued, at staggered intervals, over several years. Each time they spent the night together, they eagerly checked to see whose "thing" had grown the most. The first moment they were alone together after the accident, Seth demanded knowing whether Keith's "thing" had been damaged. That it had not was a fact which comforted both.

Sex was not the only basis for their continued friendship. As both aged, repressed conflicts with parents led to sympathetic conferences. Seth worked long, hard hours. His schoolwork, whenever he was allowed to pursue it at all, suffered. Time and again, Keith helped his friend over academic hurdles. Keith was a teacher's pet. He always had his homework ready; he always knew the answer to every lesson or question. His classroom victories, however, were not won without pain or mental anguish. Keith's devotion to reading, the major facet of his success at school, led to conflicts with his father. Leon didn't want a bookworm for a son; he yearned for a fishing and hunting companion. Keith hated both.

"Damn kid, always sitting on his ass with a book under his nose," Leon would mutter angrily. Florrie Wilson, a reader herself, viewed Leon's criticism of Keith as aimed at her. Keith's reading habits became one more piece of rope the pair tugged back and forth over an invisible line of conflict. Their monumental bouts never descended to physical abuse, but the words they screamed back and forth at one another were seared into Keith's soul. He swung like a pendulum between hatred for his father and disgust at his mother, until finally coming to rest with a profound contempt for both. Never, he vowed, would *he* marry and endure such a life.

Other problems marred Keith's existence. Growing older, he sensed differences which separated him from other boys. He suffered no physical aftermath from his accident; he was not overly frail. Yet none of the things which should interest him ever drew his attention. He did not care for hunting and fishing—Leon's passions. The animals kids hunted—rabbits, squirrels and the like—seemed tame to the imaginative Keith. Too many books he read portrayed anthropomorphic creatures. The rough and tumble games other youths engaged in frightened him. He was inept at ball games. Nearing thirteen, he was, at best, viewed as a misfit by his classmates.

Only Seth remained a close friend.

Seth, as he aged, found his hours consumed by work on the farm; but in spite of his slavery to the land, he somehow managed to be available when Keith needed him.

Of course everyone in the community knew of Keith's accident and for years after the near-tragedy, even insensitive youths overlooked traits which they would have found amusing in anyone else. During Keith's final year at the rural grade school, a new family moved into the district. The eldest child of this family—an overlarge boy—was a bully, and Keith quickly became the newcomer's favorite target. Keith put up with the taunts and threats which were hurled at him as best he could. Boys he had considered friends turned against him. Scapegoats were welcome, and Keith was an ideal one.

One recess period, Keith found himself the butt of some obscure joke. His reaction, whatever it was, was greeted derisively by shouts of "Sissy! Sissy!" from the small male furies who mocked him. The bully, enjoying his newfound popularity, seized the moment.

"Why don't 'cha fight me, sissy? 'Fraid, ain't 'cha?"

The bully and his hangers-on, finding Keith indisposed to fight them, grew bolder. One youth squatted behind Keith while the bully edged closer, finally pushing Keith over the kneeling trickster. Even while trying not to cry, Keith sensed his rage was impotent. His fear of physical pain overwhelmed his intellect, forcing him to become a pawn in the hands of fools.

Suddenly, Seth was there.

"What'da you think you're doin', Mathis?" Seth was as large as the bully. To Keith, frightened as he was, his friend's voice sounded bold and awesome.

"Tryin' to see if this sissy's gonna fight," Mathis retorted, adding, "You stay outta this."

"Leave him alone," Seth ordered. "He was in an accident."

"That was years ago!" Mathis brayed scornfully. "He's a sissy! What's it to you? You his *boyfriend?*" Mathis laughed loudly at his own, little understood joke. The others, who knew Seth well, chuckled uneasily. Seth didn't wait for further words. He swung his work-hardened fists at Mathis and the two went at it. A teacher, seeing the crowd, investigated and broke up the battle. Both boys were carted off to the Principal's office for disciplinary action. The Principal—a harried man, whose only interest was in keeping order—whipped both boys, promising more of the same if he caught them fighting again.

Riding home on the schoolbus that evening, Seth told Keith about it. The bus was only half-filled; they had the back to themselves.

Keith was ashamed. Both because he was incapable of defending himself and because Seth had been punished for rescuing him.

"I'm sorry," he mumbled, knowing the inadequacy of his words.

"It's okay," Seth replied. "It didn't hurt—much. Maybe I could show you how to defend yourself. You shouldn't let that stupid Mathis push you 'round like that."

"I . . . don't like fighting," Keith said, feeling his face redden.

"I can't be there all the time," Seth said, a little impatiently. "I could show you a trick or two."

Keith didn't say yes or no. Seth, not knowing what else to do, let the matter drop. Keith dated the beginning of his love for Seth to that episode.

Still, it was too early to speak of love. Keith, with his highly developed intellect, sensed love between himself and Seth was, somehow, wrong. Or would be considered wrong by grownups. So, he called Seth his best friend. Most of the books Keith read centered around youths who were either brothers or close friends. Having no siblings of his own, Keith gave his devotion to Seth.

Seth, having no brothers either, surrounded by what to him were only silly sisters, accepted Keith's unspoken worship as natural. If, from time to time, he felt shame because his friend did not fit in, he never said anything. They were too close. And not long after the fighting incident, they found themselves sharing another secret of great magnitude.

A few weeks after Keith's thirteenth birthday, he experienced his first wet dream. An event he eagerly reported to Seth.

3

They met in a thickly wooded region between the Rawson farm and Keith's home. There, brambles, shrubs and other growth had advanced to create an area, which, when reached, was invisible. They played in the hideaway countless times, even hiding in it a couple of times when Jeb Rawson came looking for Seth. Jeb was an experienced countryman, and he missed them. They felt relatively safe in the copse. The haven had the additional advantage of being close enough to each boy's house so they could hear themselves being summonsed by irate parents.

"Seth?"

"Yeah."

"I had a wet dream last night."

Seth was suitably impressed. "Can you shoot off?" he asked.

"Yes."

"Let me see."

Keith, resting on his knees, undid his pants, letting them fall to his ankles. He began rubbing his penis which responded by hardening at once. Seth, with sudden inspiration, wiggled around in back of Keith.

"Let me cornhole you while you shoot off," he said.

Keith, as usual, hung back. "It'll hurt," he protested.

"I'll be careful," Seth promised, spitting on his hand and

lubricating his cock. With one firm hand he forced Keith forward into a doggy position while slowly pushing his cock into Keith's asshole.

"That hurt?" Seth asked.

"No . . . not too much. Go ahead."

Seth began moving back and forth. As he did so, Keith fingered his own cock. The more he did so, the better he felt. Suddenly he gasped.

"I hurt you?" Seth demanded.

"No. I . . . shot off."

"You coulda waited. I wanted to watch. Did it feel good?"

"Yes. It feels better when you're doing that. I think."

Seth pulled out and looked at the results of Keith's ejaculation. "I thought it would," he replied complacently. His smugness vanished in a wave of youthful impatience. "I wish I could shoot off."

"Maybe it won't be much longer," Keith said, trying to comfort.

"I wonder if I could do it if I had a girl," Seth mused aloud.

"You aren't going to mess around with *girls* are you?" Keith asked, feeling his insides tighten up in an uncomfortable fashion.

"Don't you want to?" Seth countered.

"No! I don't like girls. They're hateful."

"I bet I could shoot off with a girl," Seth jumped back to his original argument. "I gotta get back to the house. I still got chores to do. See you at school tomorrow."

The episode in the copse was repeated from time to time during the summer of Keith's thirteenth year, but never often enough to suit the lonely boy. As spring and summer advanced, Seth was consumed with farmwork. Keith, too, worked away from home in the summer months, helping neighbors harvest tobacco, the area's major cash crop. He was allowed, for the most part, to keep the money he earned, but this advantage was offset by the pain which came his way as a result of being forced into the company of others.

Most youths of Keith's age were already working in the fields, or driving tractors. Keith couldn't drive anything. His family had no car; he had no way of learning the intricacies of autos or tractors. Neither was he put to work in the fields, being employed instead around the tobacco barns—positions usually reserved for women, girls, young children and old men. His sissy image remained intact. Even when Seth worked at the same place, they seldom saw much of each other. Keith was beginning to sense Seth no longer liked him very much. The times they managed to steal some moments together usually ended up in an argument.

Their friendship was further tested in the fall when Keith entered high school. The county's high school was in town. Students from the countryside were bused into the small "urban" center. This arrangement separated Keith and Seth. Given the ages of the two boys, some drift in their relationship seemed inevitable. Two things kept such drift to a minimum.

The first was Keith's nature. He hoped, desperately, that once he reached high school he would find making new friends easier than in the past. He recognized his dependence on Seth, even half-admitting to loving his comrade. Keith's glaring unpopularity with the rest of his classmates was a certainty he could never escape. Throughout the summer of his thirteenth year, he entertained fleeting dreams of entering high school and becoming popular, making the acquaintance of other boys who would admire him—if only for his mind. He soon discovered the new school was no different than his previous one. The same attitudes manifested themselves; he was as lonely as ever. The only time other kids bothered with him was when they needed help with lessons, but he saw through such ruses and refused to cooperate.

Keith's first year in high school confirmed something his mind refused to face—the fact he liked boys better than girls. For most boys, lessons took a distant second place over the primary occupation of chasing the opposite sex. Only misfits like Keith bothered with schoolwork. Between classes, the talk among boys always centered around girls. Keith hated it. He found himself looking longingly at the easy friendships between other males, gradually realizing he desired them—wanted to do the same things with them he and Seth did when they messed around. At lunchtime he always picked a spot where he could watch guys walk past. His eyes invariably turned to crotches and asses. He knew it was "wrong"; and was dimly aware of such things as "queers" and "fairies," but he refused, consciously, to admit these terms might accurately be applied to him.

The second item which preserved Keith and Seth's friendship was Seth's emerging puberty. As soon as he began experiencing orgasms, Seth was as willing as Keith to participate in physical experiments.

Their awakening sexual urges pulled them together; but the condemnation by society of their secret activities tore at the fabric of their relationship, threatening to rend them apart.

Keith was eternally complaining they were sinning by what they were doing.

"Don't you like doing it?" Seth countered.

"Yes . . . but it isn't right!"

"Who says?"

"The Bible. God."

"Bullshit!" exclaimed the young tough. In spite of his father's fanatical devotion to God (or because of it), Seth arrived at the steps of a different shrine. His young life was a continual round of work and sacrifice. He grew determined to take what pleasure he could from life. Forced by a zealous father into attending church services, Seth gained a bitter con-

tempt for the faith of his father. Somehow his mind saw through
the cant and superstition to a vision of life uncomplicated by
religion. In arguing with Keith, he never surrendered this
hard-won victory.

Their sex was good, but always rough. Neither dreamed of
kissing one another. Kissing was something reserved for
mothers and girls. At first, they agreed not to shoot off in each
other's ass. Seth, however, larger and stronger than Keith,
never pulled out in time. The closer he came to climax, the
harder, fiercer, he drove himself into Keith. After it happened
several times, Keith gave up making an issue of the matter. He
wasn't willing to admit he enjoyed it, even to Seth, but both
sensed he did. With experimentation, Keith discovered he
could climax at the same moment Seth came inside him. The
instances when this occurred became the most pleasurable of
their times together. Over a period of months, this grew to be
their accepted method of accommodating each other.

Years later, looking back over his school days, Keith
found it hard to believe the pain he experienced. Seth was the
only sunlight on a canvas of dark grays and blacks. Even his
relationship with Seth, however, led to difficulties.

Keith's mother wasn't fond of Seth; Leon was just as
quick to berate the neighbor's boy. Nor did Leon allow opportunities to pass when he might ridicule his son's lack of enthusiasm for girls, sports, and all the things "real men" were supposed to find interesting.

Once he turned sixteen, Keith could never escape his
father's derisive question, "Don't you have a girlfriend yet?
Aren't you taking anyone to the dance this weekend? When I
was your age . . . "

Stung by such criticism, Keith occasionally barked back
at his father: "What am I supposed to take a girl out in, my
bicycle?"

"You could double-date with other guys if you'd stop be-

ing such a goddamned sissy and make friends with somebody."
Leon wasn't about to counter any shift in responsibility for his
son's failures. "Seth Rawson's not the type of guy you
ought'ta be palling around with," Leon jeered, "he'll never
amount to a hill of beans."

Keith glowered. "You can't have it both ways. You hate
seeing me use my head—now you complain that Seth's not
smart enough!"

"Using your head's all very well," Leon roared. He
didn't like being contradicted. "Seems like you could be a
man at the same time! Hell, I got some sense too, you know!"

Unwilling to say what he thought of his father's mental
capabilities, Keith got up and left the table. In his room, surrounded by books he had managed to accumulate, he felt tears
of rage seep down the lines of his face. God, how he hated
them! In two more years he could leave . . .

But the thought of leaving home scared him. He knew his
parents didn't have money to send him to college and probably
wouldn't have given it to him if they had. Leon kept after him
to join the Navy. "*They'll* make a man out of you!" was the
taunting admonition. Keith didn't know what he was going to
do when he graduated. The notion filled him with undefined
terror. Knowing he would have to leave Seth bothered him even
more. He lay on his bed and pictured Seth's body. Constant
farmwork had made Seth strong and vigorous. His cock was as
big as Keith's in spite of the two-year difference in their ages.
Rolling over on his stomach, Keith wished his friend was on
the bed with him, fucking him like they did in the woods. He
wished, just once, they could do it someplace where they could
take off all their clothes and be comfortable.

He could hear his parents arguing as they finished their
meal. About him, this time. They were always yelling about
something; either money (their lack of it), or him. He got so
tired of it. Their voices poured clearly through the thin walls.

Didn't they know he could hear every word they said? Or did they just not give a damn?

"If you'd gotten a job," Florrie was complaining, "there'd be enough money to send the boy to college. God knows, *he* has plenty of sense."

"Book learning," Leon sneered. "Let him work his way through college if he's so damned smart. You always take up for him—no wonder he's never grown up. Can't make a man out of him, tied to your apron strings all the time!"

"Somebody has to take an interest in him," Florrie hurled back. "You're the boy's father—I never see you doing anything with him."

"What's there to do? Only thing he knows how to do is read a damned book!"

"Reading a book's better than having him run around with that Seth Rawson all the time!"

"At least the Rawson boy ain't a fairy. Be just our luck to raise a queer!"

Florrie lifted an eyebrow in a questioning fashion. "You don't really believe that, do you?"

"I don't know," Leon grunted, disliking having to make an admission of ignorance. "He acts like one, God knows. Maybe he'll grow out of it. I still say the best thing he could do is serve a hitch in the Navy!"

"That's your solution to everything!" Florrie replied scornfully. They went at it again.

Keith couldn't stand it. He got up and left his room. Outdoors, he ambled towards a small branch which flowed close by his home. Even his own parents believed he was queer. He tried convincing himself he didn't give a damn. Especially not if being queer meant he loved Seth. Why did life have to be so complicated? In spite of the fact he was competent at schoolwork, he wasn't much good when it came to practical problems. Everything kept closing in on him. His folks hated him, he had no friends except Seth—and Seth was always busy. The future loomed ominously in front of him, getting closer all the time. No matter where he turned, terror lay in wait. If he could only win a scholarship or something. Such things as scholarships, however, were tied to the politics of the area; he sensed *he'd* never get one. He didn't want to join the Navy. If people in the Navy were like his father, he'd hate it. And Seth wouldn't be there to help him. Life itself seemed devoid of hope; in every direction, Keith faced only emptiness and disillusionment.

Even Seth, usually so constant, was changing since he'd started high school himself. He still got Keith to help him with his lessons, but he didn't often want to do anything else.

Keith's seventeenth year was worse than his sixteenth. Life stretched in front of the young man like hell on earth.

His junior year at school made him eligible for the social event of the season—the Junior-Senior Prom—but Keith had no intention of attending. In the first place the affair was structured for the upper echelons of local society. Those with the money for all the rented suits, gowns and trimmings such an evening demanded. Keith had no such sums. His father showed no inclination to fork over the amount. Leon's avariciousness, however, did not stop him from ridiculing his son's decision not to attend the affair. Every argument Keith dragged forth, the old man knocked down—except for the one concerning the funds needed to finance such an evening.

"If you didn't spend all your money on those damned books, you'd have enough," was Leon's comment. Florrie, for once, remained neutral. She saw no reason why Keith should start chasing girls; neither did she want to provoke an argument over what was, to her, an inconsequential matter.

Keith's home life settled into such disarray he hated to return there. He needed Seth. Seth, however, chose this opportunity to begin dating girls himself.

At fifteen, Seth matched most seniors in size. He would have been a regular on the football team had Jeb been willing to give his son time to practice and play the game. Despite the fact the Rawsons' social status precluded Seth's availability to certain girls, many found him a desirable date. He was handsome in a rugged, manly fashion. He was relatively serious, not given to creating trouble like many immature freshmen. The large bulge in the crotch of his pants excited most of the high school girls in a delicious, forbidden sort of way. Knowing "nice" girls did not submit to such temptations, they nevertheless were consumed by curiosity. Many flirted with him openly.

Keith and Seth were in the hideaway one afternoon when Seth casually mentioned he had a date for the weekend.

Keith was shocked and hurt. He vaguely had anticipated something like this might happen. The event's occurrence, however, found him without defenses. He could barely mumble, "Who with?"

"Dottie May Spivey."

"That bitch!" Keith couldn't stop himself from spitting forth the epithet.

"You'd think any girl I took out was a bitch, wouldn't you?" Seth asked, not angry so much as cynical.

"I don't see what you want to go out with her for," Keith temporized, sensing he ought not have spoken so bluntly.

"Why shouldn't I?" Seth demanded. "Why don't you take out a girl once in a while? I get tired of everybody thinking you're my girl. If I wasn't able to take care of myself, I'd be fightin' half the school 'cause they'd be callin' me a queer."

"I'm *so sorry* knowing me is such a bother! I'll stop *speaking*, if that's what you want!"

"Don't be stupid," Seth snapped. "I like you; why can't we just be friends? I like messin' 'round with you, but we ain't kids anymore. It's time we started screwing around with girls. You don't *want* to be a queer, do you?"

Keith said nothing. All he wanted was to continue having sex with Seth. If that made him queer, he didn't care. He could tell Seth didn't feel the same way. Why, why, why couldn't just one thing turn out right?

"Do you?" Seth repeated his question.

"Why do you always go on about being queer?" Keith demanded suddenly. "You're the one who always said there was nothing wrong with what we were doing. If it's not wrong, then why do you care? I like you—I want to keep on liking you. I'm not interested in any silly old girls!" Contempt burst through his voice.

"Not ever?" Seth asked, eyeing him speculatively.

"No!" Keith shouted the word. "I want somebody like you, not some smelly bitch—"

He stopped abruptly. Seth grabbed him roughly. "If you ever repeat that to anybody else, I'll beat you. I swear I will—"

"Who am I supposed to tell?" Keith yelled angrily. "You're the only friend I got . . . " His voice broke and in spite of his best efforts, tears filled his eyes.

"Stop that," Seth barked, disgusted.

Keith got up and started to leave the hideaway. "I haven't got to stay here and take orders from you! If you're ashamed of me, I won't bother—"

Seth reached up and jerked Keith back to the ground. He slapped Keith's face, hard. The unexpected violence startled Keith. His tears stopped. He stared sullenly at Seth. His friend's words burned into his brain.

"If you ever tell anybody about what we did, I'll beat you so bad, you'll wish you were dead."

"You don't have to worry," Keith said, his voice deathly calm. "I'm not going to tell anyone. I don't want you anymore anyway; not if you're gonna start messing around with girls!"

He got up again, and this time Seth made no move to stop him. As he pushed his way through the bushes, Keith turned back for one last word. "Don't come around *me* if you don't get what you want from *them*! I'm not going to do it with you anymore!"

Liar, liar, liar! The word raced through his mind as he stumbled from the hideaway.

When he was far enough away from the place, Keith sat down and cried and cried. He loved Seth so much; and now Seth didn't even like him. On top of everything else, it was too much. He would have liked to kill himself, but he didn't have the courage for that. He was so afraid of everything—of living and of dying. After an indeterminable time he picked himself up and trudged home. There was nothing else to do.

4

The next few months were the most miserable of Keith's life. He stopped sitting with Seth on the school bus, a fact which did not escape the attention of the ever-present bullies. Keith had no other friends; few youths bothered to speak to him. As it dawned on the troublesome kids that Keith no longer enjoyed Seth's protection, they started picking on him with the intensity of crows after carrion.

Except for the occasions when he saw Seth with Dottie May or another girl, Keith had no notion of what his friend was doing. Seth would speak to him if they passed one another in the hall at school, or any place where not speaking would have been a deliberate snub; otherwise there was no contact between the two former companions.

Endurance comes in many forms. Keith bent, but never broke. Somewhere in the depths of his timid soul he nurtured the vision of loving a man in the way he and Seth had loved. He ached for Seth, longed for Seth, but if Seth were out of reach, another male would do. Someday, somewhere, Keith vowed, things *would* work out right.

With this unrealistic dream sustaining him, Keith made time pass.

It passed at a sluggish, painful snail's pace until one fall night. Keith was lying in bed, reading. The small lamp burned dimly by his side. A scratching sound attracted his attention, drawing him to the window. Turning aside the dull, plastic curtains, he saw a shadowy figure.

Seth!

"Get dressed and come out," Seth whispered.

Keith obeyed the summons. He longed to be strong and refrain from responding, but it was impossible for him to force his heartbeat back to normal level—impossible to keep his lonely, hungry soul from singing at the presence of Seth.

He dressed, snapped off his light and listened intently. The loud snoring from his parents' room promised security. Carefully he eased himself out of the window, leaving it cracked so he could re-enter. It was one o'clock in the morning.

They walked down the dirt road without words. Keith was by Seth's side, the only place he ever wanted to be. He dreaded words, feeling instinctively these moments of bliss could not last. The second they started talking, the mirage would collapse; he'd no doubt wake up in bed and find it all a dream.

They came to where Seth had parked his truck.

"Get in," Seth commanded.

Keith opened the door and climbed into the truck. The first thing which struck him was the smell of Dottie May's (or someone's) perfume. All the old antagonisms returned.

"What do you want?" Keith asked coldly.

Seth reached out and placed a hand on Keith's leg.

"Can't we be friends again? I'm . . . sorry about last time. I reckon I was pretty mean."

"Nothing's changed, has it?"

"I don't know."

In what was to be the first and only time during their lives together, Keith heard uncertainty and doubt in Seth's voice. He was given no time to investigate the unusual phenomenon of Seth's anxiety. Before Keith could absorb the meaning of his friend's words, Seth spoke again.

"I don't want to be queer," Seth muttered, "but . . . .I've tried it with girls. It's a hell of a lot more fun with you. I don't know what to think. Does that make me . . . make us . . . like that?" His fingers tightened on Keith's arm in a viselike grip which hurt, but Keith didn't complain. His spirit fluttered; he found himself resuscitated from an eternal blackness—he lived again!

"I don't know what it makes us," Keith replied. "I've never done it with anyone but you." Being with Seth again, hearing the words they were speaking, destroyed all Keith's self-imposed reservations. He rushed on, words gushed from him like water from a broken damn as, for the first time, he said everything he felt.

"I don't want to do it with anyone but you. Does it have to be something bad . . . just because everybody says it is? I . . . when I'm with you . . . I don't care! I *like* it with you: No! I . . . love you, Seth!" He felt his lover's grip on his arm tighten—almost unbearable pain, endured now, accepted. "Don't be mad, Seth, please. I'll be careful, I promise. Just don't—"

"I ain't mad," Seth interrupted. "I'm scared. I don't think we oughtta love each other—except maybe as brothers." It was as close as he had come in a very long time to saying he loved Keith, but it was close enough. Seth, rationalizing his own behavior, had no trouble persuading Keith to climb into the back of the truck and pick up where they had left off a few months before.

Thus their relationship revived.

Seth did not stop seeing girls, but after their late night conversation he made time for Keith, too. Their reconciliation eased Keith through the rest of high school. When he graduated a year later, it was in large measure due to Seth's renewed interest. At odd moments they talked carelessly about a possible future together. Neither could see how such a thing might be arranged, but both knew it was what they wanted—somehow.

Keith made up his mind to enter the Air Force. There was no money for anything else and he didn't want to linger around either his parents or south Georgia. Seth agreed it was a sensible decision. Keith believed Seth would be happy to have him and their secret out of the way. A belief which remained unspoken. Knowing he must leave soon, Keith vowed he would depart with their friendship intact. Then, no matter what happened to him later, the image of Seth, his love for Seth, would sustain him throughout the coming ordeal. Keith was scheduled to leave in June—a time when Seth was busy with farmwork. Keith's parents, happy at seeing the last of him, became almost congenial. In order to pass time, Keith was often at the Rawson farm helping Seth with his work. One afternoon, a week before Keith was due to take off, the day's work was completed earlier than usual. Seth suggested they go to the river for a swim. Keith readily agreed.

South Georgia, in June, possesses a beauty difficult to surpass. By June, the unrelenting sun has not yet baked vegetation brown and lifeless. Hundred degree days are not yet the rule. The Alapaha River flowed languidly along its path, looking cool and inviting, as Seth guided the old truck down a little-used path to a swimming hole both prayed would be empty. Given the time of day and season of the year, they found themselves in luck. Seth parked the truck and they undressed.

The water was refreshing but they spent little time swimming. These would be the only spare moments Seth would have before Keith left; he knew, instinctively, Keith wanted only his time as a parting gift. They emerged from the water, cooled but tense. Seth grabbed an old quilt which would be used later to sheet tobacco for market, picked up their pants and headed for a secluded spot on the riverbank. Keith followed, wondering if he dared do what he had thought about so often.

They lay down, inches apart. Their hands groped and touched and clasped. Keith hardly dared breathe, he was so completely in love with the man and the moment. If only it would never end . . . if only love—or sex at least—were not such renewable commodities. Gained, only to be lost with the passing of moments. No matter how often he was with Seth, it was never enough. Every climax demanded an encore. Now, months and years stretched forth in an endless succession of Seth-less days. Keith knew he wasn't strong enough to face them.

Keith rolled over and put his arms around Seth. Seth made no move to brush him off, as he was wont to do. Having reconciled himself with Keith, Seth tried in his own way to reach some compromise between his feelings and his revulsion at the label *queer*. When sex was over, Seth let Keith cling to him, hold him, in ways he would not have allowed before.

"I'm going to miss you," Keith mumbled.

"Miss you too," Seth answered. Then, startled, he exclaimed, "What you doin'?"

Keith was leaning on one elbow, moving his hand around Seth's crotch, touching, massaging, stimulating.

"Seth."

"What?"

"I'm scared . . . going away. I wish I didn't have to, but I do. I can't change that. No—let me finish!" Keith anticipated Seth's attempted interruption. "I . . . I want . . . today to be beautiful for us—"

"That's why I brought you here," Seth managed to get in. He was uncomfortable with Keith's intensity. Their "relationship" was bearable only if they didn't talk about it.

"I know." Softly. Then, "But . . . I want to do something . . . different. I really want to do it, but I don't want to make you mad at me . . . not today, not this soon before I got to leave."

Seth had no idea what Keith was talking about. He understood, however, the importance of the situation to Keith and acquiesced. Lifting a hand, he roughly brushed Keith's hair.

"Okay. I promise. Go ahead—do what it is you want."

Keith silently thanked the farmboy—and, for a couple of minutes did nothing. He lay down, placed his head on Seth's chest and listened to the rhythm of his lover's heart. Then, he touched Seth's cock, fingering it until the organ grew, swelled and solidified into a rock-hard projectile. Casually, Keith moved his face towards Seth's crotch. His lips tentatively brushed Seth's thighs.

In a brief second Seth understood what Keith wanted. He jerked himself into a sitting position, knocking Keith aside.

"Keith! Not with your *mouth*, for God's sake!"

"*Please*, Seth! I want to! Don't be angry, just *let me do it!*"

"It's dirty!"

"It isn't! It's part of you—and I want you in every way I can have you!"

Seth sat upright for an eternity—before giving in. He lay back on the quilt.

"Go ahead," he muttered. "I wish you wouldn't . . . but . . . if that's what you want, go ahead."

His cock had softened during the discussion. Keith lay his head on Seth's chest, letting his hand do the initial work. Seth lost his tenseness and responded. Keith touched Seth's balls, gently rolling them in his hand. His lips brushed Seth's stomach as he worked his face down until he could take the tip of Seth's cock between his lips. As the flesh filled his mouth, it seemed larger than ever. He wanted, momentarily, to stop, but the urge passed as he worked himself into a rhythmic pattern. He shifted position, placing himself between Seth's legs, finding instinctively the best arrangement. He used his hands to massage Seth's hard chest. As the action aroused

Seth, his unwillingness eased; he began moving his hips in accompaniment.

Let me be able to do it, Keith prayed—finding himself wanting, periodically, to choke.

But he didn't. The idea of what he was doing filled Keith with joy. It was a joy born more of love than physical pleasure. The joy of giving pleasure to the only person in the world he cared about. All the love of his isolated, lonely youth poured into the act of pleasing Seth.

Seth found the sensation ecstatic because it was different. Unable to contain his moans of joy, he muttered, "I'm going to shoot!"

Keith worked harder.

Seth held back. "Not in your mouth, Keith!" He tugged at the head encircling his cock.

Keith let loose his prize long enough to gasp, "Yes, dammit, let me do it!"

He dropped back down, aware of Seth's strong hands pulling to disengage mouth and cock which once more were inseparable.

Before long, a subtle shift of emphasis entered Seth's hands. As he approached climax, he surrendered himself to the astonishing feeling. Keith felt his lover's hands grasping his head, pushing it down instead of away, meshing together the two of them into one entity. As Seth's sperm filled Keith's mouth for the first time, Keith gulped the fluid, draining every drop, aware it would have to sustain him for all the countless days stretching in front of him.

Seth shuddered in limp happiness and relaxed.

Keith released Seth's cock unwillingly. He became aware of the tears which filled his eyes in protest at the unfamiliar actions of his mouth. Furtively he eased himself back down beside Seth, praying he had not ruined everything.

They lay without words.

Keith shivered when Seth stirred.

He was completely unprepared for Seth's reaction.

Seth, using his greater strength, rolled Keith onto his back and stared into his eyes. Without warning, for the first time in their lives, Seth kissed Keith on the mouth. Keith grasped Seth and pulled his farmboy to him. They kissed again, their tongues moving uneasily but unerringly, along the natural path of lovers.

When they broke apart, Seth leaned on one elbow, and, looking in Keith's eyes, stated without reservations: "I love you." And immediately had to wipe away tears of happiness.

Words were no longer forbidden.

"But I don't want to be queer," Seth explained. "I don't exactly think it's wrong, but what kind of life could we ever have together? The world don't understand people like us. It scares me. All the kids laugh at you 'cause they think you're queer—I guess you are." He grinned momentarily. "I just don't want to live like that."

"Can't we worry about that later?" Keith asked. "I got to spend four years in the Air Force. You got to finish school and figure out what you want to do. I don't want to rush you. I just need you there, Seth. Can I count on you for that? Will you be here when I need you? Will you write me and not forget me? I love you so much."

"I'll try. I'll be here . . . as long as I can."

They talked while twilight gathered.

"It's gettin' late," Seth observed. "You ain't come yet; let's take care of that. What you want to do?"

"Fuck me."

Seth smiled. He raised himself to his knees and looked down at Keith. Gently, he slapped Keith's face, back and forth.

"You like that, don't you?"

"I do when you do it."

Their sex drove them now. All else fled their minds, and when Keith was satisfied, they pulled the day about themselves and wore it like a cloak, aware of its perfection. Neither knew where the future would lead them; both now knew they wanted it to be along the same path.

5

O f all the people Keith might have chosen to drive him to the bus station, Jeb Rawson was far down the list. Seth's father always made Keith uneasy. It wasn't anything specific, only the old man's extreme religiosity. Every other word out of Jeb's mouth was about God, Jesus, and the wickedness of the world. Seth long ago learned to shut out Jeb's droning voice. Keith never could.

The Greyhound terminal closest to Keith's home was in Tilton, some twenty miles away. Jeb was going to Tilton to attend a religious conference and offered Keith a ride.

This sort of arrangement for leaving home for the first time was typical of what Keith expected from life.

Keith's parents had no desire to see their son off on his monumental undertaking. Leon was annoyed because Keith had selected the Air Force over the Navy; Florrie, attesting to her dislike of long good-byes, elected to remain at home.

Now, sitting in the truck beside Jeb Rawson, Keith couldn't believe the time to leave had arrived.

Except for the times he'd spent the night with Seth, Keith had never been away from home. The first stop on his odyssey was Jacksonville, Florida, where he would undergo a medical examination. From there, it was on to San Antonio, Texas and basic training—halfway across the country. The notion seemed unreal, as did the fact he was "grown-up." Where had the years gone? He was ill-prepared for the ordeal ahead of him. That the undertaking would be an ordeal was firmly entrenched in his mind. He did not feel adequate to cope with the new circumstances he would be struggling to adapt to. Weeks before, he had assumed a fatalism about the venture which nothing had erased.

He started as he found they had reached the station.

"Well, Keith," Jeb drawled, "hate to leave you, but I gotta git up to that meetin'. You'll be all right. Pray to God, put your faith in Him, not in men, and you'll git along fine." Jeb ambled back to his truck and drove out of sight.

The bus arrived. Keith boarded it and his trek was underway.

When it no longer mattered, Keith tried to forgive his parents their many faults. The hardest thing for him to overlook was his father's silence about what Keith would find in the military. Nothing—absolutely nothing—Keith had lived through in the tranquil rural surroundings of south Georgia prepared him for his future. That he did, in fact, survive said more about his character than he cared to admit.

The Air Force recruiter had told Keith he would be met at the bus station in Jacksonville, but like so many other things associated with the military, this too turned out to be a lie. At last, confused, Keith phoned the recruiting office in Jacksonville and was told to proceed to a hotel the military used for the Keiths of the world. There, he registered without difficulty and found himself assigned to a room with another youth.

His "roommate" was attractive; in another time and place Keith might have found the guy interesting. After preliminary questions were asked and answered, the talk turned to sex and the youth was off, regaling Keith with descriptions of a multitude of sexual conquests.

"Shit," boasted the talker, whose name was Rick, "I hadda join the fuckin' Air Force just to get enough dough to run 'round with chicks!"

On and on, until it was time for supper. Downstairs, they met other guys who were waiting for the same future. Nobody was remotely the sort of person Keith could like. After eating, the others suggested going out for a beer. Keith had never drunk a beer in his life and didn't feel this was the time to start. He excused himself and went back upstairs to the hotel room. Keith took out the two or three pictures he had of Seth and touched them lovingly. Tears filled his eyes. After awhile, he put the pictures away and went to bed. In sleep, he might at least dream of Seth.

If asleep and dreaming found Keith in a heaven of forgetfulness, the next day brought forth unimaginable nightmares.

Keith had never undressed in front of anyone other than Seth. He was immensely shy about nakedness. When he had been told he would have to undergo a medical examination, the picture which focused in his mind was that of a kindly doctor who, behind closed doors, would conduct a discreet investigation of his eyes, nose, throat and chest. The reality was considerably different.

Reality was men yelling at everyone. Throughout his military experience, Keith discovered yelling replaced speaking. The medical center was no different.

A bus arrived early at the hotel. He, Rick and ten or twelve others boarded it and were shuttled out to the military medical facilities. Once there, even know-it-alls like Rick grew subdued. A man, contemptuous of the crowd he saw before him, herded them into a large room lined with lockers.

"Undress, put your shit in the lockers and turn your keys in at the desk," he ordered. "If you don't remember your number, you'll go back to the hotel in your drawers. How many of you assholes don't have drawers on?"

To Keith's surprise, several hands rose tentatively in the air.

An orderly reached around the corner of a counter, pulled out several pairs of boxer shorts and tossed them to the offending men.

Keith learned several painful lessons that day. The first was that everything in his new environment was determined by lining up; secondly, by waiting in such lines. Thirdly, rudeness was the order of the day. Keith passed from one painful experience to another, certain each event could not be surpassed by an accompanying loss of dignity, only fo find himself proven wrong further along.

Two events stood out starkly in his memory; his ears reddened with shame everytime he recalled the episodes.

The first took place when urine specimens were required. Everyone was handed small jars and ordered into the latrine to fill them. Keith had never been able to piss when other guys were around and this time was no different. He stood at a long trough where numerous men of all shapes and sizes were lined up with their cocks in bottles, pissing. His bottle obstinately remained bone-dry. As the ranks of pissers thinned—leaving those like Keith who were problem-oriented—he finally managed a trickle which barely covered the bottom of the jar. Handing in the meagre results, he was hooted at derisively.

"Jesus!" shouted the intern. "This the best you can do . . . Wilson? This ain't goddamn liquid gold you know! Ain't enough piss here to fill a fuckin' thimble!"

Everyone laughed appreciatively. The only saving grace was that Keith was not sent back to remedy the situation.

As the line moved on, Keith couldn't believe the humiliation of it all. Nor was the worst over.

Towards the end of the afternoon, numbed by the day's

insensitivities, Keith was ushered behind a curtain.

"Drop your drawers, bend over, spread your cheeks and cough," ordered the man who was waiting. His tone was bored.

Keith, unused to the man's accent, weary fron the day's events, found himself unable to decipher the instructions fast enough.

"Goddammit, can't you understand English? Drop - Your - Drawers!" The doctor pulled Keith's underwear down to his knees, grabbed his balls and barked, "Cough!" Keith coughed.

"Now bend over and spread your cheeks."

Wildly, Keith obeyed, having no idea what was going on. As his thoughts tried rallying themselves, he felt something being rammed up his asshole.

"Not very tight," grunted the doctor. "You aren't into dildos, are you?" Keith, not knowing what "dildos" referred to, was thankful no answer seemed required. He yanked his drawers back over his no longer private parts and stumbled from the curtained area to the next line.

His first full day away from home left Keith shattered and destroyed.

On the way back to the hotel, Rick morosely told Keith he was being "held back" because he appeared to have venereal disease.

6

The best part of Keith's stint in the Air Force—other than his discharge four years later—came at the beginning. The flight to Texas. Keith had never been on a plane before and he found the experience exciting. Further, it was something he could mention when writing Seth. He still turned red with embarrassment over the pain and disgrace of the medical examination. He dared not write Seth about that episode. He vowed he would keep his letters cheerful, filled with things Seth would enjoy hearing about. Resolutely Keith tried turning his thoughts to the immediate future. He had to survive the next six weeks and sensed they would not be easy.

The plane landed and Keith boarded a bus which drove everyone out to the base where they trooped off the vehicle and were promptly herded back into a line.

Their wait this time lasted until another couple of buses rolled in and sixty men were assembled. The sixty were turned over to a squad leader. After that, as far as Keith was concerned, reality fled. It was as if, Alice-like, he had stumbled down a rabbit hole into a malevolent universe.

Keith's squad leader (whose name was Bils) walked up and down in front of his sixty men, shouting and cursing, using language whose meaning Keith could only guess at, ridiculing many of his charges and, after roughing up a couple of guys, he finally marched them off in the direction of a barracks which was to be their "home" for the six weeks of basic.

Basic training was a confusion of absurdities. Even after it was over, Keith never managed to straighten out the six weeks enough to assign any significance to them. Happily, each day was so packed with activities there was never much chance to suffer mentally. The pain of being separated from Seth was reduced to a minimum because there was never any time to think about Seth—or anything else. Keith's time was taken up in attempting to survive, adjust, and not get set back—condemned to repeat another week of the horrible routine.

Several observations, however, did stick with him.

He learned that he possessed a great deal of sexual curiosity.

There was never an opportunity to proposition anyone, and—still aflame with love and devotion for Seth—Keith never dreamed of betraying his lover. Yet as opportunities presented themselves, he managed to observe a great deal. Living in an open-bay barracks with fifty-nine other men was a unique experience for Keith. He found himself fascinated by the differences in size, body structure and sensuality. There were men whom he would have liked to know better. But they sensed his difference and, like his classmates in Georgia, ignored him.

Keith survived basic by gritty determination more than anything else. Holding his love for Seth before his mind; an eternal pledge, a religion, a god, he vowed he would not disgrace the man who was his reason for existing. By and large this motivation succeeded, although Keith's relationship with Seth, and his emotional attachment to it, was to lead the young recruit very close to the edge of disaster.

The incident occurred during the fifth week of basic.

Each week at Lackland was given over to a specific area

of training. The fifth week was devoted to a wide variety of outdoor maneuvers—running the obstacle course, night training, and other physical fitness tasks which were well beyond Keith's abilities. The things his body was forced to undergo in basic had his flesh protesting furiously. Consequently, on the field and in other training exercises, Keith was near the bottom of the squadron.

Basic, however, was composed of *two* elements. Besides the physical training, there was a great deal of classroom time. As always in areas of the mind, Keith excelled. There was various types of memory work. Security regulations which had to be memorized. Keith mastered such material within hours of receiving it—a feat which went down well with the squad leader, but not the rest of the guys.

At any rate, by superior performances in the one area, and skimming by in the other, Keith managed to progress without getting set back. The end of the six-week nightmare was in view.

In his letters to Seth, Keith believed he had managed to keep most of his misery hidden. In the first place, he wasn't sure Seth would sympathize with him. Seth had, off and on, suggested Keith should exercise, develop his body. Probably Seth would approve of the whole business. When they parted, Keith and Seth had agreed to write each other once a week. Keith would happily have penned a letter every day but realized such attentiveness would only embarrass the farmboy. Seth wrote every Sunday, his letters being Keith's salvation. Pathetically, Keith listened for his name at mail call; knowing when to expect the joyous envelope. Seth's letters were the only ones Keith ever received. Leon never wrote at all; Florrie sent him two letters the entire time he was in basic. When Seth's letters arrived, Keith's joy was so transparent that others noticed.

Lights out was at nine o'clock. On the night in question,

Keith had been assigned barracks guard duty from six to nine. Barracks guard was one of the more asinine things required of new recruits. Everyone pulled three-hour stints. Getting off at nine, Keith was given time to shower and clean up before getting in trouble for being up after lights out. He'd received Seth's letter that day but had not yet had time to read it through at one sitting. He showered quickly then stepped into the latrine (which contained the only light at night) to read and thrill once more at Seth's laborious words. The letter, as always, stirred Keith, filling him with longing and desire. He was so absorbed by it, he did not hear others enter the latrine.

Suddenly, the letter was jerked from his hands.

"What'ya know? Wilson must have a *girlfriend*! Ain't no accountin' for tastes, is there?" The speaker guffawed. "How 'bout it, Wilson? You're half-hard—must be a chick! You wouldn't be queer would you?"

Keith stared at his tormentors.

There were three of them. All rough men. They epitomized everything Keith disliked in the world. Gross, dull and unlearned, they were scornful of anything they could not comprehend. Their mission in life was harassing anyone they believed vulnerable to brute force and physical threats.

Keith was tired, disgusted . . . and afraid. But, for once, not *too* afraid. It was *Seth's* letter they held. They were too filthy to be allowed to touch anything of Seth's.

"You're supposed to be in bed," he reminded them. "Give me my letter."

"Well now, must be important if you want it that bad. Why don't you beg a little. We're so horny, we'll let you give us a blow job. Come on, faggot, suck us off and you can have your letter back."

Their faces grinned at him malevolently. Keith saw they were half-ready. Fleetingly, he wondered why they scorned

him for being a faggot yet were more than willing to let him
service them. But all he said was, "My letter, please."

The man holding the letter stepped back. The latrine was
small—room to maneuver limited. The others tried penning
Keith in a stall. They expected no difficulties with him. In a
lightning move, Keith swung his leg behind the first man,
pushed him into his friend and sent both sprawling onto the
floor. Having cleared the way, Keith leaped at the bully with
the letter. His attack, so unexpected, was successful. Angered
beyond belief, Keith swung his fists at the smirking face, hitting the guy in the eye. As the man ducked, Keith grabbed and
retrieved his letter.

"It wouldn't do you any good in the first place," he taunt-
ed them. "You have to know how to read!" They regrouped and
were lunging at him when the squad leader stepped in to see
what the commotion was about.

"Bust it up, you bastards! I'm trying to sleep. What's
your problem?"

The trio started explaining all at once.

Bils glowered at all of them. "You three go to my office.
Wilson, wait out here."

Their explanation was lengthy. Keith, tired beyond measure, could not summons fear over their accusations of his sexu-
ality. He wondered if Bils would want to read the letter. He
hoped not. He wasn't in the mood for more conflict. Suddenly,
the memory of his swing rose up to confront him. He had actually defended himself. No, what he had defended was Seth.
Their love—even if he couldn't come right out and say so.

The three finally trooped out of Bils office. They stared
pointedly at Keith but said nothing.

"Wilson!"

Keith reported to the man in the prescribed fashion.

"At ease. Tell me your side of this business."

Keith related the theft of his letter without going into the matter of insults or the trio's propositions. Bils looked at him curiously when he was finished. "That all?" he inquired.

"Yes, Sir!"

"Wilson. I'm tired. You can either press the matter or drop it. Fighting in the barracks is out. If you guys want to tangle, take it to the boxing ring." He stopped, then added, "I'll leave it up to you, since in my opinion they started the ruckus. You're only eight days from getting out of here. My advice would be to concentrate on that. Those three won't initiate anything like this again."

"I have no desire to press the business," Keith stated. "I just want to be left alone and get through with this."

"That's the smart thing to do. But then, you are smart." Bils was silent. Keith waited to be dismissed but the squad leader wasn't finished.

"Wilson, the military ain't the place for people who don't fit in. I get sixty men coming through here every six weeks. I don't have time to get to know any of 'em. All the same, I've learned to spot those who are . . . different. If you're *too* different, you won't make it. You'll always be running into nuts like those three, wanting to prove something to somebody. You follow my meaning?"

"Yes, sir."

"Good. Now, get to bed."

As he saluted and left, Keith wondered if Bils eyes were peering at him more intently than usual. Or was it his imagination. The military was a place of such total contradictions.

During the rest of his time in basic, Keith was left alone. His only disappointment came when assignments arrived. He had been told once basic was over, he'd be allowed a trip home. Another lie. He was assigned (of all things) to Air Police Training—and forced to spend another three months on Lackland. He fumed with each additional day away from Seth, but bore things he couldn't change. He knew the altered schedule was best in the long run. It would be November before he got back to Georgia—Seth wouldn't have so much work to do; they would have some time together. Or at least he hoped they would. There were times when he wondered if Seth would want to see him again. Fears haunted Keith that Seth, having months to think things over, would not willingly pick up where they'd left off. The farmboy might find some *girl*!

The Air Police training was as rough as basic. Keith found himself responding to the demands made upon his body. He never grew to enjoy physical training, but when he began seeing the responses his flesh was making, a certain pride took over. He resolved to make himself into the sort of man Seth would be proud of. Why, he wondered, had he never considered Seth's view of him before? Keith recalled the many times Seth had helped him, defended him. He reddened with shame. He would remedy the situation. If only it were not too late. As the days dwindled and his visit home neared, he grew anxious that Seth would no longer be available to him. Given this state of hesitant anticipation, he was astonished by a letter he received shortly before it was time to leave Texas:

> . . . if you haven't already told your folks when you're due back here, give 'em the wrong date. You said in your last letter you'd arrive on the twenty-fifth. Tell Florrie and Leon it'll be the twenty-sixth—that way I can pick you up and we can spend the night together. I got a surprise for you . . .

Keith wrote back, agreeing to the scheme, growing more and more apprehensive as the day of their reunion neared. Keith didn't want surprises, he wanted Seth . . .

7

As the bus neared Tilton, Keith alternated between excitement and anxiety. Would Seth like him in uniform? Would his new, improved body impress? He worried, vaguely, that Seth might feel threatened. It was only in recent days that Keith had begun trying to understand the sort of relationship he and Seth had with one another. Keith accepted his homosexuality; now his thoughts focused on the nature of their acts together. The roughness he liked; the fact Seth seemed to enjoy inflicting . . . not pain, so much as dominance. Keith feared his new physique might upset Seth, make his lover feel the same roles were no longer desired . . . or permissible. He hoped not. He'd endured too much to have Seth become troublesome in that respect. He wanted only one thing—and that didn't include arguments.

The station loomed ahead. Keith found himself nervous, sweating. Why must love be like this, he wondered? Why do I care *so much?* Yet what other way was there to care? If love was to have meaning, it could only stem from the agony and pain of wanting someone in a way which totally transcended mere indulgence, lackluster emotionalism which had no push behind it.

He saw Seth in the cluster of people waiting at the station. Seth—looking splendid. More masculine than Keith recalled. Taller, bulkier, everything a man should be. Keith grabbed his bag and stepped from the bus.

They stared at each other. Keith longed to rush forward and throw himself into Seth's strong arms. He understood, in that poignant second, what society was doing to him, to those like himself and Seth, forcing them to hide and subjugate their emotions for the sake of values not their own. The restraint grated less now, because Seth was there. Later, the feeling of oppression would return—stronger, vehement, ready to burst through the conventions others established.

"Man, you look different in that uniform!" Seth smiled and Keith felt his friend's hard hand clasping him.

"Like it?" he asked shyly.

Seth dropped his voice. "I like what's in it better. This all the luggage you got?"

"No, there's one more."

They stood awkwardly side by side, waiting for the baggage to be unloaded. Their eyes met; that their words were mundane and common, both knew and didn't care.

"I talked with your folks today," Seth reported. "Told 'em I could pick you up tomorrow. That was okay with them; asked me to dinner tomorrow night."

"You coming?"

"Doubt it," Seth said, grinning. "Couldn't hide what I feel. Your ma ain't dumb. Neither is Leon, for that matter. He just acts it sometimes."

They picked up the duffel bag Keith had checked through in Atlanta.

"Where's the truck?" Keith asked as Seth led him away from the station.

"Over this way," Seth turned down a narrow street and halted in front of an old Chevy sedan.

"What's this?" Keith asked.

"My surprise!" Seth looked almost silly. "It's mine. Ma's brother, Amos, has a garage here in Tilton . . . I've been working for him since September. He gave me this. I've fixed it up some; needs lots more work but I'll get there. Come on, get in." He laughed at Keith's astonishment. "It runs . . . really!"

Inside the safety of the auto, Seth reached his hand across the seat and gripped Keith's leg. "Miss me?" he asked.

"You know I did." Keith's words were slurred, gulped out of love and anticipation.

"I got us a motel room for tonight. Want to go there now?"

"Yes!"

They drove to the motel. Keith suspected Seth was speeding, but the concrete seemed to inch beneath the wheels.

Seth had selected their room well. The motel was secluded, the rooms detached from the office, out of sight of the road. Keith watched his lover fumbling with the key, aware that the moment meant as much to Seth as it did to him. They entered the shabby room. Keith dropped his bag, removed the hateful hat which was part of all uniforms and exited the blue coat. He snatched his tie off, haphazardly, letting it fall to the floor. He turned and moulded himself against Seth's warm flesh. Their lips met, greedy and eager. The weeks and months they had been separated fled in the explosion of their kiss. Keith sensed in the opening act of their ritual a difference in Seth: a maturity, recently gained; an acceptance now of what they were doing, where before there had been hesitation and uncertainty.

Seth pulled his mouth away. Keeping one hand on Keith's neck, he raised the other and gently rubbed the stubble of beard on Keith's face.

"Wouldn't shave for me, would you? I'll have to teach you better'n that."

"Yes, sir. What you got in mind?"

"This." Seth slapped Keith's face. Not hard, not a stinging blow, merely a tap, establishing once more the authority Seth wanted over his lover. Keith, wanting Seth in every possible way, submitted gratefully, patiently; accepting every touch as Seth—unsure where they were going—exerted his claims on Keith in ways which would make the encounter an exploration of their limits.

"You love it, don't you?" Seth muttered, his mouth close to Keith's ear.

"Yes, sir."

"Let's get out of some of this stuff—especially these damned shoes."

"Just our shoes?" Keith asked.

"Yeah. For now. I'm gonna undress you. And you're gonna undress me. I got a few more surprises in store for you."

They kicked off the troublesome footwear. Seth approached Keith, gripped him roughly by the back of the neck and pulled Keith's head down to his own massive chest. As Seth unbuttoned Keith's shirt, he whispered, "You know I love you. I don't plan on hurtin' you—not much. Anytime you want me to stop, say so. Please."

Keith looked up, his eyes moist, his heart pounding. Seth *was* different. Keith had no idea what was in his lover's mind. Nor did he care, much. He was willing to do anything, endure any ritual, to please Seth. He found his worst fear was wondering where Seth had picked up whatever notions he was planning on implementing.

"I'm all yours. I always have been. Do whatever you want with me."

Seth didn't reply. He finished unbuttoning the shirt and stripped it off Keith. Then the T-shirt and trousers; in a moment, Keith was naked.

"Now it's your turn," Seth said, his voice flintlike. He let Keith remove his shirt and undershirt without comment, but as Keith unbuckled the large belt-buckle, Seth issued instructions: "Pull that belt out and hand it to me!"

Keith did as he was ordered. Seth gripped the belt in one hand while with the other he forced Keith onto his knees. Keith pulled Seth's pants down over hard thighs. As he did so, Keith felt the belt casually moving back and forth across his shoulders. It was a strange sensation. They had never done anything like this before. Keith decided he liked feeling the leather on his flesh. Seth suddenly pulled Keith's head into his groin.

"Suck me bastard!"

Keith complied. The first time the belt struck his buttocks he started, even though he was half-expecting the blow. He felt Seth's hand on the back of his neck, tensing, exploring, trying to decide how hard was hard enough. They played the game for several minutes. Keith was careful not to bring Seth off too early. Finally, using his hand as a guide, Seth raised Keith from his kneeling position and led him toward the bed. They fell upon one another with the ferocity of passion long delayed. Seth was rough, but he never hurt Keith beyond what Keith wanted to endure. It was only after Seth entered him, that Keith understood how much he'd needed the preparations involving the belt and Seth's roughness. It was the best of all the times they'd been together.

Exhausted, they lay together on the bed, Keith in Seth's strong arms.

Seth looked sheepishly at Keith. "Did you like it?"

"Yes. Very much."

"I kinda figured you would. I liked doin' it." He clutched Keith to him. It was a minute or two before he continued. "I . . . Steve Taylor went to 'Lanta a couple of months back. Said his cousin had a bunch of dirty books, magazines. He brought some of 'em to me. They were all guys and girls but in one of 'em, the girl was usin' a belt on the guy, sorta like I did just now. I thought about it awhile and figured you might like it." He stopped, then continued in a troubled tone. "It . . . seems kinda weird. You're the one with brains—you reckon we're crazy, likin' stuff like this? It worries me a little."

"Seth, Seth! If we both like it, want to do it, what difference does it make? I love *everything* you do to me. There's no rational reason, I suppose, why I enjoy getting my ass slapped around, or hit by a belt, but I do—when it's you doing it. I daresay its because I want to belong to you in every way possible. When I get to my next base, maybe I'll meet some other guys like us, find out about these things."

"You gonna look around for another man?" Seth demanded in mock anger.

"You know better. There's only one man for me."

"I was jokin'. I ain't jealous. We need to talk about that, though." Seth shifted and looked at Keith. "I don't expect you to go without sex the whole time we're apart. You know I had a couple of girls while you were gone. I'm horny all the time. I can't help it—but I wouldn't pick up another guy."

Keith frowned. "I'd almost rather you did pick up guys instead of those goddamned females."

Seth grinned. "I know you don't like 'em. That's why I wouldn't mind—too much—if you had a guy or two at your next base. You just make damn sure they know you're taken."

"Am I?"

In a lightning motion, Seth grasped Keith, rolled him onto his back and straddled his stomach. Seth pinned Keith's arms to the bed holding him immobile and asked, "You got any doubts?"

Keith stared at Seth. "Sometimes," he answered, serious. "I . . . I love you so much . . . I couldn't stand if if you didn't want . . . if anything happened to you . . . "

"Hey!" Seth released Keith's arms and gripped his lover's face. "Don't cry, Keith. You're mine. You're gonna *always* be mine. I'm gonna stick to you till I die, and I don't plan on doin' that for a long, long time. Can't I convince you of that?"

"No." Keith whispered. "I believe you, trust you, but it's my nature to worry, to expect the worst. I look at you and can't believe you want me." He placed a hand on Seth's lips to still the protest. "I'll try doing better. Now kiss me."

It was a long time before they could tear themselves away from one another to consider the question of supper.

Seth showered first. When he returned, Keith held out a package to him.

"What's this?"

"You didn't think I'd forget to bring you something, did you?"

"Hey, you didn't have to do that. What is it?"

"A decent radio." Keith smiled at Seth's look. Seth loved country music and baseball games, neither of which he got to listen to with his parents and six sisters in the house.

"It's beautiful," Seth managed, his eyes as close to tears as Keith was ever to see them. His look was reward enough. "You shouldn'ta done it," Seth added.

"Why not? You're all I've got."

Seth clasped Keith. "That goes for me, too. You go clean up. I'll see if this works."

Keith laughed as he tossed Seth the batteries. "It does. I tried it. You can use these or electricity." He disappeared into the bathroom.

Over their meal, they discussed practical matters.

"Tampa's not that far away." Seth commented, hearing of Keith's assignment to an Air Force base in the Florida city. "Once I get the car jazzed up, I could come down there for a few days. Uncle Amos wouldn't mind."

"Sounds good to me. Tell me about your job. You never mentioned it in your letters."

"Wanted to surprise you. If I'd told you I was workin' in Tilton, you'd a wondered how I was gettin' back and forth— and I didn't want to tell you 'bout the car. Uncle Amos is okay. He never married, you know. Sometimes I wonder 'bout him . . . anyway, he's gettin' older, seems to want somebody 'round the station. He owns it, has a good business, seems willin' to teach me stuff. I might work up to a partnership or something some day." He shot a glance at Keith. "Would that bother you, me bein' a grease monkey?"

"Don't be ridiculous."

Seth was embarrassed. "I ain't smart, you know. Never was, not like you. You expect to go to the University when you get out of the Air Force. What good will I be to you, stupid, not knowing—"

"Shut up! I do plan on going to the University. I've got a pretty good mind, and don't plan on wasting it . . . but nothing matters if you're not there. I'd dig ditches or clean out shithouses if that was the only way I could be near you." Keith hurried on. "You don't understand how much I depend on you, Seth. The only way I got through basic and that damned Air Police school was by thinking about you, forcing myself to do the best I could so I wouldn't disgrace you, so I could come back to you as soon as possible." He stared at his lover. "You said before, I was yours. I do believe that. I have to, or I'd die. I'll never let you go. If you ever get ideas about leaving me, be careful. I think I'd do something . . . drastic . . . before I'd let you go. Especially if it were with a woman. I'll never give you up to a fucking female."

Keith spoke the words low, vehemently. Their intensity startled, but did not alarm Seth. Seth, unlearned in many things, understood his lover. He knew all their lives he would have to reassure and reaffirm his love for Keith. At the moment, Seth sensed both the depth and dependency of Keith's love for him. He was willing to live with both.

8

Keith passed the three-year mark of his tenure in the Air Force. Each day his separation from Seth produced a dull, steady agony. He worked hard at keeping busy, did his job well and began taking University courses in the evenings. Seth finished high school and went to work full-time for his Uncle Amos who was unreasonably generous about letting his nephew trek down to Florida. Seth and Keith's lives were moving along a path both admitted was what they wanted. Seth's folks weren't too pleased at the way their son hung around Keith, but as the farmboy was out of the house; there wasn't much Jeb and Alma could do.

The stability of their relationship, the predictability of their actions, more than anything else, signaled disaster when late one afternoon Keith picked up his phone at work and heard Seth's voice.

"Keith?"

"Yeah? Seth? What's wrong?"

"Look, man, I hate tellin' you this on the phone . . . "

"*What*, for God's sake?"

"Your folks have been killed . . . "

The shock of Seth's words took time to hit Keith. When they did, the numbness which followed came more from surprise than dismay.

Later, it was to dawn upon Keith that his unsympathetic parents, by dying as they did, paved the way for his and Seth's future. It was as if the gods themselves were on the side of the lovers. Keith—remembering uneasily that what gods dispense they can withdraw—never took the miracle of Seth's love for granted.

The disaster of his parent's death could be laid squarely on the shoulders of his father.

Leon had never purchased an automobile. Instead, he and Florrie begged rides into town with their neighbors. One such man was Ridley Spivey (father of the infamous Dottie May, Seth's first date). Spivey, more often than not, was drunk. He was in an advanced state of inebriation on the occasion Leon and Florrie asked to share a ride into town with Spivey and his numerous brood. Leon, in keeping with southern masculine tradition, hopped into the cab of Spivey's truck. Florrie climbed into the back, where she settled herself on an old cane-bottomed chair. Spivey, unwilling to pay much attention to stop signs when sober, never observed them when drinking. He happily raced past one and was smashed by a logging truck. Florrie, from her insecure perch in the truck-bed sailed like a football high in the air. Her neck broke on impact with the ground and she died instantly. Leon, tangled in the metal of the cab, died several hours after reaching the hospital.

Seth met Keith at the bus station in Tilton.

Unmindful of the busy terminal, Seth pulled Keith into his arms and held him.

"I'm sorry, man."

"I know. We weren't close, but I wouldn't have wished this sort of end on them. Tell me about it."

Seth explained the circumstances of the accident as he led Keith to the Chevy. The drive to the funeral home was filled with painful silences. Both later admitted they'd wanted to touch, but felt a sexual move at such a time would have been unthinkable. Instead they sat on opposite sides of the car, saying nothing.

"Uncle Amos told me I could take a few days off." Seth said as they pulled up outside the mortuary. "You're goin' to need somebody to drive you 'round, take care of stuff. That okay with you?"

"You know it is. I . . . appreciate it, very much. Could you . . . stay with me tonight? At the house?"

Seth looked pained. "I'd love to, but you'll have a houseful of folks. Everyone will stop by and sit up with you. I'll be there after the funerals. You can count on that."

Keith had forgotten the etiquette of funerals.

The bodies of the dead, after having been arranged in coffins, were taken to their homes and laid-out, at which time neighbors were permitted the ritual of sanctimonious tears. Until the funeral, the home of the deceased filled and overflowed with relatives and so-called friends, many of whom were people who would never have set foot in the Wilson house had Leon and Florrie been alive. Death, for some reason, erased any need for truth or honesty.

Inside the funeral home, Keith found an uncle waiting, "to be helpful."

"Awful," Henry Wilson complained to his nephew, "Just awful." Keith couldn't help feeling his elderly uncle found the situation far from distressing. It seemed instead that the oldest of Leon's siblings felt the grotesque tragedy fitting and proper. Leon was never quite forgiven for having ventured away from the South or for obtaining a job which allowed him to retire (with an income) at a relatively youthful age. And, worst of all, for marrying a Yankee.

"The family wanted me to hang around till you got here," Henry drawled in his awkward, nasal tone. "I kinda figured you might want some help with pickin' out the caskets."

Keith sighed. The next few days would give him his fill of relatives. He'd never liked most of his father's people, finding them coarse and stupid. It was time he asserted himself.

"You're very kind, Uncle Henry, but I'd rather do it myself, if you don't mind." He turned to the director of the funeral home who was hovering at Keith's elbow like a hungry spider. "Could we get this over with, please? Seth, would you come with me?"

As they entered the room where coffins were displayed, Keith had a sudden thought: "My father was a retired military man; he's entitled to a casket at government expense. Would you call the mortuary officer at the base or should I?"

The funeral director watched dollars sliding away, put on his most professional grimace and agreed to check the matter.

Left alone for a few moments, Keith grinned at Seth. "He didn't like that, did he?"

"No," Seth agreed soberly. "Your Uncle didn't like getting frozen out, either."

"Screw 'em," Keith exclaimed bitterly. "They aren't the ones who'll have to pay the bills. The sorry bunch wouldn't have anything to do with my folks when they were alive; I sure as hell don't need kinfolks around now."

The director returned, reluctantly agreeing that the military would provide a burial container for Leon, and that he, the director, would be glad to arrange everything. That matter settled, Keith quickly selected a modestly priced piece of junk for his mother, indicated which vaults he wanted and told Seth he was ready.

Back in the Chevy, Keith made a request. "Could we drive around a bit? I don't feel like going back to the house just yet. I expect the rest of the relatives will be there, snooping around . . . "

"Isn't that the best reason to go there right away?" Seth answered, more practical. "Did your folks have any insurance?"

The thought had not crossed Keith's mind.

"I don't know—about the insurance. I expect you're right about getting back to the house. Home, James!"

"Huh?"

"Never mind." Keith reached his hand across the seat and touched Seth. Seth guided the vehicle with one hand and laid the other in the middle of the auto, holding Keith's fingers between his own. The contact was comforting and necessary.

To Keith's surprise, the house was empty. He walked up and inserted his key in the door. It was the first time in his life he had unlocked the door to his own home. With no sound coming from the radio which was usually blaring away, the building projected an unreal quality. Keith walked over and switched on the instrument. Seth followed him into the house, carrying the one suitcase Keith had brought with him.

"Want this in your room?"

"Yes." Keith followed Seth.

"Hold me!" Keith exclaimed.

Seth held out his arms and Keith fled into them. Their embrace was long. Seth lifted Keith's face to his, kissing his lover tenderly, touchingly. The sound of a car pulling into the yard put an end to their tenderness. It was to be their last moment alone for three days.

Keith never quite figured out how he got through the days. There was always someone underfoot. Overzealous neighbor ladies, aunts, uncles, cousins: Leon's numerous relatives poured out of whatever holes they inhabited. Since it was the custom of the region to provide food for mourners, Keith suspected his kinfolks came by simply to partake of the funeral meats. He knew if he were ungracious his actions would be attributed to the emotionalism of the moment. He didn't want that sort of misunderstanding to take place and kept a tight grip on his temper.

On only two occasions did he vocalize his thoughts.

The first instance came when a cousin, hearing about the double deaths in the family, drove down from Atlanta for the festivities. The cousin, on welfare, was married to a woman with the unlikely name of Duzie. Duzie was a nonstop talker, covering any and every topic her feather-filled mind encountered. Her mouth flapped like hinges on a gate, from the time she entered the house until she finally left. He tried avoiding her as much as possible, but the Wilson house was not large and it was inevitable that at some point in time she would trap him.

This she did on the second night of the wake. The corpses had been given top billing in the living room. The floral offerings everyone had purchased were arranged around the caskets. Keith could not help reflecting that the room was looking far better than it ever had when his parents were alive. (Florrie had been an indifferent housekeeper.) The family cat, intrigued by the flowers, had a marvelous time shredding the wreaths to bits. One of Keith's most vivid memories of the entire three days was of the neighbor ladies trying to keep the curious animal out of the flowers and off the coffins.

Duzie ran Keith to earth at last. She grabbed him by the hand and pulled him into a corner where a couple of chairs stood vacant.

"*So* terrible, of course," she stated with a long-suffering sigh. "But it was the Lord's Will. They were taken together. God works in such mysterious ways." Keith, who saw nothing mysterious in the fact Ridley Spivey was drunk and ran a stop sign, refrained from saying so. Duzie continued to chatter as if they were attending a party, and booze rather than weak coffee was loosening her tongue. "When this is all over, you must come to Atlanta and visit with us. We got lots of room; I just

know you'd find it a blessing. Jacob and me, we go to this
church where the pastor is touched by the Spirit of Jesus. It'd
uplift you. Ain't it a shame how we all drift apart? Seems like it
always takes something dreadful like this to bring a family together. Why don't you pay us a visit? We'd just love having
you—we could introduce you to our preacher, he's such a man
of God. He'd be happy to pray with you. What a blessing
that'd be."

Keith murmured some sort of reply.

Duzie, however, pressed for a firm commitment.

"Oh, say you'll come. You know we ought to see more of
each other."

Keith eyed the woman with distaste. "No," he said with
sarcasm which was wasted, "I don't know it at all. The only
good thing I can find in Mother and Father being killed at the
same time is that it will spare me the necessity of going through
this business with relatives more than once." He rose, seeking
a different corner of the house. Duzie, for once, was left without words. A happy state which did not last long; she joyfully
spent the rest of her time complaining about Keith's rudeness.

The second instance—in which Keith forgot himself
enough to reply to an inanity—was more ominous. The incident involved one of the neighbor ladies who invariably attended wakes. She was a busybody of the first rank. Everyone in
the community agreed that if Sarah Ann Taylor didn't know
some particular breath of scandal it didn't exist. She stopped
by late one afternoon, bringing salad and fried chicken for the
table. Having deposited these items—indications of her good
will—she sought out Keith.

"Keith!" she exclaimed when she found him. "Come with
me. I want to *talk* with you."

Obediently, he followed her into an empty area of the
house.

"Sit down," she ordered, more like a prisonwarden than a

visitor.

"You're bearing up well," she stated, peering at him suspiciously, as if such fortitude were unnatural. "You're still stationed in Florida, aren't you? Tampa, I believe?"

Keith agreed this was true.

"Not married yet, are you?" she inquired, her face drawn together in a frown of fitful distress.

"No, I'm not."

"Such a shame. Florrie never got to see a grandchild. Are you engaged yet?"

"No."

Sarah Ann shook her head with muted disapproval. "How old are you now? Twenty-one? Twenty-two? Certainly time you settled down. What's the matter with you, Keith? Don't you *like* marriage?"

Keith's anger was ignited. He was tired, having gotten little sleep the past couple of nights because of the constant crowds. He'd listened to platitudes and religious asininities without a word of protest. He had, for the most part, withheld comment since the customs of death were those demanded by the community and sanctioned by his parents. It was, after all, their funeral. The bitch in front of him, however, was overstepping custom with such insistent questioning.

"No, Mrs. Taylor," he answered in a voice dripping with irony. "I *don't* like marriage. It's one of the most ridiculous institutions ever established by a gullible mankind. Look what it's done to you. I have no intention of embroiling myself in a grotesque mockery of everything any sensible man should believe." He rose and walked away, leaving the astonished woman staring after him.

At last the service was held, the burials accomplished and the crowds, duty done, disappeared. Keith was surprised at the number of people attending the final rites. He never suspected his parents were so popular. Seth had dissuaded Keith from the notion they attend and leave the funeral together. Instead, Keith was saddled with relatives for the duration of the ceremony. His Uncle Henry dropped him off at the empty house after the rituals of death were completed. The old man, after offering his aid in any matter with which Keith might need help, reluctantly drove away. Keith was finally alone.

He entered his room, got out a bottle of bourbon he had brought with him and mixed a good drink. He did not drink much, nor often, but after the past few days, felt he was entitled to indulge. He was on his second glass when Seth arrived.

They embraced as soon as the door closed behind them.

"Thank God that's over!" Keith exclaimed. "Will you stay tonight?"

"What do you think?"

They broke apart. "Want a drink?" Keith asked.

"Sure."

As they sat sipping from their glasses, Keith looked around at the messy room. Cigarette butts left by the diligent do-gooders and bits of wreaths the cat had played with littered the floor. Everything shouted the message that something must be done with the remains of Leon and Florrie's life.

"I'm going to have a hell of a time getting everything straightened out," Keith said. "I don't even know where to begin. I suppose I'd better find a lawyer. And what about the house? What should I do with it?"

"Rent it," Seth said at once. "Get some steady money out of it. I wouldn't sell it. Property values are low now, but I think they're gonna perk up before long."

"I don't know," Keith countered. "That funeral business wasn't cheap, even though I did get a casket out of the military." He smiled in remembrance at the look on the funeral director's face. Setting his drink aside, Keith got up and went into his parent's bedroom. He returned carrying a small metal box.

"They kept most of their important papers in here." Keith explained as he opened the container. "Too stingy to rent a safe-deposit box at the bank." He raised the metal lid and began shifting the papers. "Deed to the house, birth certificates —what's this?" He pulled out an official-looking document and began reading it. The silence grew as Keith sat, absorbed by the paper. After some minutes, Seth stirred.

"Well, what have you found?"

Keith looked up. "I don't know. It *looks* like an insurance policy—for twenty-five thousand dollars! And there's a line down at the bottom stating that in case of accidental death the policy doubles! I don't believe it . . . "

Seth stood up abruptly. "God! You'd be rich—"

"What do you mean *I'd* be rich? *We'd* be rich! My God, it would *free* us, Seth—"

"I couldn't take money from you."

"Don't be an ass. You're as much a part of me as an arm or leg. Of course you'd use it. Damn it, I want to build my future around you. How can I do that if we don't cooperate with each other? But I'm probably reading this damned thing wrong. Leon would *never* have had the sense to take out a policy like this. Come here and hold me—let's dream about what we'd do if it *were* true!"

9

Keith was wrong. For once in his life, Leon had done something sensible. As with all such proceedings, actually getting the money, as well as title to the house and land, took time. It was almost six months before affairs were settled. Keith, in the meantime, had nearly completed his four years in the Air Force and was working on an early discharge. He had long been of the opinion the military was no place for him. With the money from Leon's insurance and his GI Bill benefits, he anticipated attending the University of Georgia. Seth steadfastly refused to attend the University, both because he didn't want to use Keith's money and because he insisted he wasn't intelligent enough to bother with more schooling. From the beginning, the money caused friction in Keith and Seth's relationship.

Keith was determined his sudden affluence must not destroy their love. And, in time, he managed to win over Seth. In this unexpected victory, Keith found an ally in Amos Avery, Seth's uncle and employer.

Amos, discovering he was not in the best of health, wanted to sell his garage. When Keith offered to assist Seth in buying the business, they fought long and hard over the idea.

"Damn it," Seth exploded, "I'm not gonna be owned by you or anyone else!"

"Shit! You want to spend the rest of your life working for

somebody else? You can operate the damned place. Hell, I'm going to buy it, and if you want to be stubborn . . . We'll go to a lawyer and get things drawn up anyway you want. Just stop being so fucking stupid!"

It was one of the few instances when Keith prevailed. Seth insisted everything be placed in Keith's name, protection for Keith in case anything happened to Seth. Unknown to Seth, Keith turned around and made a will leaving everything to his lover. The unexpected demise of his parents had taught Keith the desirability of preparation.

The pair—so young, so in love—found their future laid out before them. Keith obtained his discharge and enrolled at the University, making sure he and Seth had a few weeks together before classes started. Seth, reconciled at last over the financial arrangements they had worked out, was better than ever at convincing Keith their destiny was bright. Yet each step towards a life together presented conflicts they never expected to encounter. The University brought Keith into contact with the fledgling gay movement in Georgia. Such exposure would bring physical temptations and philosophical difficulties. As Keith and Seth grew older and neither married (or even dated), their closeness caused talk in the community. Seth's family ceased hiding their intense displeasure at their son's continued association with Keith. Years later, looking back over this pre-university period, Keith scolded himself for not seeing the swirling tides which roared at the feet of his love for Seth. Being in love, however, rendered him sightless. Keith trekked off to the University, full of enthusiasm for the world of learning and gave little thought to the coming years, expecting them to hold peace, happiness and a growing love between himself and Seth.

10

By the early seventies, most of the nation had undergone the trauma of watching wild and raging students wrecking their universities. Civil rights, hippies, drugs—all the signs of the permissive generation—were in vogue across most of the country. Only the South, Georgia included, escaped much of the turmoil. Whether the matter in question was progress or fads, the South lingered behind the rest of the states. Therefore, when signs appeared on the University of Georgia campus announcing the formation of a gay liberation group, everyone was startled.

"Have you seen these fuckin' things?" one frat boy asked a friend. "Goddamn queers are organizing! We oughtta go to this thing and bust a few heads!"

Similar remarks floated around the school the rest of the week. Signs proclaiming the proposed meeting seldom stayed on bulletin boards more than a few minutes.

Keith was as surprised as everyone else when he chanced upon one of the notices, and the prospect of whether or not to attend caused him a lot of mental anguish.

On the one hand, he wanted to show up. The threat of violence didn't bother him; the possibility news might trickle back to Tilton, placing him amongst such a group, did. Keith sensed Seth would disapprove his involvement with such an organization. Yet the urge was there. Keith was finding university life a lonely experience. As in the past, no matter where he found himself—the Air Force, high school, or wherever—he was always alone. He did have Seth—Seth who was all he ever wanted or dreamed about—but Seth was far away: they saw one another only every couple of weeks. The easy friendships and casual acquaintances others formed were not Keith's way.

After much thought, Keith reluctantly found himself approaching the meeting site—an auditorium in the Home Economics Building. His astonishment at seeing over a hundred people seated hesitantly inside the large room was great. He took a seat, furtively looking about, nervous, self-conscious, yet inordinately pleased with himself for having dug up the courage to attend at all.

Shortly after eight o'clock, the gathering was called to order by a slight, blond-haired man. After an awkward initial few minutes during which no one ventured forth any opinions, the tension dissipated and a growing din of words erupted. Keith sat quietly and kept his mouth shut. He was amazed at the divergent number of ideas being presented. The meeting moved from high formality towards anarchy in a very short span of time. After much wrangling, three persons were elected to positions of leadership. They set about forming subcommittees. Subcommittees were going to be the working guts of the organization. On an impulse he immediately regretted, Keith found himself raising his hand and offering his services.

It was the beginning of an extraordinary learning process for Keith.

He found himself spending a couple of evenings a week with Nick Brown, leader of the group. Brown's apartment was continuously filled with homosexuals. For the first time in his life, Keith was surrounded by men like himself. Considering this was something he had longed for, the experience did not turn out to be an especially happy one.

Keith found it hard to decipher the specific problems he

had adjusting to his new acquaintances. In the first place, his judgments always tended to be sexual—which annoyed him. Simply stated, he felt many of the guys were silly. Their constant clowning around like a bunch of teen-aged girls, their titters, their calling each other by female names, all embarrassed him. On the other hand, the few who were masculine and attractive aroused his sexual interests—which made him angry with himself. In the course of working with the group, Keith learned about the vast gay underground in Atlanta. Bars, clubs, baths, bookstores, publications; the whole spectrum of things available to men like himself. It was a completely new dimension for Keith. As his awareness grew, so did his anger—anger at a hetero society which refused to recognize either the existence of homosexuals or the validity of their love. His rage increased when the campus group ran into difficulties with university authorities.

Nick Brown was the initial reason for the confrontation with school officials.

Most of the members wanted the organization to function as a social unit: to set up private parties, establish a telephone help-line, offer assistence to gays in trouble . . . any sort of service which could be arranged without raising the ire of conservative opponents or university dictators. Brown, however, insisted the organization's purpose must be political confrontation. He gleefully hit upon the notion of holding a gay dance on campus.

"Heteros jiggle all over the place," he stated. "We have the same right!"

His demands made newspapers statewide.

Battle lines were quickly formed: the university on one side, the newly-formed committee on the other. The university refused to allow the committee the use of campus facilities. Everywhere around the school, the notion of a dance for "queers" sparked derision. Brown, an astute politician, secured the services of a local attorney and challenged the university's position in court. It was all very exciting and Keith, one of the committee's more dependable members, found himself swept up in the drama.

When he paused to think about his role in the affair, Keith grew fearful. He realized his involvement might lead to severe limitations in his ability to hold jobs and function in hetero society—especially in Tilton. It was not something he should have undertaken without consulting Seth. He rationalized his silence by complaining there was never time to sit down and explain things to Seth. The conflict with the university snowballed rapidly. People were needed to carry out the committee's business. Keith continued working on the group's behalf, putting off from day to day his intentions of letting Seth know about his role in the organization.

Having secured a lawyer and challenged the university in court, money became a necessity for the committee. Fund raising activities abounded. Unable to use university facilities, private parties became the vehicle the committee used to raise money. Keith was preparing to attend such a gathering one Friday night when he was interrupted by a knock at the door.

"Seth!" Keith was stunned at the sight of his lover. "You never said you were coming up here this weekend."

Seth stalked into the room, dropped his small overnight bag and grabbed Keith.

"That's a hell of a way to say hello—didn't know I needed an invitation." He kissed Keith roughly.

"I did try phonin'," Seth complained when their embrace was over. "You ain't been home much, lately. School keepin' you busy?"

"I have been busy," Keith countered, trying to decide how he was going to tell Seth about the committee.

"With another man?" Seth asked belligerently,"or are you involved with this committee bunch?" He pulled a clipping out of his pocket and handed it to Keith.

It was a short press release which had been printed in the Atlanta papers a week or two earlier, at the start of the controversy. Keith glanced at it and handed it back.

"Do you really think I'd look at another man?" he protested, wishing he had time to prepare Seth for the committee.

"No. Not really. I do think this . . . committee business is something you'd take to. I see how annoyed you get sometimes over the way queers are treated." Seth moved to the sofa and sat down. He motioned Keith to his side. "I wish you'd have considered me before jumpin' into something like this."

Keith sat down. "I was going to tell you," he mumbled. "There was never time. I started helping out—almost accidentally—and before I knew it, we were caught up in this mess with the administration. I couldn't let everyone down." Keith's anger flared. "I knew you wouldn't want me involved, but I'm so goddamned tired of hearing us put down all the time! We've got as much right to have a fucking dance on this campus as those straight sons-of-bitches and their cunts! If things are ever going to change, somebody has to get things rolling! I don't see why I can't help out a little . . . if there's anything I can do."

Seth pulled Keith to him. His gesture contained none of the anger or violence Keith expected. "I didn't say you shouldn't help out—I just wish you'd have trusted me enough to tell me about it. I wish you'd think about the trouble it can cause me at the station." He turned Keith around and looked directly into his eyes. "I owe you too much to try tellin' you what to do, but you say you're mine; I wish you'd act like it and let me in on what you're doin'." He grinned suddenly, taking the sting out of his words. "I oughtta whip your ass, that's what I oughtta do."

"Why don't you?"

"Maybe I will, later. Right now, I want to know what I'm interruptin'."

The sight of Seth had driven all thoughts of the party from Keith's mind.

"We're having a fund raiser tonight—to help pay the lawyer we've hired to fight the university." Keith looked at his watch. "Would . . . would you come with me? I'd love to show you off. I love you so much. God! I could touch you, dance with you—"

"Don't get carried away," Seth cautioned. "I ain't into this public stuff." Drawing a deep breath, he continued. "So it's we now, is it? Okay. I'll go with you. But you know I won't fit in. I'll be uncomfortable as hell and I'll hate it. But I'll go."

They finished their preparations in an awkward silence. Thinking about the people who'd be at the party, Keith almost backed out. He knew Seth would be out of place at the gathering.

The party was barely alive when Seth and Keith arrived. It was scheduled to begin at nine, but Keith had yet to learn that homosexuals never came to life until midnight at the earliest. Was it a strain of vampirism? He never discovered. At any rate, only a few of the hard-core supporters of the committee were present. Nick Brown rushed up to welcome his most dependable lieutenant.

"Keith! I was afraid you wouldn't come!" Brown's eyes turned to Seth, devouring the large man with a hungry look of lust. "*Who* is *this*?"

Keith performed introductions. "Seth's my—a close friend," he amended—wanting to use the term *lover*, but knowing Seth would be displeased if he did.

"We're so glad to have you." Nick cooed. "Come over and have a beer." He implusively grabbed Seth's hand and

half-dragged the large man to the beer keg. Keith, watching
them, was unable to stifle some degree of amusement. Realizing Seth would be busy for awhile, Keith turned to see who else
had arrived.

"Keith!" exclaimed Kenny Watkins, a committee regular. "So *glad* you got here at last. What a *drag* this party
is—and I don't mean my sort, either." Watkins giggled and
embraced Keith. Watkins was the group's resident drag
queen. Keith found such affectations unsettling, but Kenny
was generous with his time. His flighty mannerisms and
overweight frame gave Kenny lots of time to read, which en-
deared him to Keith. The pair talked as much about books as
men.

"Who is that gorgeous hunk who came in with you?"
Kenny wanted to know.

"That's Seth," Keith replied.

"My dear! No wonder you've never brought her around.
You'd better be careful. Miss Brown would love to get her
hands on that."

Keith smiled, watching Seth and Nick talking on the
other side of the room. "I'm not worried about that," Keith exclaimed.

"Then what is worrying you?" Kenny asked.

Keith told him: "I hadn't told Seth about working with the
committee. He popped up this evening unexpectedly—there
wasn't much I could do but give him a rundown about what
I've gotten into. He's not too pleased."

"Oh, don't worry," Kenny advised, "she'll get over herself. They all do."

Keith drifted around welcoming other out-of-place gays
who propped themselves in corners like columns holding up an
old southern mansion. By the time these amenities were out of
the way, the apartment was well-filled. Keith turned to find
Seth rejoining him.

"You seem to know everyone," Seth commented. "When do you find time to study?"

"I'm doing okay," Keith protested, defensively.

Seth eyed him but said nothing.

"Come on," Keith said, "let me introduce you around."

He led Seth over to Kenny and introduced them, wincing as Kenny did his lady-like bit. As the room swelled with male flesh, Seth garnered numerous stares of admiration. Some of the better-looking members of the community came up to speak to Keith. As these were men who never bothered with him at other times, he assumed they were hoping for an introduction to Seth. He obliged.

The music grew louder and dancing began. Turning to Seth, Keith asked, "Want to dance?"

"With you? With a guy?"

"Certainly. What do you think everyone else is doing?"

"Makin' fools of themselves, if you ask me," Seth retorted. "I only dance with women."

"Well excuse me!" Keith turned to walk away. Seth jerked him back.

"You're startin' to *sound* like the rest of 'em. Goddammit—"

"Seth. I am like them. We're all homosexuals. Won't you ever get that through your head? How long are you going to keep denying—"

"Can't we get the hell out of here?"

Keith looked at his watch. It was barely twelve. The party would go on for hours yet. He sighed. "Okay. Let me make our excuses."

He was back in a couple of minutes. "Come on."

They walked to Seth's car. Keith was tempted to speak, but decided he'd already said too much for one evening. They drove back to Keith's house without a word passing between them.

11

Want a beer?" Keith asked as they entered the house.
"No, dammit, I want to talk to you."

Keith kicked off his shoes, stepped into the bedroom, changed clothes and returned to the sofa.

"Okay. Talk. I'm listening."

Seth sat down, eyeing Keith with a puzzled frown on his face. "I don't understand why you've gotten yourself involved with this madness. Is it the politics? Are you tryin' to prove something by bein' *open* about a matter you know folks won't like or understand? You always did like swimmin' against the tide. Every time you got pissed at Leon or your mother, it was over something silly. Something you could just have avoided if you'd shut up about it. This looks like the same thing to me. Do you believe this stupid bunch of queers is gonna change anything? All you'll do is get your name in the papers and destroy whatever future you may have had. That money you got won't last forever. Haven't you thought about that? What do you think's gonna happen to our garage when folks in Tilton find out you're queer? Why in the hell can't you think about stuff like that once in a while? Goddammit, I love you; I want to be with you. But I want to be able to earn a livin' too. If I mean as much to you as you always say I do, why didn't you ask me about this before you jumped into it?"

"I didn't ask you about it because I was involved before I

quite knew what I was doing," Keith responded. "Afterwards, I didn't mention it to you because I figured you'd be pissed. As you are. Why in the hell can't you get it through your thick skull that we're queers too? Just like every one of the people you saw there tonight. I don't give a fuck what those stupid bastards in Tilton think—if they've got anything to think with! I'm tired, tired, tired, of hiding, of pretending we're just friends. I'm disgusted with having to act like loving you is something sick, perverted—evil even. If you gave much thought to my feelings, you'd think about that once in a while."

They stared at each other across the gulf of the sofa.

"You think *I'm* like that bunch?" Seth accused. They're sick! That one guy—thinks he's a fuckin' woman! What kind of man is that?"

"Is there much difference between his fantasy and ours? When you compare it to some of the things we do?"

"What the hell are you talkin' about?" Seth asked sullenly.

"Do you think the way I let you slap me around is any less sick? Or the way you seem to enjoy it?"

"That's different."

"Why?"

"Hell! At least we do it in private. You like it, God knows."

Keith shook his head. "The fact I like it hasn't anything to do with the point I'm trying to make, which is all of us do things others could label 'sick' if they cared to. I'm tired of hetero society thinking they have the right to make laws against the things we choose to do. I'm disgusted by the snickering and dirty jokes our love elicits. I'm ready to tell the whole god-damned society to go to hell. I'm willing to do everything I can to hasten the day we can walk freely, hand-in-hand, down any street in America without some bloody bastard thinking it's something to laugh at!"

"That'll never happen!" Seth barked scornfully.

"It sure as hell won't if people think like you do!" Keith hesitated, then continued. "What do you think I feel like, when you say things like you've just said? You say you love me, but you never demonstrate that love—except when we're alone. You act like you're ashamed of me. You have to get physically violent with me to really enjoy yourself—shut up! I don't mind the pain—I never did. I'm not complaining about that. God knows, for whatever reasons, I want the pain, need it even. *I love you.* I love you so fucking much I'd give you up—I think—if you'd be happier with a woman. But if you love me, if you want me, I wish to God you'd get over the notion that what we do is dirty and disgusting and less than what a man and a woman do."

Without a word, Seth got up and went into the kitchen. He returned with two bottles of beer.

"I reckon we don't communicate too well, do we?" Seth asked, after a prolonged silence.

"It isn't that," Keith countered. "The trouble is, you're caught up with the practical problems of making money and getting ahead in the world. You do everything with an eye towards what people will say, how it will affect the garage, the money you make. That, plus the fact you haven't ever accepted our screwing as something natural, something *good.* Morally good. You enjoy it, but you won't admit to yourself it's natural. If I can ever get you to do that, we'd be halfway home."

"What . . . about the things we do?"

"What do you mean?"

"Before . . . you sounded like you don't like the stuff we do in bed. If I ain't satisfyin' you . . . "

"Seth!" Keith fell to his knees in front of the big man. "You do satisfy me—totally, completely, entirely. The point I was making is that the things we do, enjoy doing, would seem depraved to the people you're trying to impress in a place like Tilton. I'm trying to make you see that what we do in bed *has no significance* except between the two of us—it shouldn't be used to judge us. Certainly not by bastards in a place like south Georgia. That was my point. Plus the fact you like violence . . . . maybe in your own mind it lessens the disgust you feel over having sex with me in the first place."

"I don't feel disgust having sex with you." Seth offered the statement softly.

"Not as much as you used to," Keith agreed. "But you still feel uncomfortable in public. Like earlier, when you wouldn't dance with me."

"I . . . just couldn't. Not with all those people 'round."

"That's what I mean."

Seth swallowed some beer. "I . . . don't know what you want anymore." He shut up for a moment, then added, eyeing Keith morosely, "You gettin' tired of me?"

Keith grabbed Seth's legs tightly. "I'll never get tired of you. You're my whole goddamned life. The only thing I'm tired of is having to defend our love all the time. I'm tired of you thinking what we have is less than what a man and woman have. We have the most beautiful relationship in the world. All I want is for you to reach the point where you see us the way I do. I want *you* to see the splendor we have—I want us to be as beautiful to you as it's always been to me."

Seth did not reply. Instead he reached down and stroked Keith's face. He set down his beer bottle and dropped to the floor beside Keith.

Their kiss bespoke a passion which made a mockery of every word they'd uttered.

Seth reached back to slap Keith, then halted.

"I don't know what you want anymore."

"I want what I've always wanted—all of you, freely given. I want you being rough with me; but I want you roughing me up because you enjoy it, not because you're trying to sublimate the fact I'm not a woman. When I know you're slapping me around and getting off on it because I'm a man, a man in the same way as you view yourself, then we'll be on the same wavelength."

Seth's eyes acknowledged the words but said nothing. They began slipping into past routines, until suddenly Keith fought back, challenging Seth's strength in ways he'd never done before. The resistance startled Seth.

"Goddammit," Seth muttered between breaths, "What the hell's wrong with you now? Don't you want it tonight?"

"I want it if you're man enough to take me." Keith spat the challenge at his lover, then strained as before his eyes, the words ignited Seth into a furious, raging bull of a man.

"You come on at me with all those fuckin' *words*," Seth gasped. "But they don't mean a thing. It ain't words you need." He grabbed Keith viciously and pinned him to the floor, straddling him in total domination. "Try something now, damn you!"

Keith tried, but without success. Seth's bulk was too much. Keith lay under Seth's looming form, breathing heavily but glaring defiantly at the man above him.

Seth, grinning slightly now, slapped Keith's face. Hard. There was more pain in the blows than before, but the knowledge did not stop him as it might have in the recent past.

"You said I liked violence. By God, I'll show you how violent I can be!"

"Who are you . . . doing it for?" Keith grunted.

Seth sat atop Keith, mute. Then his hand flew back across Keith's face.

"For both of us," he said.

In a sudden motion Seth stood up and pulled Keith to his feet as well. Spinning the man around roughly, Seth jerked one arm up behind Keith's back.

"Get your ass in the bedroom!"

They entered the room, Keith dimly aware that his words

had awakened a sleeping giant. Seth was in a state.

Seth retained his hold on Keith. He pushed Keith to his knees then stepped in front of him. They faced each other, Seth towering over his kneeling devotee. Keith, visibly trembling, tentatively embraced the strong Herculean legs of the aroused Seth. He reached for Seth's belt and unbuckled it. Instead of continuing with the button and zipper, Keith carefully removed the belt.

"What the hell you doin' now?" Seth demanded.

Keith didn't reply. He simply handed it to Seth. Seth smiled grimly. "Okay," he said, "if that's what you want . . . "

12

Keith remained surprised at the passions he and Seth aroused in themselves that evening but their confrontation and subsequent fucking marked the final maturing of their love for one another.

Seth made no further attempts at limiting Keith's involvement with gay activities. The committee's victory over the University at the eleventh hour may have had something to do with Seth's acquiescence. When he saw there was some chance their love could be successfully defended, he grew more willing to make sacrifices.

Not that sacrifices were required. If Tilton's citizens learned of Keith's activities, they never mentioned it to Seth. They certainly never stopped doing business at Seth's garage. Keith managed to drag Seth to the gay sections of Atlanta from time to time, where the scenes they encountered rapidly diminished their abilities to be shocked. Seth always retained a shyness about public dancing, but after enough beer he could be propelled onto a dance floor. Their lives together deepened and expanded. Their love—having suffered the roller coaster effect of disagreements—smoothed out and began a climb which, as far as Keith was concerned, never crested, only climbed higher and higher until at times he felt dizzy from the exhalted heights of their emotions. Once in a while their happiness frightened him. It was too perfect.

Keith graduated and returned to Tilton. He sometimes wished they had left the town, but Seth's business was prosperous: Armed with a degree, Keith secured a good job. They had each other—there was no need to move to a big city where sexhunting was the major sport. Both were small-town men at heart—especially Seth. Keith bought a house. The decision not to live together (yet) was his . . . much as he loved Seth, there were times when Keith needed to be alone, needed his own space . . . and given Tilton's conservative coloration, why not play the game a little longer? Keep them guessing. In time, the lovers promised themselves, they'd move in together. In the meantime . . .

In the meantime Keith found himself walking home along the moonlit street because they had not yet moved into one house. His mind was half-alert, half still back at Seth's place. Keith's boss was picking him up in . . . four hours? An out-of-town business trip. He'd be tired, but it didn't matter. After a session with Seth, not even lack of sleep could bring him down.

Keith let himself into his house and got into bed. He set the clock and immediately fell asleep.

It was not the clock, however, which woke him. Keith seemed to have no sooner closed his eyes than a loud banging at his door jarred him awake. He glanced groggily at the clock, fearful he'd overslept. It was only seven.

He got up, slipped on a pair of pants and stumbled towards the door.

"Yes?" he growled as he flung open the panel. Two Tilton City Police officers were standing on his doorstep.

"Mr. Wilson? I'm Wayne Links, Chief of Police here in Tilton. Could we have a word with you?"

"Yeah . . . I guess so. Come in. What's the problem?"

He led the men back to his kitchen. "Have a seat," Keith invited. "I'll make some coffee."

"What's the matter, Chief?" Keith asked again, puzzled by the presence of the police on his doorstep so early in the morning.

"You're partners with Seth Rawson, over at Rawson's garage, aren't you?" Links asked.

"Yes, I am. I don't see—" Keith interrupted himself, feeling an uneasy chill wash over him.

Links was a youngish man, extremely young for one holding an exhalted position such as Chief of Police in a town like Tilton, where old age was the usual criterion for any post of social or political importance. Links, however, had impressed the citizens of the community with his fairness. The few times Keith or Seth found it necessary to conduct business with the police, they had been impressed by Links' abilities.

Now the Chief's face was serious. He and his assistant eyed Keith speculatively as Links explained their presence.

"I'm afraid I've bad news for you, Mr. Wilson. Seth Rawson was found shot to death this morning—" Links broke off, leaping to catch Keith, who, for the first time in his life, fainted.

13

Y ou okay?" Links asked, as he wiped Keith's head with a damp towel.

Keith stared at the man. He struggled to regain his feet. "I . . . I . . . don't believe you. You can't be serious. Why, I . . . saw Seth last night. Only a few hours ago. He was fine. *SETH CAN'T BE DEAD!*"

The Police Chief's hand shot out and slapped Keith back to some semblance of sanity.

"We need to ask you questions," the Chief said. "You may have been the last person to see Rawson alive. Pull yourself together."

Keith tried valiantly to stand up. The kitchen spun, the world spun . . . the words hurled at him by the invaders of his kitchen *could not be true!* He fought to reach his feet but only darkness rose before him, engulfing him . . .

As the darkness receded, Keith found himself in a bed. Awakening in a strange room, he quickly closed his eyes again. He needed time to think—find out where he was and why? But there was no space inside him for thoughts. There was only a dull, deadly ache brought back by remembering the cop's words.

Seth dead? Seth gone? It was all lies! His soul rebelled at such a notion. Tears welled up and slid out from beneath his eyelids. Someone must be playing a horrible, malicious joke on him, testing his loyalty, his love. He had just left Seth—had laid in Seth's strong arms . . . *Seth could not be dead*!

"Keith? Can you hear me?" The words urged Keith back to a reality he could not accept. He would open his eyes . . . discover it was all a monsterous nightmare.

"Doctor?" He looked at the kindly man he had visited from time to time for colds and minor illnesses contracted over the years. "What's going on? Why am I here?"

"Just a precaution" the doctor replied. "You took the news of your friend's death very hard."

"It can't be true! He's not . . . dead. *He can't be!*"

The doctor sadly nodded his head. "I'm afraid he is, Keith. I know you were very close. You've got to pull yourself together. The Chief wants to ask you some questions."

"There's nothing I can tell him," Keith muttered.

"That's as may be," the doctor said, "but apparently you were one of the last people to see Seth alive. They need to talk with you."

Keith turned listlessly towards the blank white wall. "I'll talk with them, but there's nothing I can tell them." He closed his eyes, feeling fear and a harsh throbbing in his chest which he knew would never leave. Life without Seth was worthless. There was no longer a future for him. His future was as blank as the wall before his eyes.

The questions began.

As the horror gradually permeated his soul, it seemed to Keith that the police were simply making pretenses towards finding whoever had shot Seth. The initial interrogations at the hospital were cordial. Later ones were not. Exactly when Keith became aware he was their leading suspect, he could not say. By the end of the week, however, he found himself inside a cell at the police station.

Had any humor been left him, he would have laughed at the unbelievable script the cops concocted.

"What time did you leave the deceased, Mr. Wilson?" Wasn't that awfully late for a visit? Did you quarrel? Were you aware he had taken out a large insurance policy naming you as beneficiary?"

You fools! We were lovers. Why shouldn't I stay late with the only man I've ever loved? Of course I knew he'd bought an insurance policy. My policy lists him as beneficiary. So what?

Seth's funeral—which was held in spite of his explicit written instructions—took place while Keith was in prison. Through the numbness which had enveloped him since Seth's death came the added agony of knowing he could not keep his promise and have his lover's remains cremated.

Seth's lawyer paid Keith a visit in his cell concerning the funeral arrangements. The meeting was not propitious.

"In his will, Mr. Wilson, Seth named you executor of his estate. Under the present circumstances, I feel fully justified in allowing his family to make the necessary arrangements."

Keith felt the stirrings of anger—the only feeling other than despair he had experienced since hearing of Seth's death.

"That's high-handed of you," Keith retorted. "One would expect *Seth's* wishes to carry some weight with you. He didn't want to be buried—he wanted to be cremated."

"It is my opinion that Seth was unduly influenced . . . by you, Mr. Wilson." The lawyer's distaste for Keith oozed from him like sweat. "Mr. and Mrs. Rawson have gone through enough. I am not going to subject a religious man like Jeb Rawson to the indignity of an irreligious disposal of his only son's body." The man smirked and added, "In the unlikely event you somehow convince a jury of your innocence and decide to sue me, I'll at least have done what I believe best. Under such circumstances the remains might still be cremated. Should

Seth's wishes be carried out now, the Rawsons would be without recourse later on." He stood up and pushed some papers
under the bars of the window towards Keith. "I would like your
signature on these forms. Under the circumstances, I feel you
owe the family that much."

Keith glared at the man. "You insufferable bastard! I
wouldn't sign away Seth's chances to be at rest for anything!
Get out of my sight!"

Keith was led back to his cell. He spoke no more after that
disasterous interview. When the Chief continued questioning
him, Keith remained mute. When Keith belatedly decided
he'd better hire an attorney, he discovered no one was interested in taking on so controversial a client or case. Finally he
ceased looking. Keith's hopelessness—and helplessness—
were total. Without Seth, he had no life. Better to die and
follow Seth—beloved Seth—into whatever void the future
held.

The police persisted, playing psychological games with
Keith, alternately exhibiting sympathy only to follow with hints
mocking the two men's love for one another.

For countless days, hours—Keith lost track of time—he
was dragged from his cell to a brightly lit interrogation room.
There he faced their scorn, their endless words—words which
lost all meaning in a world where he and Seth were no longer a
couple.

The jailors—fat, ribald men—baited him ceaselessly
when they brought him food. He paid no attention to them. He
seldom ate. He lay on the narrow cot in his cell for hours, staring at the ceiling and trying, without success, to unravel a cob-
web in the corner with only his eyes. The diligent spider continued her work without a thought for the man beneath her.
How, Keith wondered, could the world continue?

The cell was dirty. Cockroaches periodically scurried

across the hard stone floor. After his first few days in jail, Keith started scattering crumbs of bread on the floor for the insects. Their movements provided distractions. He lay on his stomach watching them for hours, praying they would stay, begging them silently not to abandon him to the ghosts of memory.

Their first serious love-making by the river, just before he went away to the Air Force. His return, when Seth got a room at the motel . . . so many thoughts, so many memories. Painful memories . . . recollections which under other circumstances would have been beautiful reminders of a love, pure and une-qualed, now become sullied by the charges against him, by the untimely end of love. Love ended by the bullet from a gun.

Who had killed Seth?

Keith seldom embraced the thought. During the long questioning sessions, it was the charge hurled at him most of-ten by the police.

"If you didn't kill Seth Rawson, who did? No one else, as far as we can tell, disliked the man, much less hated him enough to murder him. Only you, Wilson, benefit from his death. Benefit to the tune of a hundred-thousand-dollar life in-surance policy, sole ownership of Rawson's garage, all of Rawson's other property, which is worth a fair amount—it's all left to you. No, with Seth Rawson dead, you stand to gain a great deal of money."

Then, gradually dragging out the real relationship be-tween Keith and Seth, the police used the pair's love of one another as yet another motive for murder.

"Wasn't Rawson getting tired of you? Going to leave you for someone else, maybe? Who knows with you queers. Or was he finally going to follow his family's advice and give up his perversion, settle down with a nice girl, raise a family, like men ought to do? Wasn't that why you killed him, Wilson? You couldn't stand the notion he was going to leave you for a woman?"

Through it all, Keith uttered not a word. There was nothing to say to the ridiculous allegations spoken by men who had
no concept of the life he and Seth had shared together. Dimly,
as much as anything registered during the period of questioning, came the realization of how alien homosexuals and hetero-
sexuals were from each other. Before Seth's death, Keith had
viewed heteros as misinformed but well-intentioned replicas of
himself and those like him who, sexually speaking, were in the
minority. He discovered how false that notion was to men like
the Chief of Police and his deputies.

14

Keith was charged with the murder of Seth Rawson eight days after the crime.

Once the formal action was taken by the Grand Jury, the system was forced to dig up an attorney for Keith. Finding a man willing to represent the accused killer was no easy matter. Most court-appointed counselors refused to touch the case, citing homosexual prejudices. Finally, a young man recently out of law school, who sported a full-length beard and was viewed as a decided radical, offered to take the case. The judges in the area were afraid the bearded fool might cause trouble, but as no established attorney stepped forward to sacrifice his career for the sake of troubled officialdom, Wade Tendell was assigned the case for the defense.

He met with Keith the morning after his appointment.

Keith was led from his cell by a burly, red-faced jailor.

"Finally got ye a mouthpiece, fag. Not many folks 'round here want any part of this business. Can't say as I blame 'em," the jailor continued in a cheerful, folksy tone. "Your kind are all sick, wantin' to make it with a guy when there's plenty of pussy 'round."

The jailor had been baiting his prisoner for several days. Only Keith's total listlessness prevented his attacking the man.

Tendell was seated at a small table in the conference room. He stood up as Keith entered and extended his hand.

"Mr. Wilson? I'm Wade Tendell. I've been appointed your attorney."

Keith ignored the hand and sat down.

"That must be a big thrill for you." Keith said.

Tendell glanced at his client, then seated himself across the table from Keith.

"I'm not going to be much good to you if you adopt that sort of attitude," Tendell said with a trace of bitterness.

"Do you expect to be able to do any good in the first place?" Keith inquired.

Tendell eyed Keith alertly. "Speaking honestly, no. Not at this level," he admitted. "Everyone here has already decided you're guilty as hell. The authorities don't want to be worried with finding out what really happened. On appeal, however, any conviction will have to be overturned. The bastards don't have a shred of evidence."

"Then what am I doing here?" Keith asked.

"You're here because you're gay, were involved in a homosexual relationship with the dead man and stand to gain a lot of money from his death. That's more than enough for this bunch."

"Why are you taking an interest?" Keith wanted to know.

Tendell chuckled. "They couldn't find anyone else willing to handle the case. They don't like me very much and figured this would be a good way to damage my practice and force me out of town."

Keith's interest wandered. Since Seth's death he had concluded his was a soul cast into hell; the outcome of the mockery called justice made little difference. There was no reason he could see to change his mind now. He noted the man opposite him was wearing a wedding band—to him the classical symbol of serfdom. Keith tossed Tendell into the ranks of unregenerated heteros.

" . . . hear your side of the story. Was the gun yours? Did you know—" Tendell, seeing he had lost his client's attention, shut up and simply sat silently in the chair across from Keith. After a long time, Keith became aware of the silence.

"Are you finished?" he inquired politely, much as a waiter might ask to be allowed to remove garbage-filled plates from a table.

"No, I'm not," Tendell snapped. "Goddammit, either you killed Rawson, in which case you deserve to be here—or you didn't, in which case you owe it to him to fight them every step of the way! Was your love for one another so damned weak and pitiful you don't care? Was there nothing—"

"You son-of-a-bitch! What do you know of our love? What does any straight know about us? You sit back with your smug assurances of self-proclaimed normalcy and gloat. I despise all of you—"

"And I hate it when you bastards think every heterosexual in the world is your enemy," Tendell interrupted harshly. "I might not fuck guys but I can understand love. I won't deny humanity to any man, just because he doesn't screw the way I do. Pull your goddamn shit together and fight!"

They stared at each other. Keith turned away first.

"It's too late to fight," he mumbled, "they've already buried him."

"What's that got to do with it?"

"I . . . I promised him . . . if he died before me, I'd have him cremated. He . . . he won't let me be till I keep that promise."

"You can't keep any promises as long as you're charged with killing him. Who is the executor of his estate?"

"I'm suppposed to be," Keith said.

"Who was Rawson's attorney?"

"Charles Thompson."

Tendell grinned. "We get you cleared of these charges, you're in a perfect position to sue the son-of-a-bitch. You win, gain control of the estate . . . and if you were of a mind, and if old Thompson doesn't destroy Seth's instructions, which I don't think he will—lawyers, by nature, are too cautious —you'd be able to order an exhumation and cremation on your authority as executor." The man came back to the matter at hand. "In order to achieve any of that, you've got to fight. Now, talk to me. Give me the facts as you know them. I won't fool you. We have no chance of winning here, at the local level. Given their meagre evidence, however, it should be possible to get any conviction overturned in the State Supreme Court. Those bastards in Atlanta aren't sympathetic either, but they are sticklers for points of law. And this case stinks."

Keith stirred uneasily and glanced at his unlikely saviour.

"If . . . if you eventually won, could I really get control of the estate and . . . and have Seth's wishes carried out?"

"Yes, I believe you could. It would depend on a lot of variables, but you'd be in a hell of a lot better position than you are now." Tendell glanced at Keith. "The burial business bothers you more than being in jail, doesn't it?"

"Yes. Yes, it does." Keith whispered the words, looked away and continued. "Every time I close my eyes . . . Seth is facing me, reproaching me, pleading with me not to let him stay in the ground like that . . . filthy, decaying . . . I can't stand it."

Keith cried.

Tendell felt a shiver race across his frame. For an instant he felt a third presence in the room with them. He shook off the forboding feeling and waited for Keith to recover.

When the sobs which racked Keith gradually subsided, Tendell gently asked again, "Please, tell me what happened . . . "

Keith gulped, raised his head and in a faltering voice told Tendell of his last night with Seth.

"You left close to three o'clock?" Tendell asked, after Keith finished his story. "The police have a witness who says you didn't reach your place till quarter to four. That's one of their strongest points. What were you doing? It's only a few blocks."

"I wasn't doing anything," Keith protested. "It was a beautiful evening, we'd had a magnificent time . . . I was thinking about our life together, the times we'd had, the things we'd done . . . I just wasn't in any hurry."

Tendell seemed to accept the explanation and went on to the next point.

"You're positive the gun isn't yours? I don't believe they've managed to trace it to you. If they had, they'd have told me that."

"It isn't mine. I've never owned a gun in my life. Seth was the outdoorsman, but even he didn't own a gun. We didn't like them much."

"We'll be thankful for small favors," Tendell grunted. "Okay, you say you didn't kill him—have you any idea who did? As far as the police can determine, nothing was taken. The house wasn't torn apart or anything. Robbery doesn't appear to be a motive. If robbery is ruled out, it must have been a personal killing. And if we're going to get you off, we'd do well to have someone to replace you with—in the eyes of the authorities."

"There isn't anyone," Keith muttered. "Seth was well-liked. Oh, I suppose some people who realized we were lovers didn't think much of him, but none of them killed him."

"Somebody did," Tendell stated. "How'd he get on with his family?"

Keith shook his head. "They would have liked it better if he hadn't hung around with me so much; I know his mother and father kept after him to marry. But they weren't insistent or nasty about things. His sisters never bothered him, either. A couple of them are married—their husbands bring their cars to Seth's garage. There wasn't any friction between Seth and his family. They knew I'd helped him buy the garage and accepted the fact we were close."

"Well," Tendell said, "until we come up with another suspect, we'll simply attack the evidence they're offering. It's only because of that insurance policy and the way your business affairs were intertwined that they believe they have a circumstantial case. That, and your lack of an alibi, is all they've got. It isn't much on which to obtain a murder conviction."

"Yet you think they'll succeed," Keith reminded him.

"Yes . . . I do. I hate being pessimistic, but I understand this community pretty well. The prosecution will point out Seth wasn't robbed, that you inherit everything and that you were both homosexuals. Since you're older, and because the district attorney will want to make the Rawsons feel better about having the homosexual angle dragged into the open, he'll make you out to be the one who corrupted Seth, kept after him, set him up in business . . . and when he decided to get out of the relationship, killed him rather than let him go."

"But none of that's true," Keith protested.

"Truth is relative," the lawyer said with a tight smile. "Truth is what most people want to believe; and in this case, a jury drawn from the local populace will want very badly to believe a strong, good-looking man like Seth would have been unhappy in such an unnatural relationship. Knowing these judges as I think I do, I expect we'll get a lot of reasons to appeal. So, don't get your hopes up when we go to trial. Our chance will come after that."

Tendell gathered up the papers he had used for note-taking and stuffed them into a shabby briefcase. "I'm going to try getting a friend of mine in the ACLU interested in this case. It's such a perfect example of railroading someone, I think they'll want in. That be okay with you? If they do come aboard, it will be because it has the earmarks of a cause for gay liberation. Will that annoy you?"

"I just want to be free to keep my promise," Keith said, suddenly showing the strain of the past few days.

"We'll work that out in time," Tendell reassured him. "Is there anything else?"

"I guess I'd better make arrangements about my house. There are bills to be paid, stuff like that. Maybe I ought to rent it. Even if I'm cleared eventually, I can't very well live around here. Wouldn't want to, without Seth."

Tendell sat back down. "Okay. Give me a list of the stuff you need taken care of. I'll do it, or let my wife handle it—give her a chance to help. That's the trouble with the law, you can get caught up in a disaster like this and your entire life is disrupted, sometimes destroyed, just because society's guardians don't know what they're doing. Still, once you're cleared, you'll have that insurance."

"Is that why you're interested in the case?" Keith asked, his suspicions returning.

Tendell stood up again. "I'll overlook that. You've been through a hell of a lot; and things aren't going to improve for awhile. Just try remembering, when your hatred for the whole fucking world floods you, that I am on your side. Surely you've known some gays who were bastards. Try thinking of me as one straight with a sense of fair play."

Keith was taken back to his cell.

The spider was still spinning her web, the cockroaches still nibbling on their crumbs. The ugly grime of the floor and the scummy film of dirt left in the cell from its countless occupants remained. Nothing had changed. Neither one nor a billion heteros with a sense of fair play would give him Seth in his arms again. He felt, if possible, a deeper despair than before.

Go ahead and find me guilty . . . see if I care, he challenged them. Murder me as you have him . . . and let me join him. Without him I cannot exist.

He closed his eyes and Seth rose up before him, troubled, frowning, pleading.

You promised you wouldn't let 'em do this. Stop feeling so damned sorry for yourself. Fight 'em! Do I mean nothing to you now? Whatever it takes, you gotta find the strength to help me. I only got you to depend on now.

Seth, Seth! I have no strength! I depended on you for everything. You were my whole life. How can you expect me to accomplish the impossible? I'm lost without you.

Bastard! If I was there, I'd slap the devil out of you! You can't give in. Use me, use the memories of our love, our times together, build me into your God, do whatever you gotta do, but keep that promise! I won't release you. I won't allow you rest till you satisfy me. I loved being the strong man of our duo, but all the power and courage I used in goading you has to be yours alone now. You never accepted the fact I needed you as much as you needed me. Ours wasn't a one-sided affair. Our love was equal. Now you gotta love for both of us. Help me. Love me. Avenge me!

Keith tossed in agony and the phantom faded. He sat up, his face and shirt wet with tears. He couldn't stand it—there had to be some release from the constant pain: *There had to be.*

But if there was, he couldn't find it. His agony grew. Pain spread and engulfed him like a raging fire spurred on by furious winds. There was no escape. Keith lay still, accepting the inevitable torture he could not diminish.

15

Time ceased having any meaning for Keith. Bail was set so high he made no attempt at raising it. Instead he gave power of attorney to his young lawyer. Tendell, an eternal optimist, declared there was no need for Keith to lose everything because of his current misfortune. Keith signed whatever the man thrust at him in order that he might return to the silence of his cell.

His cell. His cubicle—where Seth was present. Every day, every moment.

If Keith closed his eyes to sleep, Seth was there berating him for giving up, urging him to fight, to live—if only to fulfill his promise. Yet without the physical presence of Seth, Keith felt drained and empty. The memories of their lives together ceased being an asset; Keith needed Seth, not the searing pain which came each time his mind pronounced the name. The days spent in the cell seemed designed to strip away the mask of love and romance in order to reveal how desperate Keith's need was for the physical man Seth had been. There was no longer any rebellion in him. Life ceased for Keith the day he heard the words that Seth was dead. What happened to the shell he inhabited no longer made any difference to him.

The trial was a farce.

It was held in a circus atmosphere, jammed with the curious who wondered if the bizarre sexual practices they had heard so many rumors about would be described in shocking details.

Tendell worked hard. At first, he urged a change of venue—a suggestion which was promptly turned down. Then he went to work on prospective jurors, attempting as best he could to select men and women who at least said they could be fair and objective. The Judge, a cantankerous old man, opposed the young attorney at every turn, but when the process was over Tendell confessed to Keith that they had a couple of people on the panel who might prove to be impartial.

"If we're lucky," Tendell commented, "we may get a divided jury. In this town, that would be a victory."

Keith made up his mind he would pay no attention to the proceedings. It was as if George Orwell's pigs of *Animal Farm* were sitting in judgment of him. Yet as the drama unfolded, he could not completely shut out all the voices which droned at him from the witness box.

There was Alma Rawson, Seth's Mother.

"Didn't you worry, Mrs. Rawson, about your son's relationship with the accused?"

"I never thought about it. They were friends. They growed up together—right across the field from us, Keith was. After Seth, the Lord blessed us with only girls. It was only natural the two of 'em would be friendly, see a lot of one another."

"But later," the prosecutor persisted, "didn't it strike you as strange that your son's . . . friend . . . would put up the money for the garage? Didn't it cross your mind that there might be something . . . unnatural . . . in the way the defendant hung around your son?"

"No, it didn't," snapped Alma Rawson. "Seth dated girls, there wasn't nothin' unnatural about him! His business arrangements were his concern, not none of mine!"

She never glanced at Keith the entire time she was in the

courtroom. When her testimony was over, Tendell whispered they had been helped by her appearance.

Jeb Rawson was a different story.

"Did your son's closeness to the defendant give you cause for worry, Mr. Rawson?"

"Yes. Yes, it did. I never did cotton to Wilson. His folks wasn't what I'd want to call good Christian folks. They didn't instill the proper respect for the Lord in him. I kept an eye on him and Seth, but a man can only do so much. I spoke to Seth, time and again . . . tol' him he shouldn't be hangin' round with Wilson. Especially after they was growed up. Didn't look right, I tol' Seth."

"And what was his response?"

Jeb Rawson's anger echoed in his answer. "Tol' me to mind my own business. Not in so many words . . . but that was the gist of what he said. Me, his own father! I can . . . "

"Yes, Mr. Rawson . . . " The prosecutor smoothly moved on to other areas. Jeb's testimony was needed, but the prosecutor did not want the father's anger to filter through and alienate the jury.

The parade of witnesses continued as the state solidified their contention that the two men were engaged in a homosexual affair, that Seth had tried to end the unhappy situation and was killed because of the attempt.

Keith's connection with the committee at the university a few years earlier was brought out and used to exemplify the defendant's perversity.

Keith closed his eyes and heard Seth's rebuke.

I told you it was dumb, gettin' mixed up with that damned bunch.

Okay, okay, so you were right. How was I to know something like this would happen?

Tendell leaned over. "Did you say something?" he asked.

Keith, not aware he'd murmured aloud, shook his head.

Letters Keith had written to Seth were introduced and read aloud to the amusement of the gathering. It was the only part of the proceedings which reached Keith. He leaned over and whispered to Tendell:

"Can't you stop this?"

Tendell shook his head. "I'm sorry, I've tried."

Keith listened as his love for Seth was held up to the town's ridicule. Their insensitivity, their mockery of all which was precious and beautiful to him, seared Keith's spirit. He would have killed them all at that moment had he the power to do so.

Fools! Groveling in your split-level mortgaged homes with your screaming kids, big cars and sanctimonious religious conventions. You dare stand in judgment of a love more sincere than any you've ever known. Your jealousy of what I've had reeks to your fucking God in Heaven! There was no marriage contract holding Seth to me, no children forcing us to remain by each other's side, no false beliefs saying we dared not separate. Only love kept us together. A love so far beyond the boundaries of your imagination, you hate us because we found it.

The trial entered a third day. In the state's attempt to prove Keith's guilt, they skirted the question of the gun's ownership, having been unable to discover how, where or when he obtained it. Neither could they find anyone able to state positively that Seth and Keith were breaking up. There was no evidence Seth was planning to leave the "strange and unnatural relationship."

Instead, the prosecutor stressed Keith's lack of an alibi, his monetary motive and the contention that the bonds between the two men were faltering. Even Tendell was startled by the weakness of the State's case. When the defense got its turn, Tendell attacked every position the prosecution had raised. Keith found himself surprised at his lawyer's emotion and ability. The man was good. He felt a flicker of hope. Might justice actually triumph? No. He glanced at the impassive faces in the jury box and knew he had no chance.

After the summations, the jury retired to their deliberations. A day passed. Midafternoon of the second day they trooped in and announced to a furious judge that they were hopelessly deadlocked. He angrily ordered them back to reconsider where their duty lay. There was no doubt in his mind; why should there be in theirs?

Tendell was ecstatic.

"We'll get a hung jury!" he exclaimed.

"What good will that do?" Keith asked, weary of the madness. "You know that bastard of a judge won't release me; I can't raise the bail he's set. We'll simply have to do the whole thing over again. Next time, you may be sure they'll see the jury is packed with their types."

"Let's wait and see." Tendell couldn't be expected to view the case in the same light as Keith. A no-decision would be a tremendous victory for him.

And, after another twenty-four hours, that was what they got.

The Judge demanded the jury be polled. To Keith's astonishment, five members of the panel had held out for acquittal.

But he was not free. Try as Tendell would, the judge would not reduce bail, nor consider a release under any circumstance. The case was a bitter defeat for the old man; he was determined to see evil, personified by Keith Wilson, punished. In the meantime, the pervert could rot in jail.

After weeks of legal wrangling, Tendell's original request for a change of venue was accepted. The irate Judge assigned the case to a nearby district controlled by a friend of his, where he could be sure the defense would find no sympathy.

Nothing changed. The search for whoever killed Seth had long since been abandoned. Seth's body lay in the ground he detested. Nightly, Keith awoke, sweating from visions and

nightmares he could not control. There had to be an end to the
terror and despair each night brought. It was to come sooner
than he dared anticipate.

One bright summer day he was jerked awake by the burly
jailor.

"Come on, fag, get up! We're finally gettin' rid of you!"

Keith refrained from answering.

In the conference room, Tendell explained the remark.
"They've decided to move you to Albany. The new trial is supposed to open in a couple of weeks, if no further delays crop
up. I'll try getting over there to consult with you as often as I
can. Believe me, I'm doing everything possible. This is turning into a classic example of legal excess. We'll come through
it yet." He grinned and added, "You might enjoy knowing that
Seth's lawyer, Charles Thompson, has approached me about a
compromise if you're not convicted. The insurance company
has been nosing around, too, making subtle offers. We're in
better shape than ever. Hang in there."

That's easy for you to say, you're not the one sitting in
here watching spiders and roaches. You're not being subjected to taunts, or visions of the one you love rotting in some goddamned hole in the ground.

Keith was handcuffed and placed in the police car. It was
the first time he had been outside his cell since his trips to and
from the courthouse for the first trial. Summer had always been
his favorite season . . . *their* season. As the car sped along, he
recalled memories of brighter days, days with Seth, days of joy
so far removed from these months of agony.

"Look at our fag," the driver jeered, peering into his mir-
ror. "So sorry to leave us, he's cryin'." He glanced at his part-
ner. "Guess he's upset 'cause he ain't had no dick for so long."

"Reckon we could remedy that," replied the other cop.
"There's lots of places 'long the way where we could stop and
give him what he's cryin' for."

Keith shuddered. Maybe he should run and let them shoot him. Death would be more welcome than accommodating these fat pigs.

Could the pair be serious? It was hard to tell. Keith kept a wary eye on the men in front, wondering what he should do if they followed through. There appeared to be little he could do. His mind was so preoccupied with the possible problem that he was paying no attention to the road. Suddenly the police car swerved to one side. Another vehicle rushed past, struck the side of the cop car and sent it hurtling down the side of a small ravine. Keith, unable to do anything else, put his hands over his head and lay back on the seat. The auto tumbled rapidly, coming to rest against a massive pine tree. One of the doors, locked when Keith was placed in the back seat, sprung open. He lay on the floor of the car dazed, trying to assess himself.

Nothing seemed broken. Gingerly he wiggled his toes, feet, hands. They all worked. Silence engulfed him. He peered over the seat into the front of the car and saw the cops were not moving. Whether dead or only briefly unconscious, he couldn't tell.

Using his feet to push open the damaged door, Keith climbed out of the car. On the road above, traffic continued zooming by without any awareness of the accident. In that instant, Keith heard Seth's voice:

Damn it, you gonna stand 'round all day? Get the hell outta here! How many chances you need?

How can I keep my promise to you if I'm a fugitive?

You sure as hell won't do me any good cooped up in a cell. That mouthpiece might get you out and he might not. You'll never be free till they find out who killed me, and they sure as hell ain't doin' anything 'bout that. Get your ass away from here!

Keith shook his head. It ached and buzzed every time he tried to reason. Well? Why the hell not?

He opened the driver's side of the car. The cop was slumped over the wheel. The key to the handcuffs dangled from his pocket. Keith reached down, plucked them from the man's pants and released himself. He rubbed his wrists, threw the keys back into the car and felt the cop's pulse. It was reedy, but steady. How much time did he have? It didn't make much difference, he supposed. He'd need some money. He started to reach for the cops' wallets when he suddenly remembered they'd put all his effects in the back of the car. He grabbed the key from the ignition and opened the trunk. It was badly bent from the tumble, but after a brief struggle he managed to raise it. He saw the bag with his clothes, ID and money. He checked and discovered he had nearly forty dollars. Not much . . . but maybe enough to keep from starving. He threw the car keys back in the front seat, checked the pulses of his captors and found them marginally stronger.

Fuck all of you. You may have me back in a couple of hours, but by God, I'm going to take a chance.

That's the way, bastard. Don't look back.

With his vision of Seth encouraging him and goading him—accompanied by a surge of anger and rage over the reaction in court to his letters to Seth—Keith ran. If he could reach Atlanta, he might be able to lose himself in the gay underground, perhaps drag himself back to some semblance of sanity. Then, someday, it might be possible to return to Tilton and discover who really killed Seth.

The thought was hollow and foolish. Keith knew if he succeeded in getting to Atlanta, and was lucky enough to remain undetected, he would never be able to return to Tilton. How could he keep his promise to Seth if he couldn't return? He seized his wallet and gazed at the photo of Seth he always carried with him.

He trembled. How could be dare hope to live again . . .

Damn it, get goin'! I'll never release you from that prom-

ise, but I always was reasonable. This is a once-in-a-lifetime chance. Take it! Make the bastards look for you. Worry about gettin' back to Tilton tomorrow, or the day after. I'm goin' to be with you, fella. Every step you take, I'll be inside your head, remindin' you of what you owe me, guidin' you with my memory, forcin' you to evaluate what you do in terms of what we had. Go! For once in your life, take a chance. This time, don't think about the risks, think of the challenge. Don't be so goddamned cautious. Go!

Keith snapped the wallet shut and jammed it into his pocket. Picking up his small bag of possessions, he trotted away from the site of the wrecked car. He fled into the summer sunlight . . . a fugitive. He had no idea if his action was sensible or not. It didn't matter. Life without Seth was worthless anyway. He might as well attempt a radical tactic for a change.

16

Keith's perception of what constituted being a fugitive came primarily from books and films. Having never run away before, he was at a distinct disadvantage. Nor did he have any idea of how much time would lapse before the law began looking for him. If the cops he'd left behind remained unconscious for a time it would be helpful, but he couldn't count on such good fortune.

He wondered if they would want to find him badly enough to set dogs on his trail. That was how most escapees were captured during their first hours of flight in the movies. If he could pick up a few supplies and head for the river which flowed past Albany, he might stand a chance.

Keith climbed up onto the road, making sure no vehicles were approaching before he emerged from the brush. The way was clear so he set off in the direction of Albany. Hitching was a risk, but so was staying in the vicinity of the wrecked cop car.

A car approached going in the wrong direction. Keith, during the first moment of his escape, began feeling the fear which would accompany him for months. The vehicle whizzed past without realizing it was passing a murder suspect. A couple of cars going his way swept past. Neither slowed down. He continued walking at a rapid rate, turning only when he heard the sound of approaching traffic.

The sixth one which came along held an aged farmer driving an ancient pickup. The venerable machine slowed and halted. Keith raced to accept the lift.

"Hot day fer walkin'," the farmer said, opening the conversation.

"Sure is," Keith shot back. "My blasted car busted a water hose and everybody 'round the house was gone; figured I'd hoof it into town and pick one up."

The farmer accepted the excuse. They drifted into a dialogue about the summer drought and the poor condition of crops. It was the sort of talk Keith had heard for countless years; he had no trouble maintaining his end of the conversation. At last the river came into view. Once past it, he asked to be let out at the first hardware store he saw. A moment's goodbye and he found himself alone again.

At the hardware store he spent a good portion of his money for rope, a knife and some fishline and hooks. Next step was a small grocery store where he bought a loaf of bread and some peanut butter. A couple of books of matches, a plastic bag and a small pot concluded his purchases. The items fit snugly into the bag the police had used to hold his personal effects and clothes. He started towards the river.

Keith glanced at his watch. Only forty-five minutes had lapsed since the accident. Suppose the car wasn't found for hours and the cops were seriously injured? He didn't believe they were, but you couldn't tell. He sighed. Given the fact they'd talked of raping him, he didn't feel he owed them any consideration, but a time might come, if his venture proved unsuccessful, when it would be to his advantage if they survived the mishap. He stopped at a pay phone and called the Albany police.

"You got a cop car disabled on eighty-two east, with a couple of injured men in it." He mumbled the words and hung up. That should help get the bastards medical attention yet allow him time to put his plan into effect. It might, he supposed, take them awhile to find out he'd even reached Albany; these cops weren't the smartest of people.

He reached the river. With any luck he could follow the waterway almost to Atlanta. He didn't plan on staying near the water the whole time, just long enough to throw any dogs off his scent. He looked at the water with a critical eye. The drought had lowered the water level a great deal, but it didn't look as if it was going to be easy traveling.

Should he wade up the riverbed barefoot and protect the only pair of shoes he had, or keep his shoes on? Decisions of this nature were hard for him to make. He sat down on the bank and removed the sturdy shoes he was wearing. No sense ruining them at the start; try it without them first, see how he made out. He rolled up his pants legs and stepped into the murky water.

It didn't take long for Keith to decide he'd made a major mistake. Nearly every step brought him to disaster, stepping on all the debris in the river. As a way of escaping, Keith felt rivers were overrated. After half an hour of hellish struggle, he was barely beyond sight of the road. Unless he improved his speed it would be the dead of winter before he got to Atlanta— assuming he didn't drown first. Much as he hated to, he climbed to the shore and put his shoes back on.

He was able to move faster with his feet protected, although once his shoes got wet they rubbed his feet, causing blisters and making progress painful. The trekking was worse because he had no idea of how far he'd advanced. Two miles? Three? After three hours, he fervently wished he'd stayed in the police car. The only sign he was making headway was the gradual disappearance of houses as he moved north. But as he left civilization behind him, the river grew wilder, travel harder. He was thirsty, but the water was so dirty-looking he dared not drink any without first boiling it. If he stopped too soon, the dogs might pick up his trail. His only option was to keep moving. Doggedly he pushed on.

It began to grow dark. He would soon have to climb onto the bank and set up a camp for the night, boil some water and eat something. Maybe he could catch a fish.

Just a few more feet, then head for that clump of trees up ahead, he thought.

He could get that far, he told himself. He forced his feet forward—and stepped into a deep hole. Stumbling, barely managing to keep his bag of gear out of the water, Keith made a lot of noise and cursed profusely.

"I ain't gonna catch no fish with you wadin' 'round in the goddamn water makin' all that racket," protested a voice in the gathering darkness.

Keith froze.

Ahead of him, moored about fifteen feet away, was a tiny boat. The boat's occupant was a man around Keith's age. He was lean and hardened, brown as a pecan hull from what Keith could see. A type who might cause trouble.

"Damn it, get the hell outta the fuckin' water! Come up here and climb in the boat. Rather have you in here than in the river!"

Keith considered the request for a second. It was more command than request, and he decided he had no real choice in the matter. Any disagreement with the fisherman would result in his being remembered more vividly than if he acquiesced. Keith reached the edge of the boat and flopped over the side.

"There's beer in the cooler," the fisherman drawled, pointing to the item in the corner of the boat. "He'p yourself."

"Got any water?" Keith asked, "I'm pretty thirsty."

"Nope. No water—just beer. Go ahead, drink all you want. Got plenty more back at camp."

Keith took a can from the cooler and popped the tab. Never had anything tasted so good. Freedom had advantages.

"That's a damnfool thing to do," the fisherman commented after a space of time.

"What is?"

"Wading up the river like that. Saw you comin' long time ago. If'n you're runnin' away, you won't git fer. Ain't cut out fer it."

Obviously an explanation of some sort was needed in a hurry, but Keith's tired mind refused to hit on anything reasonable.

"I've got a bet going with some friends of mine," he began lamely.

"Shit! You're runnin' from the law, way I see it. Don't know what the fuck you're doin' and seen too damn many picture shows." The man laughed. The sound was hard and mean.

"I ain't got no use fer pigs—you don't try cuttin' my throat, we'll git along fine."

What the hell is that supposed to mean? I don't plan on being around you that long—

Keith soon learned he was mistaken.

"How fer you goin'? Where you tryin' to git to?"

"Eventually, Atlanta."

"All the way up the fuckin' river?" The man's voice held an incredulous note.

"Well . . . "

"You won't never make it." The tone was firm. "Toss me a beer. It's gettin' too dark to fish anyways." He took the can Keith handed him and popped the tab. "I got me a camper back up a ways. Rented it fer the night. Tomorrow, I'm takin' this here boat up to Lake Blackshear. You better stay with me tonight. Nobody's gonna give a damn." He laughed again. "You sure as hell ain't gonna git to 'Lanta without some he'p."

"Suits me," Keith answered. "Don't see why you'd want to bother though. Aren't you worried it might be dangerous?"

"You? Shit! I been around. You might'a done whatever they say you done, but you don't look bad to me. I reckon I'm more of a hell-raiser than you'll ever be. You probably in more danger'n me, if'n I get tight. I like fightin' and you don't look like no fighter to me."

"I'm not."

"See, what'd I tell you." He stood up. "Come on, take the cooler, grab your shit and hop out. I'm gonna move the boat down to that there tree and lock it up fer the night."

Keith did as he was told. Watching the dark form of the boat glide towards the tree, he wondered what he was letting himself in for. The guy looked like the bullies he had put up with in high school and the Air Force. A real redneck without a brain in his stupid head. But the thought of sleeping in some sort of bed, without the danger of snakes, mosquitoes and redbugs was alluring. Any danger from the fisherman receded.

The man appeared out of the dark. "Come on," he ordered. "Reckon we gotta call each other something. I'm Jake."

"Keith."

They moved through the darkness without other words. After a twenty-minute walk, they stepped onto concrete and Keith found himself at a small campsite which advertised trailers for rent by the night. Jake stopped in front of one, inserted a key and said, "You're filthy. Wait here . . . Take off your shoes."

Keith sat on the tiny steps and removed his shoes. His feet were rubbed raw from his time in the water. Jake returned with a towel.

"There's showers over yonder," he pointed in the direction of the cubicles. "You got a clean pair of pants with you?"

"Yes."

"Wash out your shoes and come back barefoot. Maybe they won't be ruint too bad."

Keith couldn't believe how good the clean, lukewarm water felt to his tired body. Being an escapee wasn't all it was cracked up to be. He wondered if he was making a wise decision, but the hellish day, the startling encounter with his rescuer and the two beers he'd consumed on an empty stomach all contributed to make thinking futile.

When he tapped on the trailer door again, he felt marginally better.

Jake opened the door. The trailer was small, barely room for the two of them to turn around. Jake had cleaned the fish he'd caught while Keith was showering. Some of these were frying on the tiny stove.

"Reckon you can look after these while I clean up?"

"Yes."

There was no television in the small vehicle, but a radio provided distraction. The news came on just as Jake left. Keith's escape was mentioned. The officers were reported to be in stable and improving condition. Keith fried the fish and wondered what he ought to do next.

Jake returned. He had not bothered to put on his shirt, exposing a bare, hard-muscled chest. His dungarees were low on his hips, and for a second Keith felt the stirrings of urges he thought had died with Seth.

Damn it, how can I think of sex with anyone else?

Bastard! How can't you? I don't expect you to be celibate. Do what you have to do to make the road easier.

Keith was startled. He knew Seth would want him to have other men, but one like Jake? Sighing, Keith decided his new life would have to be built upon the sands of wait-and-see. In the past, he never had left anything to chance. Now, his whole existence was one big gamble. A chance he would reach Atlan-

ta free and in one piece. A remote chance he might somehow
establish himself and sort things out. And a chance, even more
farfetched, that he might discover who killed Seth, and clear
himself.

"Throw me a beer," Jake intruded upon Keith's thoughts
with his coarse voice.

Keith obliged. "These fish are almost ready."

" 'Bout time; I'm hungry."

They sat down at the small table and ate the meal in relative silence. Towards the end of the repast, Jake looked directly at Keith and asked, "You that queer that got away, ain't
you?"

Keith froze. For a brief second, he almost panicked. Then
he mentally shrugged and decided it was useless denying the
obvious. The guy already had guessed he was a fugitive, and
for whatever reasons remained helpful. Keith decided the truth
was his best option.

"Yes, I am."

Jake nodded, as if pleased by the confirmation of what
he'd suspected.

"Did you kill the guy?"

"No, I didn't."

"Why you runnin' then? They didn't find you guilty.
You might git off."

"Hell may be ice cold, too, but I don't want to find out."
Keith's bitterness flowed with his words.

"But you are queer, ain't you?"

"Yes."

"Ain't never tried doin' it with a guy. You don't like
women? For sex I mean—can't stand the bitches myself,
otherwise."

"No, women don't interest me sexually." Keith was
tense, waiting.

"What did you do, you'n him?"

What a fucking question! What the hell do you think we did?

Keith didn't like the notion of going into details about his sex life with Seth. At the same time he needed Jake's help if the man were willing to give it, and a glance at his companion convinced Keith the question was asked more out of an honest desire to know than from any sense of ridicule.

He answered the query, editing many of the intimate details.

Jake absorbed the information.

"Don't sound much different from screwin' a girl. Except for the guy who's gittin' it. Don't it hurt?"

Keith grinned briefly. "No," he answered, "not if the guy doing the fucking knows what he's doing."

Jake shrugged. "I reckon if a guy likes it, it's okay. Me, I don't know." Jake's statement made it sound as if someone had propositioned him and he had to reach a decision. Keith sensed in that instant the man was interested. Or horny.

Jake, his tongue loosened by the several beers he'd consumed, grew talkative. "I've always thought queers were sissies, but you don't look like no sissy. You ain't real tough, but you lasted longer on the river than I'd 'a thought. You got the makin's of a good body on you. Ain't fat, either. Don't like fatties." He sipped more beer and returned to his original complaint. "Women!" He spat the word, making it an epithet. "If they didn't have pussies, they wouldn't be worth shit. I reckon you think something's wrong with my head 'cause I ain't done called the cops on you." Jake grinned at Keith's embarrassment. "Hell, if they was offerin' a re-ward, maybe I would—but I ain't gonna do it fer no other reason." He grew serious.

"I ain't never liked cops. Women either, I reckon. My ma, she was a regular whore. Always runnin' 'round with some guy. The old man, he was okay. Me 'n him got on pretty good. He drank a lot—wasn't much fun then, but other times we got along okay. He'd take me fishin' out here," Jake gestured towards the river. "Hell, when I was ten, eleven, he'd bring me down here, give me a beer—he was all right."

Keith waited, knowing more was coming.

"He wasn't dumb—he knew the bitch was runnin' 'round. Once in a while he'd catch her, knock the hell outta her. Didn't do no good, though. She'd keep on screwin' 'round on him." Jake shook his head. "It what'n as if he was bad—mean to her. He worked most of the time, kept food on the table. Liked his booze once in a while was all. She took that to mean she could run 'round. Well, one night he came home 'n found her gone. He waited up till she came in. Real late it was; they started shoutin', hollerin'. He whacked her a time or two and she started yellin'. Some son-of-a-bitch called the cops. Two cars full of 'em came to the house, tryin' to break it up and that pissed the old man off real good. He was lit, and not thinkin' too straight. Got out his gun and tol' 'em to mind their own business. They kilt him."

Jake was quiet for a long time after he spoke the words. Finally he added. "That's why I hate cops. And why I ain't got much of an opinion of women. Neither one of 'em's anything but trouble."

Keith was startled by the revelations. Jake's words, in spite of the stark tale they related, helped—by showing the fleeing man that others, too, had suffered. Maybe, in spite of everything, his own tribulations would pass. Not that that would bring Seth back to him.

All actions are beyond recall. No regrets, no apologies, *nothing* could erase an act once it was placed into the mainstream of time. That, Keith thought, is where so much of what he'd studied had been wrong. In the meantime, he had to go on. He had to continue living. Could he justify himself with the bromide that "Seth would have wanted me to?" Did he have to?

Jake leaned back on the small stool and rubbed his crotch. He watched Keith with a speculative glance.

"Reckon you could he'p me out?"

Keith looked at him steadily. "I've not had sex for three months. I'd like to make it with you—if you're sure you want me to. I wouldn't want you waking up pissed in the morning. It's no big thing. If you're horny, we can give it a try."

Jake got off the stool and went over to the bed, where he sprawled himself upon it.

"I ain't gonna be pissed. I'm a little tight . . . maybe I'll use that for an excuse if'n I need one. But nobody's gonna know; I want'a see what it's like."

"Okay." Keith got up and stripped off his shirt. Then he approached the bed.

He knew better than to try kissing the man. Kissing on the lips was always the last bastion to fall. Men—many of them at least—never minded where they stuck their cocks, so long as they weren't expected to have mouth to mouth contact.

Keith started off caressing Jake's firm chest, touching the nipples which were hard and slightly projected. Knowing the guy wouldn't be used to the sensation, Keith refrained from pinching them heavily. He let his hands roam over Jake's biceps, then edged his moving fingers down to the man's levi-sheathed legs. He licked the flesh which was bare above the pants and slowly unhooked the button at the top. Jake raised himself so Keith could slide the trousers off his brown body. The fisherman's cock was hard and big. Keith couldn't believe how much he wanted it. He wished he could take the belt from the loops and hand it to the man, but decided that would be going too far, too fast.

He reckoned, however, without Jake.

Jake suddenly stood up. He was a beautiful figure of a man, and, towering over Keith, Jake's face looked mean and vengeful. Jake braced himself, grabbed Keith's head and pulled it towards his cock. Keith sucked it willingly, loving the feel of both the cock and the hands which gripped his face and neck. He stopped pulling on the cock and ran his tongue over Jake's hands. A brief look at Jake's face convinced Keith the man was not unhappy with the evening—so far, at least.

Jake's hands pulled Keith up from the floor.

"Might as well drop your pants, hadn't you?"

Keith undressed. They stood inches apart, their cocks rubbing against each other.

"You want to get fucked?" Jake asked the question as if to have something to say.

Keith nodded and said, "But let's not rush things. We've got plenty of time." He hesitated, then plunged: "I'd like to kiss you."

Jake, for a moment, seemed to think over the request, then shrugged his shoulders in agreement.

Keith backed up to the bed and lowered himself onto it, pulling Jake down to him. Their lips met, tentative at first as Jake struggled momentarily with the newness of kissing a man. Discovering, however, that the act was essentially the same with a man as with a woman, and stimulated by Keith's actions, Jake quickly surrendered himself to the pleasures of sex.

For a man who was supposed to be without experience, Jake proved to be quite adept. They found themselves restrained only by the size of the bed, which was so small. As they led each other closer and closer to climax, Keith felt a surge of strength and power pulsating in Jake. As Jake became caught up in the spirit of the game, his touch grew more competent—and rougher. Once, crushing Keith harder than he intended, the fisherman muttered, "Didn't hurt you, did I?"

"No. I like things rough."

The next hour expanded both their horizons: Keith's because Jake's whole approach to sex was so different from Seth's; Jake's because he learned how potent was the combination of sex and power, and he willingly succumbed to the lure of both. He concluded the session by furiously pounding Keith's ass, assauging a profound sexual hunger in both men. Spent and exhausted, yet filled with a deeply satisfied physical and emotional euphoria, they slept.

17

The fact he slept so well surprised Keith. It was the first time in months that he had been in bed with anyone. Jake's body was warm, pleasant to wake up next to; Keith wanted another round with him, but wondered if Jake, sober, would be as willing as he'd been the night before.

When Jake opened his eyes, there was an initial moment when Keith sensed his rescuer was ill-at-ease, but Keith reached out to arouse his companion and the uneasiness fled. Shrugging off any reservations he may have felt, Jake performed as enthusiastically as he had the previous evening.

Afterwards, Jake glanced at Keith's watch and suggested they better clean up and be on their way.

"We got a ways to go; ain't no sense lettin' the cops find you're still 'round here. Not that they're goin' to." Jake hopped out of the bed. "You oughtta let your beard grow. Time you get to 'Lanta most folks wouldn't recognize you."

Grabbing a towel, Jake headed for the showers while Keith got some coffee ready. As he drank his first cup, a sense of something close to satisfaction swept over him.

Don't get too pleased with yourself, bastard! I don't mind you screwin' around: I'm not there to help you out in that department. But don't forget, you're still a fugitive. Your future don't look too bright—and you owe me a promise. Keep things in perspective.

I will. But you've told me for three months now to pull myself together and start thinking about life . . . without you. You know better than I how much I miss you, how much I need you . . . I'm just learning I can still function; in spite of the fact I don't have you . . .

You'll always make out okay if you just remember what I tried teachin' you. Now that I'm not there to look out for you, you're gonna have to do it yourself. And for that reason . . . I'm glad you had a good time. But I am jealous.

There's no need to be. Not ever.

"What'd you say?"

Jake had returned.

"Nothing," Keith replied. "Just talking to myself. Found I was doing that a lot while I was sitting in that jail cell."

Jake nodded, adding, "Better go shower. We need to be movin' on."

In daylight, in a boat, Keith found the river less formidable. Jake cranked up the tiny motor and they chugged off.

The trip was scenic, oddly relaxing to Keith. Jake was quiet, but Keith could tell it was not an embarrassed silence. The man, with the few words he had spoken, had set Keith's mind at ease on that score.

"You in a hurry 'bout gettin' to 'Lanta?"

"No. I'm heading in that direction because Atlanta's big enough to get lost in, I hope, and it's got a large gay—homosexual—population. I expect I can find someone to stay with for a day or two."

"You won't have no trouble. Queers—what you call 'em? Gays?—don't have no reason to like cops. You'll do okay. What I figured was this: If'n you ain't in no hurry, we can git a place up on the lake tonight. Tomorrow, the next day, whenever you've a mind to, I can take you up to the north end of the lake where it flows down from upstate. We could throw a raft together—you could pole it the rest of the way up the river.

It'd be slow, but what the hell. They wouldn't be lookin' fer you traveling that way."

"Fine with me," Keith agreed. He wanted to thank Jake but sensed words would be both inadequate and inappropriate.

Having settled his affairs for the next day or two, Keith was left with a delicious sense of freedom he had not expected to ever feel again. Before Seth's death he had lived years into the future. Planning, scheming, working out what he would be doing weeks, sometimes months, in advance. He'd always scorned those of his friends who blew their money in a day, never thinking about what would happen when they were broke. And, in one sense, he still respected foresightedness. After all, had he not been vulnerable at the time of Seth's death, he would have inherited the shop and the insurance Seth tried providing. The difficulties they had sought to avoid with Seth's family *would* have been avoided. From that viewpoint, their well-laid plans were sensible.

But, as a result of the horrible sequence of events which had overtaken him, Keith was learning the value of living each day as it arrived. Never being sure he would *have* a future, there was little use in planning for it. Before being tossed in jail, he would have shuddered at the notion of having no idea where he would be sleeping three days hence. Now it was a small measure of utopia knowing he had a place to stay for the approaching evening. And the man who went with the deal wasn't bad either. He glanced at his companion and found Jake eyeing him.

"You scared, ain't you?"

"Some," Keith admitted. "But I was thinking more about the fact the next twenty-four hours are settled. I used to plan everything weeks in advance. Have schedules for this and that; now, a day at a time is a luxury."

Jake nodded. He understood.

After an hour and a half's ride, Jake pulled into a slight

cove, tree-shaded, where they got out the fishing gear and tossed their lines over the side of the boat. Jake, who had made certain the cooler was filled, tossed a beer to Keith.

Another new experience.

Drinking before noon: He and Seth never drank much at any time, trying to be conscious of physical fitness. Or at least Seth was, and whatever Seth demanded of him, Keith had sought to accomplish. Given his present circumstances it was one more debt he owed Seth. Were he not in half-decent shape he could never had contemplated escaping in the first place.

The day's pace continued in leisurely fashion. They fished in the alcove for about an hour and had a couple of beers before continuing their journey. They reached the shores of Lake Blackshear late in the afternoon. Jake left Keith with the boat while he went to pay the fee which allowed them to put the boat into the lake. When Jake returned, they ported the craft fhe short distance from the river to the other side of the spill-way. A park policeman in uniform gave Keith a start. Was this what running was like? Afraid of his shadow? Noticing the re-action, Jake offered advice.

"Don't git shook every time you see a pig. Most times, they ain't gonna give you a second thought. You look too nor-mal. Polin' up that river'll give you time to grow a beard. Do that: act natural-like if you run into a fuzz—they won't take no notice of you. Too damn lazy. If'n they was to catch you, they'd have to work their fat asses off doin' paperwork."

Keith nodded. It made sense. What made no sense to him was the position he was in. As had happened so often over the past three months, he felt almost on the verge of waking from a long nightmare. Only the dull, steady ache which accompa-nied every thought and remembrance of Seth convinced him he was awake and living a dreadful truth.

They slid the boat into the lake and Jake took off for the

camp, where he rented another cabin. It was midway up the shore of the lake: a perfect spot for lovers. As Keith moved around in the cottage's tiny kitchen, preparing some food for them, drinking from a beer can, he found himself wishing he and Seth had done something like this. They had been so damned careful. The future always had loomed ahead of them—so important, especially to Seth. There were plenty of memories, beautiful and wonderous, of their days together; but there could have been so many, many more.

Jake stepped out of the shower and sat down on the edge of the bed, wearing only the towel he'd dried with.

"Turn that stuff off and come here," he ordered.

Keith did as he was told.

Jake pulled Keith down to his side. "I know I ain't him, but I reckon he wouldn't mind. Not if'n he loved you. I liked last night. Can we do it again?"

Keith looked up into the greenish eyes, unable to fathom the man behind them. By all accounts Jake should have wanted to beat the hell out of Keith or been scornful of the situation. Jake was an uneducated redneck completely without sophistication. Yet he was helping a stranger flee the law, paying Keith's expenses and even more inexplicably, *asking* if they could fuck!

Keith drew the green-eyed face down close to his mouth where he could bite the ear lobe and whisper quietly, "You're right, he wouldn't mind. And you're damned right we'll do it again—you're one hell of a man!"

The next morning they fished the upper reaches of the lake for a couple of hours. Their patience was rewarded with three fine bass. At noon they took their catch back to the cabin, and in the afternoon, walked up to the end of the lake, where Jake looked around for stuff to use in the construction of a raft. The wooded area yielded logs which were suitable, and Jake,

using the hatchet he'd brought with him, soon had the makeshift craft ready. Keith's rope was the only other thing they
needed.

"That didn't take long," Keith commented.

"Naw, nothin' to it. Main thing is to find a decent pole.
One that won't break. We might oughtta get a couple, let you
have a spare, but it'd be in the way. I'll let you have this here
ax; then if you break the first one, you can cut another."

They tramped around the woods for nearly an hour before
Jake found what he was looking for. He cut it, trimmed away
the twigs and handed it to Keith, "Better git the feel of it, you
gonna be usin' it a hell of a lot." He grinned as he spoke.

Jake insisted Keith try the craft. Between them, they carried it down to the water's edge and Keith gingerly stepped
onto the logs. It was not very steady, and for a while it seemed
that every inch he moved forward the current swept him several
feet backward.

"Stay closer to the edge," Jake instructed. "If'n you git in
the middle of the damned river, it'll carry you back down-
stream. On the edge, the flow ain't as strong, and polin' won't
be as rough."

After half an hour of poling, Keith had reached the point
he was making limited progress. Jake laughed good-naturedly.
"The rate you're goin', you'll be back in Albany 'fore I am."

They returned to the cabin. "You fix the fish," Jake ordered. "I'm gonna take the boat and run down to the landing.
We need more beer, and I want'a get a few things for you to
take with you tomorrow."

They had decided Keith would leave the following day.
Jake only had two days left on his vacation and he would be
going back in the opposite direction.

"Don't spend too much," Keith said.

"Hell, don't worry 'bout it."

The cabin was cool and quiet. Keith, much as he hated to,

turned on the radio to see if anything was being said about him. The country stations Jake listened to had barely reported the escape. Now he was being totally ignored as a news story. It was better that way.

On the spur of the moment, Keith sat down and wrote a note to Wade Tendell, explaining the circumstances which led to his escape. The rape talk on the part of the cops furnished as good an excuse as any. Once the letter was finished, Jake could mail it back in Albany. That might throw the police investigation off his trail. They would probably be keeping Tendell's mail under surveillance.

Jake returned with a sizeable load of stuff. More than Keith wanted to accept, but he wasn't going to spoil their last night together fussing about Jake's generosity.

"You gonna be on that raft a lot longer'n you think," Jake cautioned. "The first day or two's gonna be hell 'cause you ain't used to it. You git through that, you'll make it okay."

As they sat down to eat the fish, Keith saw how much of a hit he'd made. Jake had bought a bottle of wine.

"Figured we oughtta celebrate your last night with me."

Keith didn't have the heart to say that red wine and fish were anathema, and Gallo Burgundy was hardly the stuff of celebrations. He drank it with every pretense of pleasure and found himself wishing the time with Jake did not have to end. The real celebration, for Keith, came later—in bed.

18

Jake's estimation of the difficulty in poling the makeshift raft upriver had been right on target. Three hours into the trip, Keith was ready to cry. He missed Jake; he felt guilty over having enjoyed himself so much with the man. And Seth's presence returned, haunting him with a distractive vengeance.

I know you're gonna see other guys; I don't mind that. But you sure enjoyed yourself with him. Better'n I was, was he?

Don't be a dunce! You know how much I love you; if you're going to keep haunting me, can't you tell me who killed you? Why can't you do something to make my job easier?

Am I that much of a burden? Do all our memories mean nothing?

I didn't mean that. Oh God, why did you leave me? Seth. Seth? I'm so fucking lost without you. Jake was good; he was a wonderful distraction. But you were my whole life. What am I doing out here on this damned river?

As the remorse and pain of Seth's absence filled him, Keith found it hard going on. The next couple of days tested his spirit and tenacity. He slept fitfully. The mosquitoes and bugs were a bane he'd not fully appreciated. The only consolation was that by each twilight he was so dreadfully tired, nothing could have kept him awake. He slept the sleep of the dead and if snakes, animals or anything else sniffed around him, he was never aware of it. Jake had suggested Keith try finding low-hanging branches of a tree in which to place the raft and sleep on it. The first night he'd been too tired to attempt such a solution, but later on he usually managed such an arrangement. It was always uncomfortable, but he never rolled off the raft and the raft never slipped out of the trees.

It took him nearly four days to reach Oglethorpe, a small town on the river. He poled a little ways past the town, beached the raft and walked back to get a few supplies. He hoped his money lasted until he reached Atlanta. At the rate he was going, it would take a couple of weeks. He'd not expected the trip to last so long. He and Jake had discussed how long Keith ought to remain on the river. Jake had been of the opinion Keith ought to use the waterway as far as possible.

"People won't be expectin' you to be there," Jake had said. "You can fish and git food without payin' for it."

The advice was good. Keith clung to the river. As his arms toughened and grew accustomed to poling, he made better time. He never knew how many miles he put in each day, but by the end of the journey, he figured he was approaching twenty miles a day.

Day followed day with a sameness which was both startling and calming. Keith actually found himself enjoying various aspects of the trip. Early morning were best: He normally woke at dawn. The birds which stirred about the shoreline made so much noise he could never sleep through their raucous calls. Besides, he was always in "bed" by nine each evening. As soon as he was up, he'd make a tiny fire and boil water for coffee as well as for the canteen Jake had gotten for him. Those morning cups of coffee were the best he was ever to drink. Never again would he be able to smell coffee without remembering those rich cups sipped in the green foliage of the riverbank. While his water boiled, he'd dig up a few worms and fish. Most mornings he managed to hook a couple for breakfast.

Fish had never been one of his favorite foods but they

were nutritious—and, best of all, free. By six, he was usually ready to set out. He poled four or five hours, sometimes six, depending on how his arms felt and how much progress he'd made. He rested through the heat of the day, setting out again around two-thirty or three, poling another four or five hours. Around seven or seven-thirty he started looking for a campsite. The further north he went, the harder it became finding a place which was sufficiently clear for his needs. He knew the river eventually passed beneath interstate eight-five. At that point he planned to leave the river and walk or hitchhike the rest of the way to Atlanta.

The days slipped into a dull pattern which, while uninspiring, left Keith with a lot of time to think.

Seth was ever-present. Sometimes Keith found himself talking aloud, mentally composing Seth's answers. More often, Seth's presence was less specific. It was simply there, like the shirt on Keith's back or the ragged jeans on his legs. Every facet of their relationship passed through Keith's mind at some time or another on the trip. It slowly dawned on Keith how much Seth had dominated him, not only sexually, but in all other aspects of their lives. He'd subjected his personality to Seth's—willingly, it was true—but for all practical purposes he'd been a mere appendage of Seth. Like a married woman became only a cipher compared to her husband. No name of her own, only Mrs. so-and-so.

Keith wondered if Seth realized how much he'd dominated the relationship.

Had Seth wanted it that way? Had Keith?

Keith knew he'd wanted the sexual part of it that way. He tried analyzing what it was about being slapped around, or having his ass smacked with a belt or a firm, masculine hand, that turned him on so much? Was it the man in charge? Or was it something inside himself which provided the spark of pleasure where only pain ought to have been? He never arrived at a definitive answer, but decided the need was his, not Seth's.

Why wasn't he satisfied with the basics? What was there about the other which excited him? Keith tried thinking back to how he and Seth had gotten started on stuff like that. His reflections were abruptly halted by a large tree branch which nearly flipped him over. He poled under the obstacle and decided to keep his mind on what he was doing.

But he knew somewhere along the way he wanted to find out why he so easily let other men use him in the fashion he did. That he enjoyed it, longed for it, needed it, even, he acknowledged. Why was what he didn't understand. And he wanted to understand it. He loved Seth so totally, so completely, at the time they were together that it never mattered to him why anything had been the way it was—it was enough simply being together, having Seth want him. He felt now, dimly, that by thinking his way to the reasons behind his receptiveness to Seth he could possess a part of Seth he had never touched before. And anything which kept Seth's image before his eyes was good to Keith; anything which dimmed that perfect reflection was bad.

By Keith's reckoning, it was the seventeenth day after his departure from Lake Blackshear that he saw the interstate ahead of him.

19

By the time Keith reached the end of his trek up the river, it was mid-afternoon. It was possible to go farther up the river, which was now little more than a creek, or Keith could abandon the tiny craft and take to the road. He wondered where he'd sleep if he didn't meet someone. Could he attract anyone? His beard had grown, but was ragged and wild-looking. A shower wouldn't hurt, either. Though he'd taken a dip in the river that morning, as he'd done every morning, he wasn't very clean; the water was filthy. Still, the naked plunges into the river had been fun.

With Atlanta so close, Keith knew he didn't want to spend another night in the woods. He poled along until he found a suitable landing site and beached the raft.

Gathering his gear didn't take long; most of the food was gone. He'd been living on boiled river water and fish the past few days. Only that morning he'd finished the last of his coffee.

Hitching on the interstate was dangerous. First off, it was illegal and cops could stop him. Drivers who offered rides to people like himself were usually whackos, as unpredictable as the police could be. He'd have to be careful.

The blacktop was hot. Keith moved along rapidly, stopping only long enough to stick out a thumb when he heard an approaching car. But the vehicles whizzed past. He decided he'd leave the interstate at the first side road. Hitching might be less noticeable there. A sign indicated the next turnoff was five miles ahead. A long, hot five miles. Keith groaned.

He'd walked only a mile of the five when he came upon a car pulled over to the side of the road. It was occupied by two fluttery old ladies who were consternated by a flat tire on the rear of their auto.

"Could I help you ladies?" he asked as politely as possible.

They glanced at him, at one another, at the dismal tire and both began speaking at once.

"Our tire isn't doing very well."

"We have to be in Atlanta by six this evening."

Keith found their jack and quickly changed the tire. As he worked, he chatted with the old ladies and by the time he'd finished had convinced them he was harmless. They offered him a ride into the city. Once underway, Keith almost wished he'd walked as the woman—the more vinegary-tongued of the pair—was a horrible driver. They had four near accidents before reaching the jammed outskirts of the metropolis. The ladies were due at one of the large, tourist hotels in the downtown Peachtree area.

Keith hopped out at a light on Peachtree and walked the couple of blocks to the Greyhound station on Cain Street. There, he deposited most of his gear in a locker, then phoned Piedmont Park to make sure the swimming pool was still open. At the pool he'd be able to get a shower and clean up. The park was a cruisy area; he might even be able to pick up someone, although it was too early for that. He wanted a place to stay for the night, not sex. He didn't mind—much—exchanging sex for a bed, but he wasn't interested in sex for its own sake. Not at the moment.

He left the bus station, figured out which bus went by the park and climbed aboard. After so much poling and the harrowing ride with the old ladies, the bus seemed a luxury. He'd have to be careful about riding buses as he didn't have much money left, and had no idea what sort of job he might be able to pick up while remaining safe. And if he found work, what should he do about giving his social security number? Couldn't he be traced that way? He wasn't sure. He put the problem out of his mind. He'd cross that bridge when he got a job. At the moment he just wanted a bed for the night.

The park idea was a good one. Keith wished he had a bathing suit; he could have gone swimming—in clean water for a change. Since he couldn't swim, he took a long, cool shower and changed into the clothes he'd brought with him. They were wrinkled, but blessedly clean. He dropped his dirty clothes into a bag and left the pool to walk around the park.

Piedmont Park, located in the heart of Atlanta, was many things to many people. There were numerous athletic fields where the city's amateur sports teams played their schedules. Families found the park a pleasant place. Keith knew from his own observations and the reports of friends that the homosexuals of Atlanta also got their share of use from the place—in spite of harrassment by the park police.

Keith walked past the large lake which bordered the swimming pool to the area where hustlers plied their trade. He sat down on a bench to rest and watch the antics of those around him.

The couple of times Keith and Seth had visited the park with friends had always been unsuccessful. Seth was never comfortable around other homosexuals; he came to the city only because Keith enjoyed the trip. For a few years after Keith left the university, he and Seth had visited Atlanta several times a year, but then, the journeys had tapered off. As a result, Keith knew almost no one in the city; those he did know would be fully aware of his status as a fugitive. He supposed one or two of them might shelter him for a few nights, but he wasn't too positive about that, and didn't like putting anyone in the position of having to say no.

As Keith watched, the human parade in the park picked up momentum. It was after six. The "trade" was mostly married men who—having stopped by some bar for a drink or two before going home to the wife and kiddies—had gotten enough courage to try picking up a quick trick. A fast blow job in their car; an even faster piece of action in the bushes . . . it was all so furtive and disgusting. Keith didn't understand why they bothered. Seth had found the whole business gross. Keith remembered his words: "If I thought I'd turn out like that, I'd shoot myself!"

Several cars slowed down as they passed Keith's bench. The occupants stared at him with the knowing looks of professional cruisers. Appraising his appearance, cock size, availability. He was wearing none of the accouterment identifying what he wanted. No keys, no handkerchiefs, no leather. He wondered idly if he should try making money out of the situation. He had less than twenty dollars and he'd need most of that if he went to the baths or a bar. He was thankful he still had his baths' card. Seth had always teased him about carrying it. A close friend of Keith's had presented him with the card one year as a birthday gift. An expensive gift—a lifetime membership—but the guy said he'd gotten it free by sleeping with the baths' owner. Keith didn't believe that, but he'd laughed and thanked the man, promising he'd always carry the card with him. At first, he only carried it because it had annoyed Seth.

"You go to that damned place and bring home some disease, I'll whip your ass so hard, you'll never want to get it fucked again," he'd warned. Keith had smiled and kept the card. Now it might be useful. For a fairly small sum he could get clean and get a bed (of sorts) for the night. Funny, how you never knew when something might prove useful.

Keith turned his attention back to the line of cars which were now circling the lake. Few of the men were ones he'd

want to have sex with. Such an attitude, he suspected, wasn't
going to make his job easier. He sighed. What a hell of a mess.
No doubt he could stay at one of those Salvation Army joints,
but he'd always hated the idea of them and certainly didn't
want to listen to all that religious garbage.

Now that he was in Atlanta, the options open to him
seemed remote. Was he a fool for running away?

A bit late to be thinking that, he told himself.

What am I suposed to do?

*Do the best you can. There's nothing you can do that'll
piss me off. I let you down, gettin' myself killed and causin'
you all this trouble. You think I'd throw it up to you later? Just
remember your promise when you're in a position to carry it out.
Keith, Keith, Fight 'em! Don't go gettin' remorseful, don't
start thinkin' you can't make it. You can. If only I were with
you . . .*

If you were with me, nothing else would matter.

Seth's image faded slowly. Keith felt hot tears trickle
down his face. He missed Seth so much. Needed him so much.
What in the hell was he doing here?

Gradually, Keith pulled himself together. He might as
well get something to eat. It had been a long time since he'd
had anything remotely resembling a meal. There was a cheap
but highly regarded restaurant on Ponce de Leon, right on the
way to the bar on Highland. He could walk and save money.
Picking up his bundle of dirty clothes, he started off.

On the way, he passed a laundromat and cleaned his
clothes. That move necessitated a trip back to the bus station to
drop them off. Then he ate and by the time he'd finished his
meal, it was ten o'clock. Keith began his quest for a bed for the
night. He still hadn't learned that nothing transpires in gay
bars before midnight.

The bar Keith entered was a typical cruise bar, catering to
a macho clientele. Atlanta was well-known as the drag capitol

of the South, but Keith was unable to stomach such affectations and knew he'd be unable to keep his contempt from showing. He hoped to pick up someone nice, a man who might not object if Keith hung around a day or two. He had no idea whether such a notion was valid; he was very much a novice. Was he attractive enough to interest anyone? Did relationships really begin inside these dim, dingy walls where beer and bodies mixed? Keith didn't know. He'd read a lot of books and subscribed to a lot of magazines about gay life but he'd never gone into a bar with the idea of picking up a man. Everytime he'd entered such a place in the past it had been with Seth. Seth had been there to protect him and, more importantly, to leave with him. Keith remembered swelling with pride the times he and Seth had gone out in Atlanta. Seth had been greatly admired. Men couldn't resist trying to pick up Seth. It had done a lot for Keith's ego. Now, he was on his own.

The Spur wasn't crowded when Keith pushed open the door. Feeling self-conscious, he went to the counter and ordered a beer. There were only three or four men seated at the bar. Keith took his beer and resolutely perched himself on a barstool.

The Spur was not one of the bars Keith and Seth had visited. Keith had heard about the place and figured it might attract the sort of men who would appeal to him. It had been a long time since Keith had been in any bar in Atlanta, however, and time seemed to have led to dramatic changes. He was amazed by the bartenders, who were wearing as close to nothing as possible. Some were decked out in hard hats and no shirts; the cut-off levis they poured themselves into were blatantly revealing—the seats of most were torn, allowing large portions of ass flesh to protrude. Keith wondered how they avoided being arrested for indecent exposure. Not that he considered it indecent, but he felt the city fathers would not have concurred with his opinion.

"Hello."

Keith turned as a man a couple of seats away spoke to him. The room was too dark to see if the guy was attractive but he didn't appear to be fat—one of Keith's major dislikes—so he tentatively returned the smile and mumbled a "Hello" of his own.

"You new here?" the man asked.

"Yeah," Keith said, "I'm over from Athens for a few days." Keith had decided he'd use the university town as a fictional base. He'd lived there and was familiar with it. He wouldn't get caught in a lie. By saying he'd just finished school and was looking for a job, he hoped he might get an invitation to spend a few days with someone while at the same time avoiding a lot of unnecessary explanations.

The conversation flowed well enough. Keith—against his will and nervously—kept raising his beer to his lips. He wanted the drink to last; he couldn't afford to buy very many.

"Let me buy you another brew," the man offered.

Keith acquiesed, saving his precious funds. Did it mean the guy was interested—or only generous? He had no idea.

The man, Dennis, was affable and seemed to sense Keith's uneasiness. Keith's biggest difficulty was keeping his lies from tripping him up. He decided to drop the time he and Seth had spent in Tilton and pretend for the moment that it had never existed.

Keith moved over to the seat next to Dennis. He liked what he saw. Blond hair, shaggy cut, lean body, deeply tanned. Their legs touched. Keith felt subtle pressure, an indication he'd scored on his first attempt. He felt a momentary elation. Was something going to be easy?

The bar began to fill up. Keith, plied with more beer and schnapps by Dennis, found his fears and inhibitions lessening. When Dennis pulled Keith against him for a kiss, the fugitive responded willingly.

In public, no less! I must have a whore's mentality.

His acceptance of such open displays of affection—something he'd frowned upon in the past—puzzled Keith. He decided to put it down to the drinks. He'd think about it later. None of his old beliefs seemed very important any longer. They'd not protected him and Seth. Doing all the right things, being circumspect and good citizens had gotten them a hell of a lot. A bullet for Seth and a jail cell for himself. To hell with the hetero sons-of-bitches!

"You okay?" Dennis asked, noticing the anger which momentarily crossed Keith's face.

"Yeah . . . thought I saw someone I knew," Keith lied.

Dennis made a trip to the john and Keith surveyed the crowd.

The Spur was attracting a mixed group. Two men in police uniforms caused Keith an involuntary jerk before he realized that they were gay guys pretending to be a part of some mythical force. The uniforms didn't do much for them. Once Keith had enjoyed fantasies about cops; after the past three months he doubted he could ever get a hard-on around a real cop. He also doubted he would like counterfeits.

There were men in leather—the first Keith had ever seen outside magazines. He felt a thrill of interest. When Keith and Seth had ventured into Atlanta, they generally frequented dance bars; besides, those trips had taken place before the leather fad caught fire. Seth had refused to go to leather bars, saying leather was too kinky for a simple farmboy. Keith, eyeing such men, couldn't keep his mind from considering what they did with the odd paraphernalia they were wearing. Several were without shirts, dressed in harness-like straps. There were lots of levi-clad bodies, well-proportioned and sexy. Few of the flighty, sissy-looking types were in the bar. The Spur was indeed Keith's sort of place. He felt a hand on his shoulder and half-turned to find Dennis was back. The man's warm body pressing against Keith's flesh felt very good. Their lips met in a long, lingering kiss—tongues exploring, searching for new sensations.

"Looks like they lasted longer," a voice spoke at the other end of the bar.

Keith turned to find another couple locked in a heated embrace.

"I didn't know we were having a contest," he replied spontaneously.

Dennis tousled Keith's hair and bought another round. He seemed to know half the men in the bar. Before the drinks arrived, Keith tried making his way to the bathroom.

"Be careful," Dennis warned as Keith drifted away.

Careful of what? Is he afraid I'm going to run out on him?

In the latrine, Keith found ample reason for the warning. The place was packed. Blow jobs were in progress, several men appeared to be drinking piss. Keith stared, aghast. People didn't really do these things, did they? He felt sick. He wondered, momentarily, if the hetero detractors of his world might not be right. Why couldn't these bastards keep their acts out of public areas? Much of the trouble gays experienced with straight society stemmed from people like these—exhibiting no self-control. Keith managed to take a leak without being molested and began inching his way back to Dennis and the bar. Along the way, he stumbled over two dwarf-like men—munchkins really—who were among the most out-of-place characters in the bar. Keith almost reached down to pat one of them on the head before remembering himself. As he passed by, he heard one little man proposition a guy: "Want to fuck two midgets?"

Back at the bar he was repossessed by Dennis and the feeling of being wanted surpassed his disgust over the toilet scene. They finished their drinks and inched their way through the crowd to the door. Dennis lived only a few blocks from the bar—an easy walk.

Dennis' apartment was richly and fashionably furnished.

It bespoke money and a type of elitism Keith didn't care for, but at the moment the man was more important than the surroundings.

"Would you like another drink?" Dennis asked, playing the polite host. "Some music or the television?"

"No. Just you."

They climbed the stairs to the bedroom. It was as well-furnished as the rest of the house. Keith pulled Dennis to him, kissing the man with a passion he'd dared not display in the bar. They fumbled in the dim light, assisting each other out of clothes. Dennis was finding the body beneath Keith's clothes harder, firmer than he'd expected. Tugging at the levis, Dennis pulled them down around Keith's knees. Then, lifting one of the shoes Keith was wearing, Dennis began licking it.

What in the hell can he be getting out of *that*? If he only knew where those shoes have been . . .

"You ought to wear leather," Dennis whispered, looking up from the floor with dark, intense eyes.

"I'd like to," Keith stated, wondering if the desired articles were going to pop out of a closet. He sat on the bed and placed his shoe on Dennis' crotch. The man liked it. Experimenting, Keith eased his other foot, still shod, onto Dennis' chest and applied pressure. He found the position interesting. A gladiator towering in triumph over a defeated combatant. Now if their positions were only reversed. Still, it promised to be an exciting night . . .

20

They awoke late the next morning. In the course of conversation, Keith learned Dennis worked for an airline and did not have to be on the job until late evening. A situation which precluded Keith's remaining with Dennis for a few days—not to mention the fact a certain coolness developed after sex was over. Keith, unused to bars and the casual pairings which went on there, wondered if he'd made some sort of mistake. He liked the guy and said so. The admission was a major error but Keith only learned this after making the same faux pas for weeks. Following a pleasant breakfast and several cups of coffee, Keith found himself on the street again.

What next? He desperately needed to find some sort of job. He had no idea what sort of work he should seek, but wanted something which would keep him out of sight.

In the meantime, there was the stuff he'd left in the locker at the bus station. He needed to pay for another twenty-four hours on the locker. He set off walking. It was a long way from Highland to Cain Street but maybe he'd see a job advertised along the way.

He didn't. The thing he did see along the way was a condemned building. He stood at the edge of the lot and stared at the place for a considerable time. It just might provide a place to crash for a night or two until he found work, a place to live. He moved on, keeping the old house in mind. Come night, it should be relatively easy to slip in and grab a few hours' rest.

From the bus station he took a bus to Piedmont and Cheshire Bridge Road which housed several of the gay establishments in Atlanta. Twilight wasn't the time of day to apply for jobs, but he preferred working in a gay business if possible. The baths were out that way, too. He might end up there for the night so he could kill a couple of birds with a single bus ride.

The trip caused a great loneliness to descend upon him. Everyone was hurrying to some sort of home. Keith had nothing. Growing up on south Georgia, even in poverty, had not prepared him for the emotional distress that comes from possessing nothing at all. He had barely the clothes on his back, with few prospects for gaining anything more. He remembered his books and records back in Tilton. Music had been a large part of his life. Then too, his possessions were all intertwined with Seth. Gifts from and to Seth. In the normal course of events Keith would at least have retained the physical remembrances of his lover. Now he had nothing. He supposed the lawyer would look after things, but that wasn't going to do Keith a hell of a lot of good for the foreseeable future.

He got off the bus and walked forlornly up the nearly deserted street. Families were at home eating their evening meals. Gay people wouldn't be caught dead outdoors at such an hour. Passing a small eatery, Keith noticed a sign in the window proclaiming a dishwasher was needed. He stopped in his tracks. Washing dishes might be the perfect occupation for him. It would allow him to remain out of sight and would provide some income. He shrugged his shoulders. Asking couldn't do much harm.

An enormously fat man was trying, inadequately, to perch upon a stool behind the cash register. The place was empty except for one table of customers, well away from the register. Keith approached the fellow.

"Yeah? What you need?"

"I saw your sign and wondered if you still need a dishwasher?" Keith asked.

"You?" Fatman barked. "You don't look like no dishwasher to me."

"I didn't know they came made to order," Keith retorted before he thought.

"A smart aleck, huh?" The Fatman scowled. "I pay three and a quarter an hour, need you here from midnight till eight in the mornings. We get the late, late crowd. I cater to gays—homo-sexuals in other words." He mispronounced the word in the exaggerated fashion of fundamentalist Christians. "If being around queers bothers you, you won't fit in here."

"I can handle that," Keith replied. "Make the pay minimum wage and a decent meal every night and I'll take it."

"I'll give you a meal, if you can eat the stuff. Three and a quarter till I find out if you're reliable or not."

"How long will that take?" Keith asked.

"We'll see," the man hedged.

"Two weeks," Keith stated. "Then you go to minimum."

Fatman burst out laughing. His huge belly shook so much he almost fell off his precarious perch. Keith was surprised the stool held its occupant in the first place.

"You last two weeks, you'll be here longer by twelve days than most. Okay! One night a week off. If you got preferences as to which night, we'll talk about that later."

Keith stuck out his hand to seal the bargain and Fatman took it.

"My, my! Strong bastard, aren't you? Charles! Charles!"

A tall, willowy young man appeared. "Yessir?"

"Got us a dishwasher. Take him back and show him the setup." The Fatman turned back to Keith. "Think you could last from now till eight in the morning? Things are a mess around here."

Keith nodded. "Sure."

"Good. What's your name?"

"Keith. Keith . . . Rawson."

"Okay. We'll take care of the paper work later. No húrry, till we see if you last. Go ahead and eat what you want."

Keith followed Charles into the kitchen where he found the place was indeed a mess. Was this what everything was coming down to? Keith shrugged off the feeling. The job was near enough to what he needed for the moment. Eating at the place would save him a fair amount of money; he'd never been one to stuff himself. After his first week's check he could look for someplace to stay. Best of all, he wouldn't be visible.

He set to work with a vengeance. Simply having something to do was a welcome change. He was tired, but it was obvious the Fatman didn't care if the "help" helped themselves to coffee and the like. Keith had the cook fix him some food and he consumed several cups of the strong black coffee. By the time midnight approached, Keith had gotten the kitchen into a sort of order. It was soon apparent that he was expected to do more than simply wash dishes, but he didn't mind. The Fatman waddled back to the kitchen once or twice and seemed impressed. On occasion Charles tried coaxing Keith out of the kitchen into the public area but he avoided promptings. Charles, forever embued with the dream of meeting "Mr. Wonderful," flitted about the place trying to arrange a tryst for when he got off. Inevitably, the assignations fell through. Keith discovered that every evening at work was filled with a litany of complaints from the unfortunate Charles about men who never materialized.

Eight o'clock in the morning arrived faster than Keith expected.

The Fatman made no effort at learning anything about

Keith, a fact which surprised the fugitive.

Keith was hanging up the apron he'd been wearing when the Fatman stuck his head through the kitchen door.

"That's it for this time. You didn't do too shabby, Keith. Am I gonna see you tonight?"

"Of course," Keith replied, startled. "But not quite so early."

Fatman chuckled. "Good! I'll get more info about you then. You in any hurry to provide me with Uncle Sam's tax data?"

"Nope. Just as long as you remember the hours I put in."

Fatman nodded. "You work like this all the time, I'd be a fool not too. See you tonight—unless, of course, you'd like to come home with me."

Keith couldn't believe his ears. He wasn't in the mood to fight off the guy. A glance at his new employer convinced him the proposition had been made in jest—sort of.

"I'd better get some rest." Keith said, evasively. "See you later."

He stepped out into the bright sunlight. He felt dirty, greasy, and in great need of a shower, but didn't want to go to the baths at this hour. After a moment's uncertainty, he decided to check out the abandoned house he'd noticed the night before. Anyplace to collapse would be fine. Fatman, rather smelly and unsavory himself, probably wouldn't object too much if Keith wasn't the cleanest person in the world.

Keith was too tired to walk back to the abandoned dwelling; it was too far. He hopped a bus and was quickly back on Piedmont where he walked the few blocks to Ponce de Leon and the ramshackled building. The place was tree-shaded; it should be cool.

Not only was it tree-shaded, but towards the rear of the place, shrubs and bushes had grown to such a height they offered some protection as he slipped in. The back door was locked with a hasp and padlock, but a window was open, the panes shattered and laying about on the floor. Keith hopped over the window sill and found himself inside the dilapidated structure.

The house was in bad shape—so bad Keith almost decided against staying in the place. It wouldn't help if the damned roof toppled down on his head, a feat it seemed capable of doing at any moment. Having nothing else to choose from, however, he reluctantly opted to stay. He searched around and found a spot which appeared safe. In the corner of one room he discovered a rat-eaten mattress and dragged it over to his choice of a resting place. He hoped the bedraggled bundle of cotton wasn't infested with bugs. Without further consideration, he tumbled onto the thing and promptly fell asleep.

The rest was precious. Darkness had fallen by the time Keith opened his eyes again. Fearful at first that he had overslept, he raced to a window and peered at his watch. It was nine o'clock. He had slept nearly twelve hours. He slipped out of the house and caught the bus to Cheshire Bridge and his job.

Fatman was behind the register. Keith greeted him, asking if he could sit down for a few minutes and have some coffee. With a wave of his hand, the man grandly agreed. They talked a bit. As before, few people were in the place. Keith was surprised the restaurant could operate on only a late night business, but he remembered how crowded it had been and supposed it wasn't all that hard.

When the last customer got up and paid his bill, Fatman left the register and came to the table where Keith was drinking coffee. The gargantuan man gingerly slid his bulk behind the table, attempted without success to make himself comfortable and asked Keith a chilling question.

"Don't suppose you got a food-handler's card, do you?"

Keith froze. Damn! A complication he'd not thought about.

"No. Do I have to have one just to wash dishes?"

"Yep. I'd never be able to convince the Health Department you won't be serving food, too." He eyed his employee thoughtfully. "You don't want to apply for one, do you?"

Keith stared frankly at the man. "No, I don't."

The Fatman hunched himself forward. "Okay. Let's talk business. You appear to be the kind of man I can use. I don't, however, feel like paying minimum wage. I don't like paying all those goddamned taxes, either. If you're willing to work for me without having your pay reported, I'll pay you three bucks an hour without deductions." He rummaged through a sheaf of papers. "For purposes of your health card, you'll be . . . John Clark. How's that sound to you?"

Keith shrugged. "Fine with me, if you can get away with it. What about a day off?"

Fatman pulled the papers back together with a grunt of satisfaction. "Monday or Thursday's best for me: My sort of customers don't eat out as late on those days—nights; rest of the time, we're pretty busy. I oughtta close one day a week, but never have. Ain't open all that many hours anyway."

Fatman rolled his shoulders. "Trouble with you being off at all, is, how do I find anyone to fill in? Getting any kind of help around here is a never-ending chore. These flighty queens bounce in and out of this place like it was Caesar's Palace or a one-night stand. Most of 'em use this joint till something better comes along, or because their unemployment runs out. I know that."

Fatman glanced at Keith with a shrewd stare. "I suspect you're willing to work here 'cause you're running away from something. Possibly something involving the law." He held up a hand to forestall any protest from Keith. "Don't deny it; and for God's sake don't confirm it. Whatever you're up to, I don't want to know. I judge men on what I can see—mostly—my evaluation of their character. You're a good-looking stud, you even appear halfway serious about your work."

Fatman tried edging himself out from behind the table. "I

don't mind some fun and games while you're here. You get a chance to pick up someone, go ahead—just make sure your job's taken care of. When we're busy, customers don't like waiting for their food because we're out of clean dishes."

Keith nodded and watched with some amusement as Fatman finally escaped the table. People began coming in; Keith did some mild cruising as he drank coffee and watched the goings-on in the cafe. A few minutes past eleven, he decided he'd take pity on the rest of the help and headed for the kitchen and his dishpan.

The next two days passed with a sameness which became almost comforting. Keith continued using the old house, hoping he could crash there until he received his first check. Or cash, as it turned out. Fatman didn't believe in evidence. One day Keith used part of his meagre remaining money to go to the baths and get cleaned up. He now owned only the clothes he was wearing, having lost his other outfit by oversleeping and not returning to the bus station locker within the alloted twenty-four hour period. Fearful the police might discover the stuff was his, he let it go. The clothes were the only things he would have liked to have.

His sixth day of sleeping in the old house almost proved his undoing.

He'd anticipated staying there another day or two. Fatman was going to pay him the following morning; the money would be more than usual because of the overtime he'd put in. Fatman had indicated he was stingy about pay, but when he'd reported Keith's total hours for the week, they'd almost argued.

"That's an awful lot," Keith said.

"You worked 'em, didn't you?" Fatman almost fell off his stool.

"Yeah, but we only agreed on the first night's overtime; the rest of the evenings, I came in on my own. Besides, I'm eating a lot here. And drinking tons of coffee."

Fatman waved that aside. "Makes no difference. I like your enthusiasm. The fact you weren't doing it for the money is all the better. Take what I offer. You'll need it."

Keith had said no more. As a result, tomorrow, he hoped he would have enough money to try looking for a place to live. He walked around the now-familiar path to the back of his temporary refuge and crept through the window.

He made a quick inspection of the house. Something he did each morning. As usual, everything was fine. He went to the old mattress and fell asleep.

He awoke, when someone shook him.

"Come on fella, wake up. You can't sleep in here. There's plenty of places to crash if you're in trouble."

Keith jerked awake. A cop was kneeling over him.

Unreasonable fear was the only emotion which raced through his body. He tried taking in the situation at a glance and saw only one thing: The cop had unhooked the top of his holster—in order to be able to draw the weapon if need be.

Keith, feigning drowsiness, suddenly moved in a single motion and yanked the weapon from its resting place. "Stand back," he ordered harshly. "Don't come near me. I'll use this if I have to." He flipped off the safety, indicating he knew something about the use of a revolver.

The cop, pale, tried reasoning with the man before him.

"Come on, give that back. Don't do anything foolish. You're not in any real trouble, yet, just sleeping here. Hell, if you're down on your luck, I'll help you find a place—"

"Shut up! You pigs wouldn't help anybody. I don't need that kind of help!" Keith, keeping his eye on the cop, reached down and picked up his shirt and wallet from the mattress.

"You're wrong," the cop said, quietly.

Keith looked at the man for the first time. Really looked at him. Even without the well-fitting uniform, the man would have been splendid. For a second, Keith felt a surge of emotion.

Goddammit, get your mind out of his pants, you fool! This man can have you back in jail in a minute!

"Come on, fella. Give me back that weapon and let's talk things over. You don't have to sleep in a joint like this. There's places in the city—"

"Stop!"

The cop had taken a tentative step towards Keith. He halted.

They stared at one another. The man's features etched themselves on Keith's mind.

"I'm going to back out of here. If you show yourself in that hallway before I'm away from this place, I'll shoot you," Keith warned.

"You don't look like a killer to me," the cop stated. He appeared ready to step forward.

"Then don't try making me one," Keith told him. "Stay right where you are."

Keith slowly backed out of the room, then raced down the hallway to the rear of the house. He stepped out of the window, swiftly removed the bullets from the gun and dropped the shells at the base of the window. He wiped the weapon clean of his fingerprints before tossing it back through the window. The sound of the gun hitting the floor ought to give the cop something to think about. If he was too dumb to look for it, that was his hard luck. The cop's motorcycle, parked in front of the house, indicated he was by himself—a stupid thing for him to have done in the first place. Keith's heart was pounding as he hurried up the street as fast as he dared without attracting attention to himself. A few blocks from the run-down house, he saw a laundromat and ducked into it. Fumbling with some change he bought a Coke and walked to the back of the place and sat down. Swear poured from his body. He found he was trembling.

21

B rad Evans mentally kicked himself. He should have called for reenforcements. But it was half an hour until shift change and nobody took the old lady's complaint seriously in the first place.

"Somebody's sleeping in that condemned house on Ponce de Leon," she'd said. "Been doing it a week now. I've watched him coming and going. Can't you people do something?"

The desk sergeant yearned to tell the woman it was better for the man, some old drunk no doubt, to be off the streets rather than sprawled across the sidewalk. He kept his mouth shut, however, and ordered Evans to detour by the house and check out the place on his way back to the station.

Evans had noticed at once that the weeds were trampled down. Somebody was using the house. He pulled his weapon and cautiously made his way around to the back, where the open window gave mute testimony as to how the tramp gained entry. Not that anybody gave a damn—the place was going to be demolished soon. If, in the meantime it provided shelter for some hard-up fool, well . . .

Brad climbed over the sill, and as a precaution, kept his weapon in his hand while searching the house. Keith's "bedroom" was last on the tour. Brad pulled up short when he saw the sleeping form.

The heat of summer had forced Keith to remove his shirt each day. He would have liked sleeping naked, but couldn't be certain someone wouldn't climb into the place—just as he'd done. Keith confidently believed he would hear anyone long before they reached his bed. That he had not was due to the fact Evans moved cautiously.

Evans stared at the form, and a great sense of pity welled up within him. The man on the ragged mattress was handsome. He'd expected an old wino, not some young demigod. Brad slipped his weapon back into its holster and fought down an urge to simply melt away and report finding nothing. His additional impulse of wanting to kneel and touch the handsome male body—awaken the sleeping prince with a kiss—annoyed him so much that Evans abruptly decided he'd be brisk.

I was a fool!

The thought filled Brad's mind as Keith edged towards the door. Evans was disgusted with himself. He'd behaved unprofessionally, allowing private feelings of pity and lust to outrun his reason. Now, having indulged in a second's worth of charity, he was in a pickle. Watching the exquisite sleeping form, who'd have thought the guy was crazy?

Explaining the loss of his revolver would take some doing!

Damn! And only half an hour before he was supposed to go on three-day break. Losing a weapon would take hours of paperwork—maybe days.

He snapped out of his self-pity and moved towards the hallway. He peered out but saw nothing. A thud startled him, slowing him momentarily. Advancing slowly, he neared the open window. Intent on watching for the fleeing man, he almost stepped on the weapon. Brad stared at it unbelievingly. He reached down to pick it up but the thought it might have the guy's prints on it made him cautious. He couldn't believe a simple vagabond would return the weapon, which could be sold. Replacing the pistol on his side, he noticed the bullets were missing. Incredible. Deciding he'd wasted enough time, and certain the man was gone, Brad climbed out of the window. Laying at the base of the window sill were his bullets.

Shaking his head, Evans gathered them up and headed back to his motorcycle.

At headquarters, he glossed over the incident.

"Somebody's been using the place to crash, but they weren't there. Have a patrol check it out for a night or two."

The desk sergeant made a note for the evening shift and Evans prepared to sign out. Before doing so, he stepped down the hall to the fingerprint department.

"Chuck? Got a minute?"

"Sure Brad, what's up? You're just getting off, aren't you?"

"Yeah. Look, could you see if yoou can lift any prints off my weapon?"

Chuck Wood, one of Evans' closest friends on the force, looked both puzzled and amused.

"I can do it, but what's the point? You didn't lose it, did you?" The last was delivered with an ironic grin.

"Could we just do it?"

"Okay, okay." Wood got out the stuff he needed and went about the job. It didn't take long. When he finished, he turned to Evans and appeared annoyed. "What are you pulling? There are no prints on here—not even your own. Whose were you expecting to find?"

"You're sure?" Evans persisted, unable to believe his ears. His spine tingled. If the guy hadn't wanted his prints discovered, it could only mean he was wanted—wanted for something serious. Damn! Evans picked up the weapon and started backing out of the room when he remembered the bullets.

"Chuck? I hate to bother—"

"What now?"

"You suppose you could check six bullets?"

Wood groaned but held out his hand, covered with a cloth.

"Let's have 'em," he barked.

Wood worked diligently for a few minutes, "Okay, here's one. Let's run yours." After a brief comparison, Wood looked up and smiled without humor.

"This one's not yours. Would you mind telling me . . . "

"Later. Now, could you try finding out if it's in Records anywhere?"

"You don't want much, do you?"

"It's kind of important. I'm starting break today. Going down to the coast but I'd like knowing what you get on this first. I don't have a phone down there. I could call you at home tomorrow."

"Go turn in your gear," Wood said. "I'll call you this evening if I get anything. What time you leaving?"

"Around ten. I wanted to nap first."

Wood nodded, thoughtfully. "I suppose you don't want anybody else in on this, do you?"

"No."

"In that case, make it tomorrow. I'll have to do the work myself. Call me when you wake up. Find a phone down there somewhere if it's that important to you. Otherwise, wait 'till you get back."

Evans agreed, turned in his weapon and left the station.

He drove to the condo he'd purchased with money from his parents' estate, his mind filled with a great many conflicting notions.

If the man were wanted, why hadn't he fired the gun? At the very least, why hadn't he kept the damned weapon? Guns were worth money. Brad remembered the way the guy looked before he'd awakened. That memory was as disturbing as any of the other aspects of the incident. Evans reflected—as he had done many times during the past couple of years—that he was going to have to do something to resolve that situation. Either give up guys (not that he'd made it with many) or leave the force. He was tired of the conflicts.

Brad let himself into the house and immediately slapped a cassette into his machine. Music helped relieve the tensions of the day. Nothing helped with the nights alone.

He napped. Shortly past ten that night, he got into his car and drove south towards the Georgia coast where he owned a beach cottage—the only thing belonging to his parents which he had retained. The taxes and upkeep on the place were a burden, but having it there, knowing he could run to it when things got rough, made it worthwhile. His superiors didn't like it—he was often at th cottage and unavailable when the myraid tasks, for which they loved recalling troops, came along.

The drive was uneventful. Brad pulled onto the wild patch of land an hour before sunrise, fixed a drink from the stock he kept on hand and let the pounding sea soothe him, ease his pain. When the sun was well up over the water, he went to bed.

It was past two before Evans woke. The heat was bad. He stepped out on the patio and watched the endless surge of water to shore. After coffee, unable to put the incident of the day before out of his mind, he drove a half-mile to the nearest phone booth.

"Chuck? Brad here. What did you find out?"

Wood's voice came over the wire clearly. Low, insistent.

"Listen to me, Brad. I don't know what the hell you're up to, but drop it. Do you hear me? Drop it. You, of all people, don't need this sort of association."

Evans was puzzled. "I take it you matched up the print with a name?"

"I sure as hell did."

"Well for Christ's sake, whose was it?"

"Remember that case a few months ago down in Tilton? A guy was accused of killing his male lover? The case you said looked like a frame-up?"

"Yes, what about it? Don't tell me—"

"I'm telling you. That print on your bullet belonged to the escaped killer, Keith Wilson."

Instead of feeling terror, as he supposed he should feel, Brad only experienced an excitement over the fact the guy was gay.

"*Accused* killer," he reminded Wood.

"Whatever. He'll be convicted if they ever catch him and you know it. Brad, for God's sake be careful. You know I don't give a fuck about your personal life, but you don't hang around enough women for some guys in the department. Leave this mess alone."

Evans thanked Wood for the information and hung up.

Goddamn! Coincidence? Evans didn't much believe in coincidences. Besides, he didn't want to believe the call which sent him to the old house had been mere chance. Fate. It had to be. He recalled the man on the mattress. The image of Keith filled and overwhelmed him. Back in his car, he got out the map and found Tilton. Not far at all. He could be there in a couple of hours.

22

Driving to Tilton, Brad thought carefully about what he was doing. Chuck was right—by involving himself with the case, he was getting into a sticky situation with the department. If they accused him of being gay, they'd have to prove it —or make him mad enough to admit it. Neither scenario did much for his future as a cop. Well, he'd wanted to leave the force for a year or so anyway. The only thing which kept him in uniform now was his desire to save enough money to get by on until something better came along. He had that much already.

Putting aside his personal involvement for the moment, he turned his attention to what he was going to do when he reached Tilton. First he ought to make an attempt to contact the attorney who'd handled the case. Brad couldn't recall the man's name, but hoped a glance at the phone book, under attorneys, would jar his memory. If that failed to work, he knew any local lawyer could provide the information. An all-purpose auto stop loomed ahead. Brad pulled in and walked briskly to a phone booth.

Tendell, Wade. That sounded right. Evans dialed the number.

"Mr. Tendell?"

"Speaking. What can I do for you?"

"I'd like some of your time if I may, about the Wilson case. You did handle it, didn't you?" Brad was evasive. No sense saying too much until he gauged what sort of man Tendell was. At the time of the trial, the lawyer had firmly asserted his client's innocence—but that might have been a ploy.

"Keith Wilson?" Tendell's voice took on an edge of excitement. "Yes, I did. Do you know where Keith's at? Have you a message from him? Listen, I'll be glad to talk with you. Now? Later?"

Brad grinned at the phone. The lawyer sounded eager; the policeman had been prepared for a brush-off.

"I'm in town now." Brad told the attorney. "But I don't know my way around Tilton. I'd like to talk with you. A conversation might point me in a direction which could prove helpful."

"God knows Keith needs all the help he can get!" Tendell exclaimed. "Care to come to my place? Or would you prefer something else?"

"Your place sounds fine," Brad assured the man. "Give me directions."

Twenty-five minutes later he was pulling into the driveway of a modest but neatly kept house. Wade Tendell almost burst out of the door as soon as he spotted the car.

"Come in, come in," he said, sticking out a hand. Without waiting for an answer he led Brad into the dwelling.

"A drink?" Tendell offered. His wife had discreetly disappeared. Brad nodded an acceptance and waited for the man to fix it. The lawyer was bursting with a curiosity which was barely held in check.

Drinks in hand, they sat across from one another, each taking the measure of the other. Brad spoke first, feeling the initiative was with him.

"I've followed the Wilson case from the time it first hit the newspapers. I ran into Wilson in Atlanta a couple of days ago—" He could see that news hit the lawyer—and that renewed my interest. I don't know what you can, or will, tell me about where things stand presently, but I'd be interested in hearing how the case is going, whether you think Wilson's guilty and if anything has been overlooked which could be helpful if looked into."

Tendell answered at once. "The idea he's guilty is absurd. I've never seen a person more broken up over the death of someone. Keith loved Seth Rawson—and whatever you might think about their type of love doesn't in any way change that fact. Keith would *never* have killed Seth. For the moment, the case is at a standstill. Until Keith is recaptured there is little which can be done. He was a fool running away like that—but I can't say I blame him too much. Of course once he's recaptured he'll be convicted. That's a foregone conclusion in my mind. I can only hope the appeals process will overturn the conviction. There is no real evidence pointing to him. The fact he has no alibi and stands to gain considerably from the death of his friend is what led to his arrest. If he were not a homosexual, he'd never have been arraigned and tried. Running away, however, will make the appeals process harder. The only thing which would really help is finding out who did kill Rawson. The Tilton police haven't bent over backwards to do that, although they have done more than one might expect under the circumstances." Tendell stopped, run-down for the moment.

During Tendell's speech, Brad made up his mind. When the lawyer stopped talking, Brad got out his wallet and handed over his police identification. Tendell's eyes shot up on seeing the card. Brad told him about his recent encounter with Keith.

"Oh damn," Tendell groaned, "another charge."

"I didn't say anything about the episode at headquarters." Brad said. "So there wouldn't be any new charges over that."

Tendell took their glasses for a refill. As he mixed the

drinks, he shook his head. "I'm grateful for your information of course, but I don't understand your interest in assisting someone who could quite easily have killed you."

"You said he hasn't killed anyone," Brad reminded the man.

"So I did. And I'm convinced he didn't. But you have no way of knowing that."

Brad smiled. "Maybe I'm simply grateful he didn't shoot me." He hesitated, then added, "I'd like to help, if there's anything I could do. If you'd go over the case with me, maybe I could make a suggestion or two."

It was Tendell's turn to smile. "That's fine with me. Let me step out to the kitchen and tell the wife. We weren't sure who might turn up." He started out the door, then turned and asked, "Have you decided to stay in town for the night?"

"Yes."

"You're welcome to spend the night here if you'd like. Tomorrow, if anything comes to mind, I could introduce you to the Chief of Police, Wayne Links. I think he'd cooperate."

While he waited for Tendell's return, Brad reflected there had to be some way of proving Keith didn't kill Seth, even if it was impossible to discover who had. He'd been involved in too many cases himself not to be aware of countless loopholes. He was deep in thought when Tendell returned with his wife, whom he introduced to the policeman. The three talked for a few minutes, after which Mrs. Tendell excused herself to go prepare a meal. The two men leaned back and Tendell narrated the case for Brad. When he finished, Tendell settled himself comfortably on the sofa and waited.

Brad slowly digested the information he'd just heard. The power of policemen to latch onto the wrong man was awesome. In Keith's case the homosexual angle—combined with a strong monetary motive—made it so easy to stop investigating.

"Who will get the garage and insurance if Keith's convicted?" Brad asked at last.

Tendell raised an eyebrow. "Seth's parents, I suppose. Seth's will left everything to Keith, as well as providing elaborate instructions for his own funeral. Seth's lawyer, Charles Thompson, refused to follow those instructions, claiming that Keith's arrest negated his rights in the matter. By law, Keith should have been in charge—or the deposition of Seth's body held in limbo until after the trial. Thompson's in an awkward position if Keith's acquitted—and he knows it. I'd love suing him. Keith was more upset over his friend's burial—Seth wanted to be cremated—than over being charged with the crime. He'll fight Thompson on the will business." Tendell returned to the matter at hand. "But surely you don't suspect Seth's parents?"

Brad shrugged. "If Keith didn't kill Seth, somebody else did—unless the man committed suicide, which under the circumstances seems out of the question. What did the Rawsons think about Seth's homosexuality? Were they aware of it before the murder? What was the opinion of the community?"

"At the trial, Mrs. Rawson avoided the issue. She wasn't overly hostile to Keith. Her husband, Jeb Rawson, was. He's a typical moral majority religious zealot. He harshly condemned Keith at the trial. They must have suspected something even before everything came out. Jeb indicated he knew and had expressed his disapproval. Alma, Seth's mother, simply said her son's 'business arrangements' weren't any of her concern. Keith and Seth were circumspect: They lived in separate houses; neither was effeminate. Seth, in fact, was one hell of a man. Strong, muscular, would have been a damn good football player for the high school if Jeb had let him play. I suppose the community as a whole knew but didn't give a damn as long as they didn't flaunt the affair. And they didn't, though I suspect that was more Seth's doing than Keith's."

"So Seth's parents get the money if Keith is convicted?"

Brad asked as Tendell nodded. "Did anyone check Jeb Rawson's whereabouts at the time of his son's death?"

Tendell shrugged his shoulders. "Frankly, I don't know. It never crossed my mind. I doubt it would have entered the Chief's head either. After all, Keith was supposed to inherit."

"Yes, but did the Rawsons know that?"

Tendell nodded his head. "They'd have known about the garage; that was a partnership. Keith put up the money for it when his parents died. A partnership was the most sensible arrangement. The Rawsons wouldn't have expected to get the garage."

Brad went off in another direction.

"What about the gun? Tracing the weapon seems the easiest solution. If it didn't belong to either Keith or Seth, whoever used it must have brought it with them. Which means they had to get it from somewhere. Records concerning gun purchases are inadequate, but there's always a chance a record might exist. Especially if the thing were picked up in a pawnshop or used gun shop. Did the Chief look into that?"

Tendell nodded.

"He checked the pawnshops around town and had the Sheriff check those in the county. There was no record of such a sale. But I doubt the Chief sent the serial number out of the area. Did you people in Atlanta get anything on it?"

"I don't know," Brad admitted. "Nothing would have been done about it if we had. We don't have the manpower. I could do something like that on my own when I get back. Could you get me a picture of Jeb Rawson?"

Tendell grinned. "You've already picked out your scapegoat, haven't you?" he asked. "Yes, I can. The reporter who covered the trial for the local paper snapped tons of pictures. He's bound to have one of Jeb. I doubt he'll mind giving me a print."

They discussed the case until it was time to eat, then

found they could not leave the topic alone, even at the table. By the time Brad was ready to retire for the night, he and the Tendells had established the basis for a firm friendship.

The next day, Tendell introduced Brad to the Chief of Police, Wayne Links. Brad expected some antagonism from the official but found almost the opposite.

Brad and Tendell had concocted a tale to account for Brad's interest in the case. Links seemed not to care why the Atlanta cop was interested. Links was determined to be helpful.

"I've never been completely at ease in my own mind that Wilson was guilty. He lessened my concern by running away like he did, but what the hell. If I were queer in this town, I'd probably run too. I can tell you this much," Links clenched his fist and pounded his desk for emphasis, "If he hadn't been queer, the Grand Jury would never have brought in an indictment on the meagre evidence we had. I was surprised they did." He willingly gave Brad the serial number of the weapon and a photo of the gun.

Tendell, hesitantly, broached the matter of checking up on Jeb Rawson.

Links looked amused.

"Trying to lay it to the old man, are you?" His smile disappeared. "I don't know as I ever did question Jeb. Now it's been so long nobody will remember." He stood up, leading the pair from his office. "Tell you what, Wade," he said, "I'll do what I can. Discreetly. The community is very sympathetic towards Jeb and his wife—their daughters. It was, is, an ugly mess. Folks wouldn't like having us pester the Rawsons. But I'll see if I can't find out something—while being careful at the same time. But I'm afraid you're far off the mark there," Links added to Brad. "Jeb would be too scared of going to hell to shoot anybody." The Chief chuckled at his joke and bid his visitors good-bye.

Their next stop was the newspaper office where, again,

Wade Tendell got what he wanted: a photo of Jeb Rawson. It was a crisp, clear portrait, one Tendell insisted looked exactly like the old man. By noon, Brad was ready to leave. He shook hands with Tendell as he climbed into his car.

"You'll let me know, won't you, if you find anything?" the lawyer asked.

"Certainly," Brad assured the attorney. "But don't expect much. There are, literally, thousands of places in Atlanta where a man could pick up a gun. I haven't got that much time and I'll need to be discreet myself. Besides, if the weapon was bought in Atlanta, it could be months, if ever, before I find out anything. The chances of some clerk remembering who bought it get more remote with each passing day. On top of that, I've got the additional job of finding Wilson. He doesn't look like he used to—has a full beard. I'd seen pictures of him at the station, on television during the trial, and I didn't recognize him. Between checking on the weapon and trying to run Keith to earth, I'm going to be a busy man."

"Would it help if I came up some weekend?" Tendell offered.

"No. It will mostly be a matter of luck." Brad waved to Tendell and headed towards the interstate. A few hours at the cottage would have been welcome, but Brad now had a lot to do in Atlanta. The sooner he started the sooner he might discover something useful. And he'd remembered something he'd not mentioned to the eager young lawyer. As he'd bent over Keith in the old house, the smell of grease and kitchen odors had clung to the guy's clothes—indicating he might be working in a kitchen someplace. With that as a clue and the certain feeling Keith would have turned to the gay community—both for a job and as a refuge—Brad hoped it would only be a matter of time before he found his man.

23

Keith drank his Coke; slowly the trembling stopped. Damn! A narrow escape. He hoped to God he'd wiped all his prints off that gun. All he needed was a bunch of goddamn cops looking for him all over Altanta. The police in Tilton probably knew he'd reached the city; but in Atlanta he was only another fugitive. Cops in the metro area had too many other problems on their hands to worry about him.

Glancing at his watch, Keith saw he had time to run over to the park and shower before going to work. If he bought a pair of shorts he could wash his clothes and let them dry in the sun before going to work. He'd give it a try. Cautiously, he made his way from the laundromat to the bus stop, keeping a wary eye out for the cop—any cop. Safely on the bus, he allowed his mind to consider how good-looking the pig had been. Wonderfully broad shoulders; nice face. Keith grimaced. Just what he neeeded, getting moon-eyed over a goddamn cop. He'd had enough of them to last a lifetime.

He got off the bus a couple of blocks from the park and visited several small clothing shops before finding the kind of shorts he wanted.

"Would you care to try them on?" smirked the clerk, making an obvious play.

Keith grinned. "No," he said. "Not unless you get off soon."

The clerk—a small-framed, tired type—turned fearful, shocked that his make-believe invitation was being taken seriously. Keith still looked too much like rough trade to be successful when it came to picking up store clerks. Both accepted the clerk's protestation of a "previous engagement" to ease them past the matter.

Everything, Keith thought as he walked to the park, is a game. If I could just accept the fact that life is a damned game —that we're all fucking pawns, pushed around by invisible hands, hands without feelings or compassion—it would be so much easier to endure.

But he couldn't. He didn't believe in gods and didn't accept the notion that an impersonal universe could stand in the way of his own individual achievement. Yet his present difficulties seemed so prearranged. The very sort of embroglio a god would dream up. Keith took his shower, washed out his pants and shirt, then found a place to sun himself for a while. If he couldn't sleep, he could at least watch the queers.

The cruising area by the small lake didn't interst him this afternoon. He might be able to rest there on a bench, but the steady stream of traffic would be distracting. He turned instead towards a small hillock, past which were the greenhouses. At one time the greenhouse section had been a choice spot for picking up guys—but park officials put a stop to that by fencing the area and locking it at night. There was, however, a pleasant grassy knoll situated between the swimming pool and the greenhouses. Keith went there, found a sunny spot, spread out his clothes and tried relaxing.

He didn't sleep. Actually, he'd slept nearly as much as he ever did before the cop woke him. But the warm sun made him feel drowsy so he closed his eyes and relaxed. He wondered if he were adjusting to life as a fugitive. Was it something anyone ever got used to? Always fearful, always looking over one's shoulder—never trusting anyone? He sighed and

opened his mind to the persistent image of Seth which hovered
on the edge of his consciousness.

*You're doing okay. Today was a fluke. Somebody prob-
ably saw you goin' in that house and called the cops. Once you
git a place of your own, you won't have that problem. Hang in
there. You're gonna make it.*

Seth! Seth! I miss you so! I don't know how long I can
keep doing this. I'm not cut out for this sort of life. The running, the fear, the lying. How can I see you, hear you so plain-
ly, yet not have you? If I could only join you, if we could be
together just one more time . . .

*Knock off that nonsense! I'll always be a part of you—
your memory, your life, even your future. But you gotta look
beyond me. You gotta do two things for me: Keep your promise
as soon as you can, then let me go—find someone else who'll
love you as I do, as I did. I want only happiness for you and
peace for myself.*

Keith stirred and resolutely tried turning his thoughts to
his present situation, weighing pros and cons, hoping something useful might result from such action. It didn't. Finally
he opened his eyes and surveyed the scene around him.

A couple of unattractive men had taken up positions on
either side of him. No matter which way he stared, one of them
smirked at him, hoping to catch his eye. He shuddered, hoping
his situation never became so bad he would have to have sex
with such men. He failed to see why men who were obviously
gay, and aware of the praise good flesh garnered, permitted
themselves to grow fat and gross-looking. One of the pair was
married, but had removed his ring, leaving the telltale mark
gleaming like a beacon on an otherwise tanned hand. The other
probably was married too. Neither could have been over forty-
five, but bloated bellies hung over their belts like a pregnant
woman, minutes from the delivery room. Why did they persist
in chasing men, Keith wondered, facing inevitable rejection—

or, even if gaining a momentary sexual acceptance, finding it laced with scorn and disdain? Keith felt his clothes. The shirt was almost dry, but the jeans had a ways to go yet. He closed his eyes and willed the pair away, as if they were wraiths to be banished with a thought.

Since the nature of their lives permitted them only a certain amount of time to devote to frenzied cruising activities, both men left when it became obvious Keith wasn't going to respond to their overtures. In their place appeared a more youthful prospect. Handsome and tall, he was a type Keith could accept. Keith gazed at the newcomer with an interested look in his eye. The man responded.

"Hi. Sun hot enough for you today?"

"Yeah. It's pleasant, though."

The man stared intently, then asked, "You got time to fuck?"

You're certainly direct.

"Maybe," Keith said aloud.

"Come on." The man got to his feet.

Keith raised himself to one elbow, in no hurry to rush off anywhere. The warmth of the sun made him lazy. Horny, but lazy.

"Where you live?" he asked, stalling for time to make up his mind.

"Oh, I ain't got time to go home," the man said. "Let's step down one of the trails."

"You mean here in the park?" Keith questioned. "In public?"

It ain't public," responded the man. "Lotsa guys do it. Nobody gives a fuck."

"I give a fuck," Keith replied with some acerbity. "A cop or the park police could come along any time. If it isn't worth going someplace private, it isn't worth doing at all." He lay back down. "I'm not into public sex."

"Suit yourself." The man strolled away, certain he'd find someone else who was more eager and less demanding.

Keith let the man slip away. The urge to indulge in public sex was one of the things he least admired about fellow gay men. Back in Tilton, he'd always been annoyed at the blatant displays of affection between men and women. Watching women sitting close to "their men" while driving around, you'd think they were Siamese twins. Heteros were always kissing and slobbering all over one another in public. Part of Keith's disgust stemmed from society's double standard. If he and Seth had tried anything like that, the bastards would have raised hell, probably arrested them. As far as Keith was concerned, watching hetero mating rituals was just as annoying, just as sickening. Feeling as he did, Keith was willing to agree that gays and straights ought to refrain from such displays. He shook himself, hoping to toss off an approaching feeling of gloom, and got up. His clothes were dry enough to wear. He walked to the bathroom by the tennis courts.

The toilets were another area in the park where cruising took place. Not that Keith considered sticking his cock through a glory hole, but there was plenty of that going on in the park bathrooms. As fast as attendants closed up one hole, another materialized. He entered the restroom, closed the door of a stall and swiftly stepped out of his newly-purchased shorts and pulled on his nearly dry jeans and shirt. As he was zipping up his pants, a finger began wiggling in the hole which was carved out of the wall. He ignored it. A hissing sound started up. What would happen, he wondered, if he bent over and bit the finger? How would the john explain a chewed finger to wifey? Or for that matter, what if the man stuck his cock through the hole and someone bit that? Keith grinned to himself. If he had a magic marker, he'd be tempted to entice the man's dick through the hole so he could draw a smiley face on it. That would be a surprise. Since he had no marker, and was not in the mood to decapitate a cock, he ignored both finger and hissing, and left.

It was too early to report for work, so he decided to make use of the time by looking for a place to live. He was getting paid tonight and he'd noticed signs advertising places by the week or month. The area around the park contained many expensive apartment complexes, but there were others which were dilapidated and rundown and apparently rented for what he could afford.

Keith stopped at a couple of places, inquiring as to availability and price. He was slowly making his way towards a third, when the door of the building burst open and a man and a woman raced down the steps. Behind them scurried an incredibly old woman, bellowing at the top of her lungs and pelting the pair with bits of food.

"Out, out! I ain't a'gonna have a bunch of pigs in my place. Ye git the hell outta here." A piece of rotten apple tumbled down at Keith's feet and jiggled fitfully before coming to a halt.

On reaching the pavement, the man turned and picked up a rock to hurl at the irate woman.

Keith stepped up and grabbed the upraised hand. "Knock it off!" he ordered. "She's older than you."

The man swung at Keith, who blocked the blow and tripped the guy.

Finding himself unable to extract revenge, the man and his girl friend disappeared down the street, mouthing obscenities.

The old woman stared at their retreating backs.

"Sons-a-bitches! I oughtta had better sense'n to rent to 'em." She turned and stared up at Keith. "Thanks, young'un. Not that I needed no help. That fool was so doped up he couldn't a' hit me." Her wrinkled face broke into a misshaped grin. "I appreciate it all the same."

"You're welcome," Keith said. "Would you happen to be the landlady here?"

"That I be. Why? Ye lookin' fer a place?"

"Yes. I was hoping to find something inexpensive. I only need a bedroom."

"All I got's what that pair left. Ain't paid me nothin' fer three weeks. Place looks like a pig's been wallerin' in it. Ye come back tomorrow—I'll have it cleaned up some."

"How much you asking for it?"

"Two hunnert a month."

"Is it quiet? I work at night and need to sleep in the day-time."

"Yep. Most folks 'round here's night people—one sort or 'nother. It'd be fine fer you. Big room, with a tiny kitchenette, even a shower of its own. Furnished, too—if'n I can clean up their filth."

Keith grinned. "Tell you what," he said. "I need it in the morning. If you'll let me pay you a week at a time, starting tomorrow, I'll come up and clean it for you—if you provide the stuff . . . I don't have a broom with me."

"I usually git a bit more by the week," she said hesitantly.

"You said you didn't get anything out of them for three weeks," Keith reminded her. "I'll pay promptly and clean it up for you; besides," he added, "if that rock had hit you, you might have ended up in the hospital with a big bill to pay."

She crackled. "Ye convinced me. Come on. I'll git the stuff you'll need. Where ye work?"

He told her.

"Fer Fatman!" she exclaimed. "Hell, I know him. Knowed him all my life. Ye work fer him, ye gotta be all right. Must be queer, too." She took the sting from the epithet by adding, "I oughtta know'd better'n to rent to anybody else. That pair what just left—trash. Nothin' but trash. Ye guys take better care of stuff."

24

Finding the tiny apartment was a stroke of luck. It took Keith the better part of two days to make the place livable, but once cleaned, it wasn't too bad. Best of all, it was affordable. And the building was in a predominately gay neighborhood.

A month went by. Two. Three. He found himself surviving. It amazed him how little a person needed. He usually put in some overtime at the restaurant. Fatman began depending heavily on his dishwasher. After the promised two weeks he gave Keith a small raise, and another after the third month. The only disadvantage with acquiring Fatman's confidence was the request to run the register from time to time. Keith was the only one Fatman trusted with the money. Unwilling to flatly refuse, Keith tried keeping the times he worked out front to a minimum.

Slowly his funds accumulated. Keith spent very little. He almost never ate anywhere except at the restaurant, keeping only a little food in his apartment. He missed music so much that he broke down and bought a decent radio from a local pawnshop. Atlanta had a multitude of radio stations and they helped ease the pain caused by the loss of all his records and stereo equipment. The library and used bookstores provided him with material to read. Passing a cop on the street no longer made him want to run, although the image of a certain cop remained planted firmly in his mind.

At first Keith feared his landlady, Lucy Whitman, would become a nuisance. She developed a fondness for him and chattered away every time he passed her around the building. When she needed a favor, she turned to him. This proved to be to his advantage. One day while searching the basement for something the old lady wanted, he ran across a set of weight-lifting equipment left by a delinquent tenant and conned her into letting him use it. Lifting provided an outlet for his excess energy and, momentarily, took his mind off his own predicament. It also improved his appearance to such an extent that his trips to the bars grew more successful.

Successful from the standpoint of leaving with some hunky number. None of his encounters, however, lasted beyond a trick or two. This facet of gay life in Atlanta made him question the subculture. What were they doing to themselves? Was sex in and of itself the end-all and be-all of every good-looking male? He went to the baths a couple of times after moving into his apartment, but on his second visit contracted his first dose of VD, which caused him to swear off the tubs. The disease left him feeling dirty and common. For a few weeks he stopped doing anything, but his need of physical contact was too strong. Hoping to relieve tensions he started frequenting the leather bars, trying—not altogether subconsciously—to find a man capable of satisfying him as Seth had.

Keith was discovering Atlanta had sex for all tastes, both basic and bizarre. The city's reputation was that of "drag capital of the South"; but having no interest in drag queens, the show bars didn't attract him. Neither did the preppy hangouts. In his search Keith was drawn to three or four particular bars. The Spur, which he frequented at first, attracted a nice crowd: a few leathermen, some ersatz cowboys and some guys in uniforms of one sort or another. Nothing too extreme. Keith was comfortable there, but two things pushed him towards more radical bars: The men he picked up in the Spur seldom were interested in more than one-night stands; and they were not, by and large, into anything other than basics. As months passed, Keith discovered his version of kinkiness had a firmer grip on him than he cared to admit. After weeks of wavering, he decided to try the city's premiere leather bar, the Cellar.

The Cellar had a wild reputation which Keith soon discovered was well-deserved. On-premise sex was the name of the game. There Keith witnessed his first fist-fucking performance. Both parties seemed to be thoroughly enjoying themselves, but Keith almost lost all the beer he'd consumed. The bar's rest room (modeled after the barracks latrines he'd known in basic) was full of guys drinking piss. At first, Keith wanted to walk out and pretend it was a bad dream. Still, he had no right condemning others since he wanted full freedom to engage in his own brand of offbeat behavior. Tolerance, he was learning, did not come easy.

Keith's uneasiness was evidently very visible. He ordered a beer and stood off to one side taking in the scenes in front of him. It was unlike anything he'd ever viewed before. The back room and bathrooms contained blatant displays of raw sex; the main bar area catered to the costumed seekers of thrills. Guys wearing studded leather collars were led around like dogs by their "masters." Keith felt stirrings of something akin to anticipation at the sight of such arrangements. What would it feel like, playing such a game? Did he really want to know? All he was sure of was that it would take a special sort of man to get him into such gear.

After a couple of beers, however, the bar seemed less radical. Keith's acceptance of it grew; he decided another drink was in order.

"I'll buy you one."

The words were spoken by a man who'd moved in next to

Keith. It was more like a command than an offer but Keith
nodded. He had learned by now that the offer of a drink did not
automatically imply spending the night.

The order was taken by a sexy waiter wearing next to nothing
—plus leather suspenders and a hardhat. Keith turned, giving
a frank stare of appraisal at the man who was buying his beer.

The guy was older than Keith, in his early thirties: muscular arms and shoulders; a stomach which was flat, hard and
rippled. A leather vest did little to cover the man's upper anat-
omy. His nipples, excited by their continual brush against the
vest, were taut and erect. His lower region was encased in levis
so tight they could have been skin on a sausage. He showed a
substantial box.

"You're new here," he accused Keith. Again, his words
were not a question so much as a statement of fact. His look
was just short of insolent.

"Is that a crime?" he asked.

The man grinned. The response changed his entire appearance. He was very attractive. "Only if you don't know why
you're here," he replied. "Do you?"

"I guess so," Keith answered. He knew he ought to be
more positive, more assertive, but the truth was he wasn't sure
what he was doing there. He wasn't sure he knew what he was
looking for. He shrugged, mentally, and opted for honesty—in
a milieu where honesty was not easy to come by.

"Did you come to gawk or to get picked up?" the man
asked.

"To get picked up—if I meet anyone who interests me,"
Keith answered.

"What sort of limits you got?"

Keith felt uncomfortable. "I guess I'm pretty much into
basics," he responded.

The man looked shocked. "Nobody who's interested only
in basics comes to the Cellar! You gotta be a little kinky or you

wouldn't be here." His voice softened slightly. "Come on, I've done just about everything and heard about it all. You won't faze me, no matter what your scene is. If you're looking to get started, I'm a pretty fair instructor."

Their drinks arrived, giving Keith time to consider his answer. Once more, honesty seemed his best option.

"I am into basics; but I don't mind—I enjoy—a bit of roughness along the way. A belt slapping my ass feels good; a hand across my face from the right guy, stuff like that . . . " Confessing his peculiarities struck Keith as absurd. One did not have conversations like this. These sorts of things were never spoken of; they simply, sometimes, took place in dark and sterile rooms, where they might, afterwards, be forgotten.

The man nodded. "And the idea you like it embarrasses you, doesn't it? No, don't answer—" he interrupted Keith's attempt at protest "—I can tell you're ill-at-ease talking about it. You shouldn't be." He swigged from his beer bottle before adding. "I'd like to trick with you. Think you'd trust me enough for a night together? I've not had a night of basics in so long, it would be novel for me."

"I'd hate putting you in an awkward postion," Keith said. He liked the guy's looks but didn't care for the conversation. Had he made a mistake coming to the Cellar? Maybe he wasn't ready for the type of men who frequented the place. Maybe he would never be.

"What's your name?" Keith added as an afterthought, thinking how impersonal cruising was; he'd spilled all his secret perversions long before wondering who he was telling about his innermost desires. What a screwy world.

"Mac," the man answered. "And no position's awkward for me; either physical or mental. I like you—you're different. If you want to go home with me, we can leave."

Keith shrugged. What could he lose but his life? "Where do you live?"

The address was on Monroe Drive, close to Ansley Mall, an area familiar to Keith. It presented no difficulties, so he accepted. They finished their beers and left, with Mac leading the way. As soon as Keith agreed to their leaving together, a subtle change in the relationship came into play. Mac at once assumed the position of leader, of commander. Keith wondered what *he* was supposed to do.

The drive to Mac's place was silent. He was busy driving and Keith, unsure what he ought to say, kept quiet. The evening was not turning out as he'd expected—which only served to prove, to Keith's mind at least, that he was looking for something special. He wasn't certain what it was, but hoped he'd recognize it when he stumbled across it. Mac, while attractive, wasn't striking the right chords. The man's sexy magnetism was contagious, however, and by the time they reached his house, Keith found his expectations rising.

Mac led Keith into the kitchen.

"Let me fix something to drink, then we'll go up to the bedroom. You want music?"

"No. It would be superfluous."

Mac nodded. "You're perceptive. If we can't carry on in such a way that we think we're hearing music, we're in bad shape. You want beer or something else?"

"Beer's fine."

"You're easy to please—as far as drinks go." Mac churchkeyed the top off a bottle and handed it to Keith. He mixed himself something with a generous shot of bourbon in it, then turned and put his arm around Keith's waist. It was the first time they'd touched. Keith's found the hand firm, masculine and warm. Mac squeezed the flesh on Keith's hip and half-turned, half-pushed his guest towards the stairs.

"Let's go."

They climbed the stairs arm in arm. The bedroom was large and sparsely furnished, with only a king-sized bed and dresser. Mac pointed towards a door.

"There's the john if you need it." He went to a closet and fumbled around for a few moments. He approached Keith carrying several accouterments.

"Come here."

Keith put his beer down and advanced towards Mac. Only a very dim light illuminated the oversized room. The walls appeared to be a dark blue; the drapes and bedspread were either a deep hue of blue or black. Everything combined to make the space eerie, not quite real. Keith felt he was living a dream, a shadow moving unattached through someone's mind. Mac's strong arms and hands belied the dream-like aspect of the moment.

Mac pulled Keith towards him and they kissed deeply. Mac was tremendously strong and gripped Keith in a hard, rugged grasp. The leather vest exuded a stimulating odor. Carefully, they made their initial moves. Mac grabbed Keith's shoulders and pressured him to his knees. Kneeling in front of the man, Keith pulled Mac's thighs into his face, nudging the swollen crotch with his mouth. He fumbled with the belt buckle and loosened it. The snap was easy; so was the zipper. Mac cupped Keith's head with a hand and jerked it upward. With the other, he slapped his worshipping acolyte. Not too gently. The sound of hand against face-flesh echoed harshly in the quiet room. Keith unlooped the belt and handed it to Mac. Mac gripped the instrument, slid it across Keith's back and under his arms, then used it to pull Keith to his feet. Holding the belt with one hand, Mac used his other hand to pull Keith to him for a kiss. Their mouths met in a hungry embrace which, like a spark on dry hay, engulfed them both, unleashing their passions.

Mac unbuttoned Keith's shirt, loosening the belt across Keith's back only long enough to let the man slip out of the garment, then the belt tightened again, biting into Keith's flesh; uncomfortable, but with a compulsion all its own. In seconds Keith stood naked in front of Mac. He lowered his head and took one of Mac's hard nipples between his teeth, while allowing his tongue to brush the leather vest. He stroked Mac's cock with one hand and tugged Mac's levis with the others. Once the pants fell past Mac's thick thighs, Keith dropped to his knees, ready to work on the stiff cock with his mouth. It was then he heard the first cries.

For a time he paid them no mind, too entranced by the man he was working on. Gradually, however, the sounds could not be ignored.

"Help! For God's sake, somebody get me out of here!"

The words sounded pitiful, weak. Clanking sounds, chain-like, dimmed the pleas while urging their authenticity.

Mac now removed the belt from around Keith's back and was dragging it up and down Keith's spine. Occasionally he allowed it to play down between the crack of Keith's ass. Tantilizing without doing anything. A louder cry from—the next room?—demanded Keith acknowledge it.

He stopped sucking Mac's cock and looked up at the towering man.

"Am I supposed to ask what that noise is all about?"

"No!" Mac was brusque. "That isn't part of our game; it's none of your business."

"I think a cry for help from another person would be anyone's business," Keith answered, not sure whether the sounds were real or fantasy. If they were fantasy, what was their purpose? Keith found them distracting.

"Not these people," Mac replied.

"Are there actually people here? Chained up?" Keith asked the question disbelievingly.

"Certainly," Mac snapped, irritated. "They're my slaves. They want to be my slaves. Their only complaint is that they aren't here in your position. They've disobeyed my orders and I'm punishing them. Disobedience must be punished." He looked at Keith, but the light was too dim for Keith to read the glance. "Slavery's not your scene, so keep out of it. Don't judge others by your weakness."

Keith's mind raced. Was Mac telling him the truth? Were there men in another room, chained, pleading for help? Or were the sounds part of some macabre tape, being played in order to test aspects of Keith's own personality? Was Mac getting off by placing Keith in the position of condoning something he disapproved of? Keith didn't know—and suddenly found himself not caring either. Whatever was going on, it was taking place outside the rules of any game he wanted to play. Continuing to mess around with Mac would only compound the situation. Keith wanted out. He started to stand but found Mac's hand pressuring him back to his knees.

"Ignore them," Mac warned in a cold voice. "They're not your business. You wouldn't want to join them, would you?"

In a swift motion, Keith knocked Mac's hand aside. "Is that a threat of some sort?" he asked as he rose to his feet. Without waiting for an answer, he continued, "because if it is, it isn't effective."

"You planning on doing something?"

"Yes. I'm getting out of here. I don't understand why sex has to be such a goddamned enterprise! It's supposed to be a pleasurable activity. An end in itself. Without wives, kids—even without love, if necessary. I enjoy the embellishments I foolishly mentioned to you. But when the frills become more important than the main dish, forget it. The time comes I can't get my rocks off without the sort of orchestration you need, I'll retire and become celibate. I wouldn't have minded all this even, if you'd told me. But no, you drag it in unannounced and pretend it's more than it is. I'll forego this trip, thanks."

"You're certain it's a game, are you? Certain you can walk away?"

"Yes. To both questions."

Mac shrugged his shoulders. His leather vest gaped wider, exposing his beautiful torso. The sounds from the room beyond grew pitiful. Keith felt his resolve wavering. Were there people chained, needing help? Could he ignore the possibility?

He balked at the notion. Looking around the room, he located his shirt and pants and put them on. The whole business was either a test of himself or a way for Mac to get his kicks. Either possibility was too much for him.

"You're really going to leave?"

"That's right."

"What about them?" Mac nodded towards the next room.

"*Them* is a recording, or some such trick—gimmick I should say—as far as I'm concerned, the whole thing's in terrible taste. Hell, I'm all for everyone doing their own thing, but you knew what my thing was before we got here. Then you come along and pull something like this! I not only don't like it, I'm in no mood for it."

Keith checked his pockets to make sure he had everything he'd started with, then headed for the door.

Mac stepped in front of him. "You forget—it's up to me to determine if you leave or not."

Keith glared at him. "I hate to disagree with you, but it's not up to you to decide. Either you step aside or I'll knock you out of the way."

Mac looked as if he wanted to take up the matter, then he shrugged and moved aside.

"Want me to drive you home?" he asked, morosely.

"No thanks, I'll manage. It's not far."

Minutes later, Keith was back on the street. His relief was tempered by the fact he'd been stupid enough to leave the bar with Mac in the first place. Not that there'd been anything to indicate Mac was a nut, but all the same, Keith understood the risks of the game he played. And there were legitimate dangers. When society pushed a group of people as far as it did homosexuals, there was always a possibility that some would snap. Keith always felt he could spot the few who might; his run-in with Mac made him wonder.

He tried putting the episode out of his mind. The evening was pleasant; he'd enjoy walking home.

His mind wandered. In spite of the late hour and the unsettling incident, caution was not paramount in Keith's thoughts. Seth was. The loneliness he'd experienced since his lover's death, the emptiness which filled him most of the time, sometimes threatened to overwhelm him. Rationally, Keith knew it was important that he continue searching for another man. No one would replace Seth; it wasn't a replacement he was looking for. He was looking for someone to make the loss bearable, the pain less intense, the loneliness more endurable. He wanted someone to love.

Cars whizzed by on Monroe Drive. Atlanta was a city which seldom slept. Keith paid them no mind. He was tuned out, feeling so safe, he did not notice the approaching cop car. It drove past without alerting him to danger. He had, more or less, gotten over his fear of arrest each time he saw a man in blue. The screech of brakes, as the vehicle spun round in the street and headed towards him, woke Keith from his reverie.

As the distinctly marked vehicle neared him, Keith saw the face which was so vividly etched across his brain. That damned cop! The sight was all Keith needed; he sprinted forward and dashed down an alley. The car, swerving recklessly, followed.

Brad Evans couldn't believe his luck. Months of frustration made him determined. He almost forgot the reasons he wanted to talk to Keith, so eager was he to catch his quarry. As Keith raced away, however, a sense of the situation returned to Brad.

Calling over the car's loudspeaker, he sought to reassure.

"Keith! Stop running! I only want to talk to you! Stop running!"

The sound of his name chilled Keith. The son-of-a-bitch knew who he was. Keith ran faster, ducking down one alleyway after another, scurrying over obstacles, and, at one point, scaling a small wall. Halting for a minute to catch his breath, he heard no footsteps behind him. He dared not relax, however, and continued his desperate race, keeping to back streets and out-of-the-way sections of the city. After forty-five minutes, feeling he'd eluded the cop, Keith made his way back to his apartment. He showered, then lay on the sagging bed, scared all over again.

The cop knew him! How in the hell had that happened? Had he missed a fingerprint on that damned gun? He should have kept it, not tried being a nice guy. Being a nice guy never got him anyplace. Never got him or Seth anyplace. The cop was so damned good looking. Keith had not wanted the bastard to get in trouble over the loss of his fucking weapon. Keith reached for his wallet and turned to the photo of Seth. He felt his eyes burn as tears welled in them. Wasn't he over crying yet? Would he ever be? Was his life going to be one continual nightmare of running? He ought to leave Atlanta. The cops obviously were looking for him. What chance did he have of outwitting them for very long?

What chance would he have elsewhere? At least here he had a job and a place to stay. If he'd just work and keep close to home for awhile, maybe they'd give up looking for him. God knows, they had enough to keep them busy; Atlanta was presently being proclaimed "murder capital" of the South.

Even as he thought it, it didn't sound like much of a life. Holding Seth's picture, Keith knew he must somehow escape his present dilemma—find some way of clearing himself, then find a man he could love. Only in a relationship could he realize his greatest potential—and that was a goal he owed himself. It was time he worked at finding a way to stop being a fugitive.

25

Brad Evans was pissed. So close—and the bastard got away! Keith had outsmarted him a second time. Well, maybe outsmarted was too harsh a term. If he'd called in, gotten reinforcements, done the things he'd normally have done when pursuing a fugitive, they'd have gotten the guy. Brad didn't want to catch Keith that way. He wanted to capture him in a way that would make it possible to invite the man home with him, or out for a drink—a situation which indicated Brad was a friend, not a cop out to bust him.

Evans got back in his car and continued his rounds. It was a quiet night, for which he was thankful. The past few months had exhausted him—and his patience as well.

In Atlanta, he'd gone the rounds of gun shops and pawnshops, trying to find the one which sold the weapon used to kill Seth Rawson. So far, all he'd done was lose sleep and waste gas.

The news from Tilton was more encouraging.

Every week or so, Brad phoned Wade Tendell for progress reports. The first month had been devoid of anything remotely resembling progress. The last time they spoke, however, Tendell had been excited.

"I swear to God, Brad, we've finally gotten a break!"

"You're kidding? Has Keith been in touch with you?"

"No, nothing like that. Links finally stirred himself a bit.

I can't blame him much, for taking his time—he's got to be
cautious. It wouldn't do for folks around here to get the idea he
was going after the Rawsons—which he isn't unless one of
'em's guilty. Anyway, what he learned is that the night of
Seth's death, somebody left the Rawson farm. Jeb's old
pickup is on its last legs. You can hear it a mile away. A neighbor of his, an old lady name of Mary Spivey, wasn't feeling too
well that night, Links says. She got up to take some medicine
and heard Jeb's truck crank up. A few minutes later, it rattled
past her place. That was at three in the morning. Links asked
Mrs. Spivey how she happened to remember the date and she
said it was easy, because it was the same day the news got
'round about Seth's being killed. Fixed the date in her mind
real well."

"So Jeb could have been involved!" Brad exclaimed.

"Well," Tendell hedged, "it's going to take more than
Mary Spivey's word about seeing Jeb's truck go by to get
things moving in the direction we'd like, but it is a beginning.
Links followed up Mrs. Spivey's information and learned Jeb
was in Waycross that day, attending some sort of religious
gathering. He's famous for that. The meeting, however,
didn't begin until nine in the morning. No reason for him to
have left Tilton so early. One man recalled Jeb wasn't feeling
well that morning. Maybe he was tired."

"You're right—it's not much. but it is a beginning. Now
if I can just find something about that blasted weapon!"

"That's the main thing," Tendell agreed. "If we can tie
that weapon to anyone other than Keith, I believe we can get
the charges dismissed. As I've said all along, they don't have
much of a case in any event. I know it's a lot of work but if
you'll keep checking on that gun . . . "

Brad assured the lawyer he would.

And he did. Whenever possible, he'd check as many
places as time permitted, asking about serial numbers and gun
sales. It was tiring and unrewarding. At the same time, he tried

half-heartedly to find Keith.

Atlanta, however, was such a sprawling city. There were too many places where Keith could work and hide out. Brad thought about going to the gay bars, but that solution was a last resort. He might be spotted by someone from the department which would open a whole new can of worms. If they discharged him for being queer, he wanted it to be after he'd used his authority to find that weapon's origin, not before. He concentrated on looking for the gun seller, letting the search for Keith lag.

There were other reasons for not going all-out in an attempt to find the fugitive.

If Brad found Keith, he'd be breaking the law himself if he didn't turn the guy in; and there was no way he was going to do that. Besides, he'd admitted to himself he was infatuated with his image of Keith. The sleeping man on the floor of the old house, coupled with the devotion and love he was learning existed between Keith and Seth Rawson filled Brad's dreams, lulling him into daydreams where he and Keith were lovers, where it was he and Keith . . .

And when it got down to cases, Brad doubted Keith could ever care for a cop. Or, if his profession didn't prove to be a handicap, there would be something else. By finding the gun's source, Brad would be providing a way of approaching Keith along a path not fraught with the problems inherent in his job. Not that he'd have the job long, once what he was doing came out. He'd already started making plans for leaving the department. He'd had enough of it. The pettiness, the paperwork, the regulations geared not for effectiveness but designed instead to give some men power over others. Brad was in good financial shape and had offers for other positions. If he could interest Keith, they might do something together . . .

He wanted the man. There was no doubt in his mind about that. And he feared rejection.

Walking back to the police car after Keith had gotten

away, Brad wondered what he'd have done if he'd caught the
guy? Pleaded with him to trust a cop? Forced him to return to
the condo and screw? Every image the policeman conjured up
ended in disaster.

Fate, however, seemed ready to bring the men together.
Two days after chasing Keith, Brad was driving home from
work and passed the Fatman's diner. He'd debated on going
to breakfast with the guys but decided against it. He swung
onto Cheshire Bridge Road, knowing instinctively that many of
the shops were gay oriented. As always lately, when in a gay
section of the city, he kept his eyes open. One day . . .

And it happened.

He stopped at a traffic light; his eyes roaming around. In
the restaurant at the corner, a beard caught his eye. Keith!

Horns honking behind him jerked Brad back to the now
green traffic signal. He drove on, turning around as soon as he
could. Across the street from the eatery was a parking area, a
gas station and telephone.

Brad stood by the phone booth and stared at the
restaurant. It *was* Keith at the register. An elated feeling swept
over the cop. As Brad watched, Fatman waddled into the din-
ing area, spoke to Keith and after a couple of minutes installed
himself behind the register. Was the fugitive coming or going?
Brad stepped into the phone booth, looked up the number of
the place across the street and dialed the digits.

Fatman picked up the phone.

"Yeah?"

"Is Keith still working?"

"Yeah. He oughtta be gettin' off in a few minutes. You
wantta talk with him?"

"No, that's okay. I'll catch him at home."

Brad gently hung up the phone. Now, to wait. It was quarter till eight. The shift must end at eight. Would Keith leave by
way of the back entrance—or the front? The minutes ticked by
with a slowness that defied description. Brad waited.

But should he wait? Should he try talking with the guy today? Now that he knew where Keith worked, shouldn't he first try to find out who'd sold the weapon? Have something solid to offer the man in the way of hope? If he talked to Keith now, would the guy leave his job, flee the city? Brad wondered if he could convince Keith it was safe, their knowing one another, that Brad wasn't going to arrest him. Maybe it was too early . . .

There were, however, Brad's interests to consider. He wanted to talk with Keith—now. He wanted the man seated across from him, in his own house, at his table. Maybe, if he were lucky, in his bed. He would risk it.

Keith emerged from the kitchen without his apron, told Fatman good-bye, opened the door of the restaurant and stepped out into the hot, sticky air. Without looking around, Keith walked in the direction of the bus stop.

Brad stepped quietly behind Keith and grabbed his arm in a firm, secure grip.

"If you try running again, I swear I'll whip your ass."

Keith turned. For a moment his eyes contained the frightened stare of an untamed animal caught in a trap. Then he shrugged his shoulders.

"Third time you're lucky. And persistent."

"Damned right I am. Will you come along peacefully?"

A small smile tugged at Keith's lips. "You asking me? No, why should I? If I get a chance to get away, I'm going to take it. Didn't bring your cuffs with you, did you? Or your weapon?"

Brad looked serious. "Damn it, I never said you were under arrest. I just want to talk with you. That's all I've ever wanted." Which wasn't exactly true, but it was close enough for now.

Keith was puzzled, confused—and still frightened. His uncertainty caused him to react angrily.

"You expect me to believe that? Goddammit, if you're

not arresting me, let me go! Why the hell should I want to talk to you?"

"I said *I* wanted to talk with *you*. Can't you spare me a bit of time?" Brad bit his lip, adding, "Please."

Keith found himself weakening. The guy's good looks were enough to tempt God himself. His diffidence was the perfect blend; Keith knew he was being the biggest sort of fool, but he wanted to go with the guy.

"Can I leave after we talk? Are you telling me you're not going to take me in?"

"That's exactly what I'm telling you."

"I don't believe it." Keith stared intently at the man. "Is that a promise?"

"Yes, on one condition."

"What's that?"

"Promise me you won't take off if I let go your arm. I can't take you far this way. It's uncomfortable for both of us."

"I promise," Keith muttered, after a long pause. They glared at one another for a considerable time. Brad released Keith's arm, ready to tackle him if the man started running. Keith didn't. Instead he rubbed his arm and said: "Actually, I enjoyed that. Maybe I shouldn't have promised so quickly."

Brad grinned and grabbed Keith's arm again, but not so violently.

"Okay, if that's how you want it. Let's go!" He led Keith to his car and opened the door.

"Get in!"

Keith slid into the auto and watched as Brad walked around and climbed under the wheel. They sat there silently for a minute. Then Brad started the vehicle.

"Where're we going?" Keith asked, feeling certain the police station would be their inevitable destination. He was a fool to trust this man.

"Will my place be all right?" Brad spoke quietly, calmly.

"It's your show," Keith responded. "I'm just along for the ride. I hope."

"You won't trust me?"

"No! Why the hell should I?" The last was belligerent.

Brad nodded. "No reason. You can trust me, but you've no way of knowing that. Yet. Truce?"

"Okay."

They said no more. Brad pulled into the designated parking spot at his apartment after a ten minute ride. Silently they got out and walked up the steps. Brad opened the door and let Keith enter ahead of him. As the policeman closed the door, Keith wondered if either of them knew what they were doing.

26

Having "captured" Keith, Brad was uncertain what he ought to do next. Brad didn't want Keith returned to Tilton until there was ample evidence to clear him, and he sensed any physical relationship could only come after the case was over. Brad knew instinctively that any sexual action before then would forever compromise any chance of love. Their time, if it were to come, would be only after Seth was no longer a living presence for Keith, but a ghost at last at peace.

Brad led his guest into the apartment's spacious den. "Since we've both just gotten off work, I could offer you a drink? Would you like anything?"

Keith shook his head. "I don't drink much. Maybe some coffee, if I'm going to be here a long time; otherwise, milk."

"You're anxious to leave?"

Keith shifted position. "I don't know what's going on. You obviously know a lot about me. You know I'm wanted. You know about the murder, about my escape. Why should I trust a cop? You want the truth? Yes, I'd rather be someplace else." Seeing the hurt look which flashed quickly across Brad's face, Keith regretted his words. Anger at his own feelings followed, replaced immediately by remorse and exasperation. This guy was nothing to him. What difference did it make if he spoke his mind?

Unaware his feelings were showing so transparently,

Brad tried to be businesslike. "After our run-in at the old house," he explained, "I took an interest in your case. You didn't get your prints off all the bullets." He grinned briefly, noting Keith's look of consternation. "I'd followed your case in the news. When you didn't shoot me in the house or keep the gun, you got my interest. Most criminals would have kept the weapon and pawned it. I got a friend to check for prints. That's when I found out who you were and that you were wanted." He paused, wondering how to frame his words. "I never believed you were guilty in the first place. I was down on the coast when I learned who I'd stumbled across in that house. I was close to Tilton, so I drove over and talked with your lawyer, Wade Tendell. And to Chief Links. Tendell defended you. Links himself admitted the case was weak. With their agreement, I've been looking around up here, trying to find where the gun which killed Seth came from."

Hearing Seth's name mentioned by Brad affected Keith. He couldn't have said what it was that touched him—maybe the warmth Brad put into the name or the man's evident awareness of the role Seth played in the drama. Whatever it was, Brad gained Keith's attention.

"It's a bit late for that, isn't it?" Keith protested. "No matter where the gun was purchased, you think some clerk will remember who bought it at this late date?"

"Maybe—maybe not," Brad said. "If the guy who bought the gun was out of the ordinary, the clerk might remember."

Keith, suddenly alert, stared at the splendid man before him. "You think you know who killed Seth?" He asked the question tautly, unable to believe that even a small part of the nightmare might be ending. No list of suspects had ever crossed his mind, in spite of the fact all Tendell ever harped on was finding a name to substitute for Keith's.

Brad looked uncomfortable, aware he'd said too much.

"I don't want to build false hopes," he said, looking

away. "There's no evidence against anyone else—only a supposition on my part, substantiated by a couple of things Links found out. I'd rather not name names."

Keith became furious. "What the hell kind of game are you playing? I didn't ask for your fucking help! I didn't come begging you to solve the goddamned case! If you've found out who killed Seth, we . . . I got a right to know who it is."

Brad's face tightened. He knew in a sense that Keith was right, but all the same he wasn't going to be drawn into saying more than he should. Instead, he asked, "Would you talk with Tendell if I get him on the phone? He is concerned about you."

Keith shrugged. What difference could it make? "If you want."

Brad dialed the lawyer's home, found Tendell had already left for the office and reached him there. They talked several minutes. Keith only half-listened. He was busy trying to figure out what the hell was going on. After a while, Brad handed the phone to Keith.

"Yeah?"

"Keith!" Tendell's familiar, eager voice bounced in Keith's ear, flooding him with memories and familiar sensations. "How have you been? Damn, you pulled a slick one. Links and the Albany cops figured they'd have you back in a day or two." Tendell's laugh carried over the line. "When they didn't succeed, they tried blaming me and the wife, said we must have helped you get away. Took me a week to convince Links I was innocent! That letter you sent helped. You *are* all right, aren't you?"

"I'm fine." Keith's mind briefly fled over his journey up the river, the days in the house where Brad had found him, the sheer hell he'd gone through. Yeah, he was fine, just fine. "You know this guy, then?" Keith asked Tendell.

"Brad? Of course. Listen, he's been a big help. We're on the road to clearing you, getting the guilty party behind

bars. And once that's out of the way, all the rest of the mess
can be taken care of. Seth's will can be reinstated, you'll get
the insurance plus interest, be able to handle Seth's burial
arrangements any way you want. You did still want to follow his
instructions, I suppose."

"I do. More than ever!"

Tendell's sigh carried over the wire. "That's gonna piss
off a lot of folks around here, but what the hell, you've got a
right. You know I'll stand by you. We'll get Seth's lawyer,
Thompson. You can bet on it."

"Who did it?" Keith asked, his voice low, intense.

Tendell abruptly shut up.

"Who was it?" Keith repeated.

"Didn't Brad tell you?" Tendell asked, playing for time.

"He wouldn't."

"Maybe he's right," Tendell answered. "We don't have
any proof yet; none at all. You, of all people, know what it's
like having false accusations leveled at you. Couldn't we let it
ride till—"

"No!" The word contained only ice. "I've got a right to
know!"

Tendell capitulated. "We have reason to believe it might
have been Seth's father."

Keith, momentarily stunned, reached behind him for a
chair, found one, and sat down.

"Hey! You still there?"

"Yeah . . . yeah, I'm here." Keith cleared his head.
"I . . . sort of . . . expect you're on the right track. I never
believed Jeb would be that violent, but he didn't care much for
Seth. And he hated the fact we saw so much of each other.
Jeb's religious notions pervaded everything he did. Seth and I
couldn't stand all that garbage and the old man knew it, especially after Seth and I bought the garage. It makes sense, sort
of. I'll bet he was looking for me, though."

"What do you mean?"

"He probably expected to find me there that night. If it was Jeb who came gunning for someone, you can be damned sure he was after me. I bet he hoped to find us in bed together." Keith forgot for a moment he was talking to a straight man and that a cop was listening.

"Why would he shoot Seth, then?" Tendell asked.

"There's no telling. They might have gotten into an argument. Jeb would have had to offer some sort of explanation as to what he was doing there so late at night. Remember how vehement he was at the trial? If Seth goaded the old bastard and Jeb shot him he'd blame me in some twisted fashion. The Rawsons all blamed me, anyway."

"Listen," Tendell urged, "help Brad any way you can. He's promised not to take you in—not until you're ready to give yourself up. That won't be until I think we can win. Of course this is all unethical, and I'll swear I've never spoken with you if anyone asks me. Brad's in the same predicament and he's done a great job. Trust him, Keith."

"I don't understand all the interest," Keith said sullenly.

Tendell backed away from the question. "He's been a one-man saviour on the case, Keith. I don't profess to know all his reasons, but goddammit, he wants to help. Don't be so suspicious. He's a fine guy."

"Okay, okay, I get the message. I'll try." They hung up.

Keith sat back in the chair, thinking over the information he'd just been given. He was only dimly aware of Brad's presence in the room. Keith was back in Tilton, seeing Seth, listening to him talk about his family, about Jeb. Keith focused on what he knew of the old man, of his own relationship with the fanatic; he found the idea that Jeb might be Seth's killer acceptable. He looked up and found Brad standing over him, offering a drink.

"Why did you do it?" he asked.

"Do what?" Brad responded.

"Get mixed up in this mess. Your department won't be pleased having you involved with a queer. They'll no doubt suspect you of being one. Guilt by association."

"They think so already," Brad answered. "I've never said I wasn't."

"Are you?" Keith asked, feeling the conversation turning into a strange, trance-like play on words. It must be the brandy. He was not sitting in a cop's house, asking him if he was queer. Certainly not a man like the one in front of him.

Brad shrugged his massive shoulders. "Who knows? I've made it with guys. Women too. Lately, I've not bothered with either. I've never felt labels made a hell of a lot of difference. I centainly don't give a damn who's screwing who. If both parties are happy, it's none of my business."

The answer didn't satisfy either of them. They were sparring with one another. Both knew it. Keith, however, had no idea why. That the policeman might have some ulterior motive for involving himself in the investigation, he accepted—in spite of Tendell's strong words of praise. The past hour or so had sent Keith's head spinning around like a circle. Did the cop's admitting he'd made it with guys mean he was interested? Keith was too tired and too confused to consider the implications right now. The guys he'd picked up in bars were just that. This man's looks, his attitude, what Keith knew of his personality, were the stuff of which another exceptional love affair might be constructed. And, in spite of the fact he would have liked someone around, a friend, a comrade, Keith wasn't ready yet to replace Seth with anyone.

Brad was unhappy knowing he wasn't being honest. He wanted Keith—wanted him in the worst way. But Brad had sense enough to understand Keith wasn't ready for such a disclosure. He might never be. And, until Keith was cleared, thoughts about love were premature. So, for the moment, they spoke at cross-purposes.

"Would resting here today bother you?" Brad asked, shifting topics and emphasis. "There are things I'd like to go over with you, concerning Jeb Rawson. At the moment, however, we're both tired. My guest room's made up. It's comfortable." He grinned briefly. "No cop would dream of looking for you *here*," he added.

Keith handed the brandy glass back, empty. "Why not? My place isn't air-conditioned, I'll sleep better here."

Brad led Keith upstairs, showed him the shower and the guest room. As he left, he grabbed Keith's arm again. Friendly, jocular. "I'd appreciate your hanging around if you wake up before me; if I'm up first I may go out and check a few more gun shops. Can I count on your being here when I get back?"

Their closeness pleased Keith. He didn't understand what was happening, but a message was coming across and it spelled something precious.

"I'll be here," he said. Brad moved his hand and turned to go. Keith reached out and touched the firm flesh of Brad's muscular forearm.

"Thanks," he said.

Brad nodded and left the room. In the kitchen, he did a few chores while Keith showered, cursing himself for the giddyness he felt. After the shower stopped running he went upstairs himself. If nothing else ever happened, at least he'd had a moment of crystal beauty. Who could want more?

27

Keith woke with a start. At first he couldn't remember where he was. The room was too cool, the bed too comfortable. He glanced at his watch. Six o'clock. He'd not slept so long in ages. Awareness returned. The cop's house.

At least I'm not in jail. Yet.

An unfair thought. Tendell wouldn't recommend anyone who'd betray him, and Evans seemed a nice enough guy. Too nice. Keith felt the stirrings of desire and choked them off. When he got free, when the complications with Seth's estate were behind him, then he'd think about the future. Right now, the past's grip on him was too strong. One-night stands were fine but he couldn't think about the future when the present was so dark. The fact Keith already was connecting his future with Evans told him that he was almost in love.

A damnfool notion!

If Evans expected praise for getting Jeb Rawson convicted of his son's murder, he was in for a shock. Nobody—with the exception of Keith, and possibly the Tendells—would be pleased with such results. Replacing a queer with a fine, upstanding family man like Jeb, a pillar of church and community, simply *would not do*. In the eyes of the community, Keith's sin rose like smog above all morality, all decency, all justification. No, there would be no accolades from the good people of Tilton for Evans even if he succeeded.

Yet that fact apparently didn't count for much with the cop.

Keith got out of bed. One thing he'd learned as a fugitive was not to think far ahead. He was due at work in a few hours, that was enough future to consider. He glanced in the bathroom, found it empty and took a fast shower. Dressing afterwards, he wished he had clean clothes to wear. His shirt and jeans smelled like Fatman's diner. He shrugged. He hadn't asked to come here. He pulled on his pants, left off his shirt and went downstairs.

The place was empty. In the kitchen he found a note:

> Keith: I'm going out to check a few shops.
> Make yourself at home. There's food in the
> fridge, the coffee machine's ready to go. Use
> anything you want. I'll be back around seven.
> We can go out to eat, if you want. Brad.

Keith folded the note and placed it in his pocket. He plugged in the coffeemaker and looked around. The makings of a decent meal were in the refrigerator. The sudden urge to cook came over him. It was ages since he'd done any real cooking. His place didn't lend itself to culinary artistry; besides, he always ate at the diner. He found the stereo system and picked out some records. Evans had good taste. Keith had not listened to a record since his arrest. As music filled the house, he realized how much he missed his possessions. He returned to the kitchen. The meal he was throwing together was well underway when Brad returned.

God, he looks so tired. I wonder if he slept at all?

"I hope you don't mind, but you did say—"

"It smells wonderful," Brad answered before Keith could finish. "And I mean it. It's nice to come back and find the place . . . lived in." He glanced at the clock. "I'd love a drink but I guess it's too close to time for work. I have to be there at eleven."

"This will be ready in fifteen minutes."

"Time for me to clean up then." Brad mounted the stairs and disappeared into the upper level. When he returned, he looked only marginally more awake.

"You couldn't have gotten much sleep," Keith stated, handing Brad a cup of coffee.

"Enough." The answer was sharp. Brad realized it, grinned sheepishly and apologized. "Sorry. Didn't mean to bark at you; it just gets discouraging."

"I don't see why you keep on with it. It's a waste of time."

Brad shook his head impatiently. "Damn it, the evidence has to be there, somewhere. *You* didn't kill him, did you?"

Keith turned to stone. "No."

Brad was contrite all over again. "I am tired. You know I didn't mean that the way it sounded. What I mean, goddammit, was if you didn't then someone else must have. And the means of proving someone else did it has to be out there. I mean to find whoever it was." His belligerence communicated the right note to Keith and after a moment, both relaxed. The meal was generally free from tension. They talked of other things, letting the case simmer in the background. Keith found himself able to tell Brad about Seth, something he'd not been able to do with anyone else since Seth's death. There had never been anyone he could trust. Now, it wasn't so much a question of trust as the fact Brad knew the history of the business.

"I've got to get dressed," Brad said at last, putting aside his coffee cup. "Where do you want me to take you? You working tonight?"

"Yeah. Just drop me off at the diner. I go in early lots of times."

Keith cleaned up the dishes. When he turned around, at Brad's return, he couldn't help starting. Somehow, when they'd been eating, it had been so easy forgetting what Brad did for a living. The uniform changed all that. Brad filled out the clothes wonderfully well. But that gear—the billy club, the holster, handcuffs—all suggested unpleasant things to Keith. The clothes themselves reinvited suspicion.

Brad saw the withdrawal, but was too tired to fight it at the moment. He'd expected as much. Since everything depended on clearing Keith, he couldn't get too excited right now at the obstacle of distrust. The drive to the diner was somber.

"I'd like to see you again," Brad stated. "You know that." He stopped the car. "Would you come back to the house? Can I phone you here?"

"Sure," Keith answered.

"Keith?"

Keith stared at the cop.

"Yes?"

"You won't take off, will you? You've got my promise. I won't betray you."

Keith softened. "I know that . . . I guess. But I can't help being apprehensive. Be patient with me. I won't leave town, I promise. At least, not without telling you first. What if somebody else spots me? I'm not going back to jail, I can tell you that much."

Brad scribbled down a number and handed it to Keith. "Call me. Call me and let's just talk. If anyone else spots you, call me at once. At home or the station. He took the paper and added the second number.

Keith pocketed the numbers and nodded in agreement. He watched longer than he should as the car pulled back into traffic and disappeared.

Fatman was behind the register when Keith entered the diner. He motioned to his dishwasher.

"That a cop I saw you with?"

Keith nodded.

"You ain't in trouble are you?"

Keith shrugged. "Not so's you'd notice." He smiled, adding, "Don't worry, I don't plan on leaving you looking for help again."

Fatman didn't appear relieved. "Look," he said seriously. "I like you. You've done a damned good job here. I've known all along you're runnin' from something. I don't know what it is; I don't care. I hate to think of you leaving—I've had the easiest time of my life with this place since you've been here. But hell, I know you won't be here forever. You're too good for this joint. You get in trouble, let me know, will 'ya? I got a few connections in this town. I might be able to help."

"Thanks. I will." Keith went on into the back, but was shortly summoned up front to run the register. His mind kept returning to his meeting with Brad. By the time he was back in his apartment, the whole episode seemed a thousand years old.

Keith lay on his bed holding Seth's picture, conjuring up the presence of his lover. Instead, the face of the cop came between them. He laid the picture aside, overcome by a great melancholia.

It shouldn't be like this. What sort of guy am I? Seth is my whole world. I can't let him go. I can't.

But how long could he mourn? How long would Seth have wanted him to mourn? He knew the answer to that—Seth would have demanded nothing. Once his promise was carried out, Keith would be free. Even the promise might be foregone were it truly impossible to fulfill. That was the beauty of Seth—he never demanded the impossible. He had been so generous, so full of love . . .

I'm so tired of seeing you cling to my memory, as if I were able to comfort you. As if we had a future. I don't want you forgettin' me completely. I know you won't anyways. We had

*too much together, and it was so damned good. You couldn't
forget, but don't idolize me. Don't make me a god. Why you
sittin' 'round here mopin' when you could be with him?*

Seth, Seth! I'm frightened. He scares me!

*Cause you know he's what you need. He'll help you git
over me and you can't stand that notion right now. I think your
stupid ideas about sufferin' are keepin' you from thinkin'
straight. You sure you ain't enjoyin' layin' about, playin' up
your great tragedy? My memory won't keep you warm at night.
It won't make love to you. It won't relieve your tensions. Put
your love for me in perspective. Brad can't take what we had
from you; he wouldn't want to. I babied you too much. I kept
you in my shadow more'n was good for you. Your growth these
past months has been great. Honor my memory now—become
the man you can be, the lover you oughtta be. Love him. Don't
be afraid of happiness, don't let our enemies convince you happiness ain't possible for us. Fight'em! We had a right to our
love; you and he have the same right. Fight for it!*

The days immediately following his encounter with Brad
left Keith pensive, tired and uncertain. The forces fighting inside him pulled in several directions at once. Memories of Seth
conflicted with desires and thoughts of Brad. Fear of arrest and
prison floated upwards in his mind and could not be dismissed.
Fatman saw something was bothering him and offered Keith
additional time off, but Keith declined. He couldn't have
stood any more hours in his apartment. Brad phoned one night
at the diner, suggesting he and Keith have dinner together, but
Keith put him off. The last thing he needed was the temptation
of Evans.

It was during this time Keith finally learned, he thought,
the reason so many gays indulged in indiscriminate sex. Sex
was a relief. He reached the point he wanted a man, any man,
who could distract his mind from everything except male flesh.
Cocks and balls and asses and pecs. The faces blurred; Keith

remembered lengths and sizes but not names. Submerging himself in sex was so completely out of character, Keith didn't feel like himself any longer—which, he supposed, was what he wanted to achieve. Waking up in strange beds, looking into the eyes of men he would never see again, released him from the restrictions of remaining faithful to Seth's memory while being tempted by Brad.

Becoming a whore solved so many problems. The pursuit of men prevented Keith from thinking. He had reached a point where thinking was counter-productive. Action was all that mattered and the only acts he could engage in, safely, were sexual. In the back of his mind reason kept hissing that such behavior couldn't go on forever. Keith agreed. He wouldn't keep it up *forever*, just for the time being—until his life sorted itself out, until some of his problems were resolved. He was tired of facing life with all the burdens he was carrying. Without Seth to share them, protect him, guide him, he was empty. The suggestion that Brad might help him, listen to him—love him?—became an affliction too great to be borne. Once he admitted such a solution might be possible, he once again became vulnerable. He'd succumbed to love once, giving his soul to Seth. From that encounter he'd emerged bleeding and torn. The wounds were still raw and ugly. He was not yet ready to consider happiness a second time.

28

Just as Keith began using a steady diet of faceless men to hold his problems at bay, the Atlanta Police Department embarked on a campaign to clean up the city—from a moral point of view. The approaching November contained elections —always a propitious time for attacking queers. Arriving at work one evening, Keith found the diner buzzing with news that the baths, only a couple of blocks away, had been raided.

"It was awful!" Charles exclaimed in his high-pitched voice. "Really! The pigs were too much! We've simply *got to do something*!"

Keith was mildly surprised. More by Charles' vehemence than by information of the raid. He had always expected something of this sort to happen. When a fearful society got tired of something, overreaction was bound to occur. Atlanta, while tolerant in many degrees, was still controlled by the morality of Baptists who long ago had sold themselves into slavery to a god of restrictions. They couldn't allow *excesses* or their whole world would crumble. Raids were to be expected; it was a part of homosexual life in the South.

"It's election time," Keith reminded the outraged waiter. "Once November has come and gone, they'll get over themselves. They couldn't have been too serious about it, or they wouldn't have raided the baths in the middle of the afternoon. Nobody in this town ever goes out until midnight or later—they couldn't have arrested many customers."

Charles conceded this was true. "I think they arrested five old men and the employees. But that's beside the point. We've simply got to do something!"

Charles' view was shared by a surprisingly large segment of Atlanta's gay community. The next two days brought a furious turmoil in the ranks of the city's gay people. Legal advice was obtained, lawsuits filed and a protest march planned for the approaching Sunday. The raids had been loudly praised by the city's religious community, so the Atlanta Committee On Alternate Lifestyles (ACAL) decided a parade down Peachtree Street, timed to coincide with the termination of Sunday church services, would be a fitting idea.

Marching permits were denied at first. Court action put a stop to that. The delay, however, allowed all parties to mobilize their adherents into angry cadres which threatened to flood the streets with violence.

Keith reflected a long time before opting to join the marchers. Had he not been "wanted," he wouldn't have hesitated for a second. He was disgusted by the raids, was tired of the bullshit gay people were daily forced to put up with from the rest of society. There was, however, a very real danger that he might be recognized. The entire parade route would be infested with cops. Did exposing himself to possible arrest make sense?

Reason said it didn't; emotion demanded he join the protestors. Too many people with too many excuses failed to take a stand. Besides, Keith rationalized, with so many people around he'd be just another face in the crowd. Straights thought all gays looked alike; he wouldn't be viewed as an individual in any case. All eyes would be on the drag queens of whom, if past parades were any indication, there would be an abundance. Keith decided to risk it.

The atmosphere was tense. All week before the Sunday

march, the diner was a beehive of rumor, speculation and giggly hopes of meeting "Mr. Right" at the demonstration. Fatman agreed to close the diner so everyone who wished to do so could participate in the event.

The parade moved out on time—a miracle in itself. The crowd was larger than Keith had anticipated, numbering around fifteen hundred. A sizeable turnout for a conservative southern city. He buried himself in the middle of the marchers and felt safe.

By twelve-thirty the loud, colorful crowd swung onto Peachtree Street and immediately found themselves confronted by numerous religious zealots, standing on the sidewalk outside their churches, carrying placards condemning lesbians, homosexuals, communists and other groups considered worthy of vilification. One sign attacked "Humanists" as "agents of Satan." Keith noted none of the religious folk bothered to condemn fascists or Republicans, groups with much in common when it came to depriving citizens of freedom. Unhappily, freedom was alien to the religious mind in the first place.

The initial signs of violence surfaced at the Ponce de Leon-Peachtree intersection, close to the Fox Theater. As the marchers drew abreast the venerable building, rocks, bottles and assorted other debris rained upon the parade. The leaders of the march protested to police, who were standing on the sidelines observing the scene with a strong, visible sense of disapproval. The men in blue made no move to counteract the waves of missiles which were beginning to assault the line of protestors.

Scuffles broke out as gay men left the line of march and headed after bottle-throwers. Cries of "We've had enough!" rose from the demonstrators and mingled with screams of "Purify America," coming from religious fanatics. Keith felt a wave of exhaultation sweep over him. At last—to fight the bastards!

Three burly toughs were attacking a pair of hand-holding gay men. Keith pushed forward and joined the melee.

All the pent-up frustrations and disgust he'd felt for years fueled Keith's fists. All the hatred he felt over ridicule swept aside his reason. The years he'd been forced to listen as mindless fools screamed hatred of homosexuals, while at the same time chanting torpid praises of "God," "family values," and "love," culminated in one magnificent gesture of retribution. The men he aided, no longer outnumbered, forced the brutes who'd attacked them back into the herd from which they'd emerged.

But peace was irreparably shattered. Gangs of teenage Christians swarmed out of side streets, attacking the marchers in a concerted attempt to scatter them and break up the march. And, in part, they succeeded. The protestors, however, were not about to abandon their positions without a fight. In a matter of minutes, famed Peachtree Street became a swirling mass of fighting men and women. Only when it became clear the queers were not going to be rapidly beaten and dispersed did the police move in to halt the violence. The action by Atlanta's finest was directed almost exclusively against gay men and women. Swinging their clubs vigorously, the cops waded into the maze of bodies with enthusiasm and after several minutes achieved what the attackers could not accomplish on their own.

Keith, defending himself and several other guys, did not at first notice the involvement of the police. When he did, he muttered to those around him, "Come on, head down that side street. We can't fight these creeps and cops too!"

The same idea dawned on the rest of the protestors, who were now in open flight. Cops ran them down, arresting those they could get their hands on. Keith was ready to race away, when he noticed a leader of ACAL struggling with a uniformed man. Anger welled up, blinding him to everything else. He grabbed a bottle from the ground and headed for the pair. The cop saw Keith coming and raised his nightstick but could not swing it effectively while holding his prisoner. He swung and missed. Keith slammed the bottle against the policeman's wrist, knocked the club away and thrust his fist into the cop's jaw. The man staggered and released the ACAL leader.

Keith pulled the guy to his feet. "Let's get out of here!" he shouted.

Other policemen, seeing one of their number falling, raced to his rescue. Keith stood for a moment rooted to the spot.

Brad!

They stared at one another across the sea of surging bodies, each unable to believe the other was there. The rescued gay man pulled at Keith, drawing him back to reality. Keith ran down the narrow street. Gunshots echoed behind him and a searing pain scorched his arm. Was this how it was all going to end, he wondered? Was Brad so loyal to the force he'd shoot him?

"This way," gasped the man Keith had aided. "I think we can get away."

The ACAL leader knew his way around. Keith followed, feeling pain and warm, sticky blood dripping from his arm. His breath came in short, quick gasps as they ran and ran. Finally, hearing no pounding footsteps behind them, they slowed down.

"I think we've made it," Keith's companion said. "Damn, man, thanks a—Hey, you're hurt!"

"Somebody started shooting," Keith muttered. "I don't think it's too bad."

"We gotta get you medical help. Come on, my place isn't far from here. I know this doctor I've tricked with. I think he'll look at it. I'm Ralph, by the way—Ralph Stapler." The way he added the last name struck Keith, despite the pain in his arm, as ludicrous.

We're so used to tricks and bars and baths, Keith thought, we don't even remember our full names half the time. It was a bitter notion. What the hell was he defending?

"Keith Raw—" Keith started offering the name he was working under at the diner but stopped. He was tired of farce and hiding and being hunted. "Keith Wilson," he said. "I'd shake hands but it hurts."

Concern showed on Ralph's face. "I'm sorry, man. God, what a fucking mess that turned into. I can't understand what happened. Atlanta's never been a violent town before. We've always had a good relationship with everyone. I can't believe this day!"

"That's one of our problems," Keith answered sourly, "nobody wants to believe it will happen in their town."

"But we've gone so far out of our way to show straights we're no danger to them. They've no reason to feel threatened," Ralph protested. "We're just like them—"

"Goddammit," Keith exploded, "We're not *just like them*! In the first place we've got more sense and tons more ability than ninety percent of the sons-of-bitches! I'm tired of hearing gay leaders spouting this drivel about us wanting, or needing, their fucking approval in order to exist. The only thing I want, and the reason I participated in this mess, is to get *justice*! We've got the same rights as any other citizen of this country and that's the only thing I give a damn about getting across to them. As for their approval of us and who we sleep with, they can take that and shove it up their asses!"

Ralph, uncertain how he'd unleashed the storm of Keith's words, changed the subject.

A hurried fifteen-minute walk brought them to Ralph's apartment. Once inside, Ralph led Keith to the bathroom and removed the bloody shirt. An ugly gash oozing blood presented itself to the two men.

"At least there's no bullet in it," Keith said. "It just grazed me. If we can stop the bleeding and put a bandage on it . . . "

"Stay here and wash off," Ralph ordered. "I'm going to phone Paul—that's my doctor friend."

Keith did as he was told. Using an old washcloth, he cleaned away the blood but as quickly as he wiped one blot away, another appeared.

He was still at it when Ralph returned.

"He's coming over. Don't worry—Paul won't say anything to the authorities. He says we're on all the networks. Says the television stations are having a field day. Let's find out."

Ralph went into his den and turned on the television. Keith, holding a towel to his arm, trailed into the room.

The media was having fun. The Mayor was on the scene, with various councilmen and, depending on which district they represented, the elected representatives were either deploring or praising the police. It was obvious a split was developing among the political factions. Television crews, at the beginning of the violence, reeled off footage of film showing the bottle-throwing episodes as well as the subsequent behavior of attackers and police. Reminiscent of the attacks by police departments on war protestors of an earlier decade, a couple of newsmen began calling the mess a "police riot." The latest "Battle Of Atlanta" seemed capable of raging for days on the tube, if not in the streets of the city.

Paul arrived. He was a prancy man, given to uttering exclamation points. His eyes roamed Keith's body but he seemed to know what he was doing, medically speaking. He stopped the bleeding, applied salve to the wound and when it was obvious it had stopped running blood, bandaged it up.

"It's going to be *so sore* for a few days!" he exclaimed,

"But you'll survive! I'll leave this tube of salve and a few bandages so you can change it. Maybe you'd better come by my apartment later this week and let me look at that arm. We don't want it getting infected, do we?"

Keith agreed an infection would not be welcome.

"What do I owe you?" he asked.

"Oh don't worry about *that*!" Paul exclaimed. "Let me do my little bit for the movement! I could never get out and march like you *men* do! My Scarlet O'Hara matrons would never darken my office doors again!" He tittered, kissed Ralph and departed in a flurry of exclamations and expressive sighs.

Keith used Ralph's phone to call Fatman and let him know he'd be out for a couple of days. "I got shot," he explained, in answer to Fatman's inquiry.

"Oh goddamn! You all right?"

"Yeah. Considering I was shot. It's only a flesh wound —my arm. But it's going to be too sore to wash those dishes."

"Okay. Come back when you feel up to it. You can still stop by and eat if you want to."

Keith thanked him and hung up. After a few minutes conversation with Ralph, he made his excuses and left the apartment. Keith was tired, his arm hurt like hell and he was angry and annoyed. He supposed he'd have to think about Brad's presence at the goddamn march. He should have known Brad'd be there. If only he'd not seen him.

Keith reached his apartment. His arm hurt, but did not start bleeding again. He awkwardly undressed and tumbled onto the sagging shabby bed. With an effort he blotted out the hellish visions of the past few hours and fell into a troubled sleep.

An insistent knocking on his door, hours later, recalled him to consciousness.

"Just a minute," he yelled at the visitor. He supposed it

must be old lady Whitman; no one else knew where he lived. Keith pulled on a pair of shorts and gingerly slid his sore arm into a shirt. He flung open the door.

Brad stood there. Unsmiling, almost sullen. They stared at each other. Keith felt all his fury returning.

"What do *you* want? Didn't you get to bash enough queers at the demonstration? I should think—"

"I didn't spend half an hour convincing your boss to tell me where you lived," Brad interrupted, "to come here and listen to this kind of bullshit. Can I come in or not?"

"I don't have much choice, do I?" Keith turned on his heel and headed for the center of the room. Brad reached for him.

"Goddammit—" he began.

"*Ouch!*" Keith screamed as Brad grabbed his wounded arm. "Watch it, you sonofabitch!"

Brad dropped Keith's arm. "Sorry. You seemed to like it before."

"That was before your fucking goons shot me!"

Brad stopped. "Are you serious?" He didn't wait for an answer but started pulling off Keith's shirt. "Let me see."

"There's nothing to see," Keith replied stonily. "I've had it looked after."

Brad removed the shirt anyway and glanced at the bandage, then glared at Keith. He shook his head and moved to sit down in the only chair in the room.

"I thought you were afraid of getting picked up? You sure didn't use a hell of a lot of sense participating in that sort of madness. The doctor who dressed this will report it. You don't think you'll stay free long pulling stunts like that, do you?"

"The doctor won't report it," Keith answered in an angry retort. "*He's* queer, too—and some of us stick together. I was there because it was important! I'm tired of the shit we have to put up with. You fascists are out to get everyone who doesn't agree with you—totally, completely, one hundred percent.

According to your philosophy, there isn't room in this world for all of us. Well, it's my country too, and I'm going to fight for it!"

"Do I get to say anything?" Brad asked, quietly.

"I don't give a damn! I saw you there! What the fuck is there to say?"

"Yes, I was there. I was there doing the job I was hired to do. Namely, trying to protect you assholes."

"Protect us? Some fucking protection you were! I'm tired, my arm's sore. Go back and join your queer-bashers! You apparently think as they do. Don't worry, I won't expose you. But can I count on your still keeping quiet about me?"

Brad's mouth tightened in anger. "I don't make empty promises. I stand by what I said."

They glared at each other. Keith was angry and annoyed at himself because Brad mattered so much. Brad wondered how he could make the man across from him see that his uniform and his respect for law and order need not preclude his heart from feeling a love which in spite of the obstacle course both were erecting was growing stronger.

Brad moved towards the door. "I'm going. You need to rest. I guess I do, too. I'm sorry . . . I . . . I'll be in touch."

"If you want," Keith agreed, his tone careless and uninterested. What did it matter?

Brad closed the door and left. He drove back to his own place, his mind a turmoil of conflicting ideas.

Physically, he ached for Keith. But it was obvious Keith would never settle for an invisible love affair. Brad, when he visualized a life with Keith, had done so from the point of view that No One Would Know. He'd never reflected on the situation before, and as he did so now, he could understand some of Keith's anger. At the same time he wasn't sure he could handle anything like a public proclamation of something as private as a sexual orientation. Life was so much simpler when No One Knew.

29

The violence surrounding the gay march led to repercussions within the police department. An investigation was launched into why guns were drawn and fired. The few men arrested in the raid on the baths were released. Most cops were disgusted over the episode. Their general animosity towards homosexuals rushed to the surface, spilling over in their conversations during the days immediately following the demonstration. Brad tried remaining quiet, but the time or two he voiced the opinion that it didn't matter who people slept with, he was jumped on.

"Goddamn faggots! It's unnatural! They oughtta be exterminated."

"Fucking sissies!"

"How the hell can you alibi 'em? Shit, you ain't one, are you Evans?"

Brad kept his cool. At the same time Keith's image rose up and challenged all his convictions. If he loved the guy, and he thought he did, why didn't he defend his love? Why was he sitting around keeping his mouth shut while everybody was laughing and joking, telling fag stories?

It wasn't fear. He didn't give a damn about the job anymore. So why didn't he, when presented with the opportunity, answer that, yes, goddamit, he *was* one of 'em?

Picturing such a scene sent chills through him. He began to understand the courage which was needed when one admitted to the world he was queer. The overwhelming hatred, disgust and fear which routinely was directed at homosexuals in society had never seemed real to him. He'd always believed *he* was different. Those dirty terms, the disgust and ridicule other men directed towards effeminate cocksuckers didn't apply to *him*. Accepting the fact he was vulnerable, Brad gradually understood Keith's anger.

His days at the station house became nightmares. Only one thing kept him going—the search for the weapons seller. Every waking moment he could spare went into that hunt.

One afternoon—tired, having slept only a few hours—he walked into a pawnshop. The questions he asked had become so routine he could have carried out the operation in his sleep. Sometimes he thought he was asleep.

"Have you sold a weapon with this serial number in the past year?" he'd ask, handing over the numerals.

The clerk in this instance was a seedy-looking man whose features were redeemed by bright, jumping-bean eyes. He picked up the paper and glanced at it. Walking down the counter he pulled out a ledger and peered through it.

"Any notion when the sale might'ta been made?" he asked Brad.

Brad gave him a date a couple of months before Seth's murder. He turned and looked around the place. A grunt from the clerk spun Brad back around.

"Ha! Figured there was something funny about that ol' bastard," the clerk said, a smile lighting up his dismal face.

"You . . . *sold* it?" Brad whispered, unbelievingly.

"Yep. Tol' my ol' woman at the time that fella was a'gonna be trouble." The clerk peered at Brad. "You see, he didn't know what he wanted. I could'a sold him a machine gun, if I'd a'had one."

His hands shaking noticeably, Brad drew forth the portfolio of pictures he carried with him.

"Could you look at these and see if you remember who

bought the weapon? Could it have been one of these men?"
Brad offered them fearfully, unable to believe he may have
reached the end of his search.

The clerk flipped through them carelessly. He stopped
when he came to the photo of Jeb Rawson.

"Him, it was. I got a good eye for faces. Gotta have, in this
business. It was him."

After the realization of what he had found hit him, Brad
almost collapsed. He cautioned the man to keep quiet and returned to his apartment. As soon as he was inside the door, he
raced to the phone and called Tendell.

"Wade? I've found it! It's a positive ID. Absolutely perfect!"

Brad sensed he was babbling, but he didn't care. After a
few minutes he calmed down enough to explain what he'd
learned.

Tendell's shout of glee almost burst Brad's eardrum.
The lawyer agreed to contact Links and get the ball rolling.
When they hung up, Brad felt better than he'd ever felt in his
life.

He wanted to celebrate! He wanted Keith!

The thought of Keith—of what Keith must have gone
through, an ordeal which might be reaching its conclusion
—sobered the policeman. It wouldn't be fair to raise such
hopes, only to have them dashed again. How anything could
keep Keith from being cleared, Brad didn't know, but he'd
seen strange things happen in the past—and with this case
centering on a homosexual affair, he didn't want to take any
chances. He'd wait—if it killed him.

Links didn't waste time. He called Brad the following
day, and arrived in Atlanta the day after that. Which was when
Brad's troubles began.

Once Links turned up, there was no way Brad could keep

his involvement in the matter out of the limelight. His superiors weren't pleased. Links, Brad and two men from Brad's department interrogated the pawnshop clerk who stuck by his story and identification. When the clerk was dismissed, Links turned to Brad.

"I'm satisfied. I'll get back to Tilton and pick up a warrant. Once the case gets back in the news, I expect we can issue some sort of statement and see if we can't lure Wilson out of hiding. He's probably here in Atlanta somewhere."

"What can he expect?" Brad asked.

Links shook his head. "You got me. He's got the escape charge to clear up, but as he wasn't guilty in the first place, I can't imagine many judges not going along for a dismissal of the escape charges." Links chuckled, adding, "Any judge who gets obstinate now will have Tendell to reckon with. I suspect they've had quite enough of him down my part of the state. Wilson ought to be freed without any difficulty."

"When he comes forward, is he going to be able to get released without excessive bail this time?"

"I don't see why not." Links prepared to leave. "You want to join me in making the arrest? Wouldn't be one without you."

Brad, glancing at his Captain, decided it was time for a showdown.

After Links left the office, Brad turned to listen to the inevitable lecture.

It wasn't long in coming.

"Dammit, Evans, I don't know what to make of this business. We don't like having our men messing around in an independent fashion like this. Haven't you got enough to do without racing around trying to clear a goddamned queer. Just what we need—another faggot loose to march up and down Peachtree, giving us more headaches!"

"Doesn't the fact he's innocent mean anything to you?" Brad asked. "I thought we were supposed to be upholding justice."

"Justice, hell!" the Captain exclaimed. "The only justice we're interested in is keeping law-abiding citizenry relatively safe and able to go about their business. Goddamn queers break the law by their very natures. They oughtta all be out of circulation. Hell, if you've got to crusade for justice, looks like you could pick somebody decent to help out." The Captain's eyes narrowed as he pulled a cigarette out of a pack on his desk and lit it.

"You need to find yourself a woman and learn to have some fun on your off-duty time. We don't need men going off on their own, using their authority for personal projects. I can tell you, the Major will take a very dim view of all this."

"I suspect the press would take an even dimmer view of your attitudes on justice," Brad told the man, in a voice he kept as calm as possible.

"What the hell is that supposed to mean? Are you threatening me?"

"Yes. I want to be in on this case the rest of the way. I want to be down there when Links arrests that old bastard. I want to be in charge of Wilson when he turns himself in. I'll make a deal with you: You go along with me, and when this business is over, I'll resign. If you don't—if you, or this department gives me any flack, you'll be sorry."

"You son-of-a-bitch! I oughtta take your badge right now! Why the hell should I go along with you? You run to the press with what I've said, I'll deny it; say you misunderstood. Something like that. You'll be the one who's discredited."

"Maybe," Brad agreed without rancor, "but the suspicion would always be there. The public, parts of it at any rate, wouldn't like thinking their police officers don't give a fuck about justice and fairness. There'd be a stink to get rid of you.

Instead of being a member of the inner circle around here, being considered for a promotion and all that, you'd be on the way out. Hell, you don't need me to explain the politics of this department to you. You've got every nuance down perfectly. Which is another reason you'd do better going along with me."

"What the hell you mean?"

"As I've suggested, you make my path on this case easy, I'll resign the day Wilson's cleared. You don't—well, I guess I'll go public about being a goddamn queer like Wilson —and let the public know how the police harrasses the homosexual population of Atlanta. And rather than resigning when you bastards try kicking me out, I'll get a lawyer and fight you every step of the way. Hell, I might even win. I've got a decent record—"

"Get out of my sight! I . . . I . . . " The Captain found himself speechless. His rotund face grew livid digesting the information Brad was handing him. When at last he recovered, he glared at Evans as if he were viewing some disgusting serpent or insect and said: "You're the type of perverted bastard who would pull a stunt like that! It'll be worth it, getting rid of you without a hassle. Don't report back here. I'll get special orders cut for you, so you can work with your little pansy. And by God, the very second that faggot's cleared, you better have that resignation on my desk! Or I'll come after you! Now get the hell out of here!"

Brad turned and without undue haste, left the Captain's office. For the first time in a long time, he felt free.

30

The Sheriff of Tilton County led a parade of vehicles towards the Rawson farm. In the car with the Sheriff were Links and Brad. Behind them was Wade Tendell, and he was followed by another car from the Sheriff's department, carrying men to implement the search warrant Links had obtained.

The small band of autos stirred up a dense cloud of dust as they turned onto the dirt road which led, after a time, past the house in which Keith was raised. They bumped slowly on around the curved trail towards the Rawson place. The summer had been unusually hot and dry. The corn in the fields was burned almost to the tassles. The men in the cars were silent, each thinking their own thoughts. Brad, drinking in the peacefulness of the countryside, wondered what it would be like living on a farm with Keith, just the two of them, telling the rest of the world to go to hell. The Sheriff pulled into the large, tree-shaded yard which surrounded the Rawson home. Unlike a city house, the yard was of dirt, and swept. It resembled photos Brad had seen in books of the old South. Or paintings on exhibit at the museum. Everything he was seeing looked like an ancient snapshot from fifty years past. As the Sheriff's car stopped, a girl of about fifteen emerged from the house onto the large, shady porch.

"Howdy, Rachel," the Sheriff greeted the girl. "Your Pa or Ma around?"

"Yessir, they're in the kitchen. Won't you step in?"

"Reckon maybe you'd better ask your Pa to come out here for a minute if'n you would."

After a moment, Jeb came out of the house onto the porch. Behind the screen door, Brad could see the form of a woman moving around uneasily.

"Come in Sheriff, pull up a chair." Jeb greeted his visitors cheerfully. "Rachel didn't say you'd brung a posse with you. What can I do for you?"

The Sheriff slowly led Links and Brad up the steps to the porch. Tendell remained in his car, a mute witness to the proceedings. The other car's occupants also remained where they were.

"Jeb," the Sheriff said, shaking his head. "Seems like the Chief and this here officer from 'Lanta have come up with some evidence connectin' you to the death of your boy, Seth. They was wantin' to talk with you 'bout it."

As the Sheriff delivered his words, Brad heard a muffled gasp from the woman who lingered behind the screen door. The gasp was followed by soft weeping.

Links stepped forward. "Mr. Rawson, we have a man who has positively identified a picture of you as the person who purchased the weapon used in killing your son. I have a warrant for your arrest, as well as an additional warrant to search your home. We don't want any trouble, but . . . " He left the rest of his words unspoken.

Jeb Rawson said nothing for a long time. Brad found the scene to be one of unbearable tension. The Sheriff was not happy being a part of the tableau. Links stood waiting for his statements to elicit some response. The muted sobbing of the woman created an eerie music to a noiseless, real-life photograph.

"Never meant to kill Seth," Jeb said carefully.

The Sheriff interrupted again. "You ain't got'ta say

nothin' Jeb, without havin' a lawyer present." Brad supposed
this corresponded to a reading of the man's rights.

Rawson waved the words aside. "Don't matter. Reckon
the Good Lord meant this to happen. I leave everything up to
Him. Figured if'n He wanted things brought to light, He'd see
about it. Always trust the Lord. You can't go wrong that way."
Jeb looked into the distance for a second then turned back to
his visitors. He ignored Brad and Links, directing his com-
ments to the Sheriff.

"Never meant to kill Seth," the old man repeated. "Seth
was led astray by that devil, that Wilson boy." Jeb's eyes took
on a glint of intractability. "He was the one I wanted. Seth was
a good boy, til Wilson got a'holt of him. My boy was good. I
taught him the ways of the Lord. But he was led into perversion
and filth by Wilson. I meant to do away with Wilson. Set my
boy free. Knew he'd come back to the Lord if I just removed
that devil. I happened to be in 'Lanta—we was havin' a meetin' of the Brotherhood of Deacons one weekend back in the
spring—I passed by that there pawnship and saw them guns in
the winder. The vision of what I had to do appeared in my head.
The Lord directed me. I bought the gun and come on back
home. Put it away fer a time, tried talkin' to the boy. He
wouldn't listen. Too set in his evil ways. I . . . never believed
he'd commit such abominations. Just thinkin' 'bout what him
and that Wilson must'ta been doin . . . " The vision so horri-
fied the old man that he stopped speaking for a minute.

When he resumed his narrative, he was strong-voiced
and fanatical.

"Couldn't let it go on. Folks in town knew what they was
doin'." Jeb looked at the Sheriff. "You know that, well as me,
Sheriff. People was good to me 'n the wife. Didn't want to
shame us or the girls. Wouldn't never say nothin', but they all
knew. I couldn't let it go on. They was sinnin', their lives was

an affront to the Good Lord. That Wilson—always over at my boy's place. Or Seth over at his'n. I figured I'd just slip over there one morning, early-like. Catch'em in their wickedness. That's what I was a'gonna do.

"But I was late. When I got there, Wilson was already gone. Seth came to the door, not wearin' nothin'! He reckoned it was . . . Wilson come back. The words he used! Filth! I was shamed! My own flesh 'n blood! Standin' 'fore me, naked; shamin' me before the Lord! Not repentant! Not sorry for his wickedness—he exhalted in it! I . . . shot him. I meant to kill Wilson, but when I saw how far into sin Seth had fallen, I saw both of 'em would have to be destroyed.

"After everybody took to figurin' it was Wilson what done the killin', I felt like that was the Lord's way of tellin' me I done right. Reckon He's got other plans fer me, now. He's gonna destroy Wilson some other way."

Jeb stood up. "I'm ready, Sheriff. Always been ready. What else was it you was lookin' fer? Said you had a warrant? I ain't plannin' to hinder you none."

Once Jeb was in the Sheriff's car, the Sheriff was given the bill of sale for the gun which Alma Rawson had discovered and hidden away.

"You knew all along?" Links asked the woman.

She nodded, wiping her tear-stained face with an apron.

"I knew," she whispered. "I heard him when he got up that mornin'. It was early. Too early for him to be startin' off to the meetin'. Then, when I heard Seth was dead, I knew. I found the paper a few days later." She looked from one man to the other. "I couldn't say nothin', I just couldn't!" She started weeping again.

"What'll they do to him?" she asked after her renewed tears slackened.

"Don't know," the Sheriff told her. "Just don't you worry

too much, Alma. I'll look after him real good. So will Wayne if he's put in the city jail. Just you try pullin' yourself together. The girls are gonna need you now."

As the cars drove away with their prisoner, Brad got into Tendell's car.

"Not very pretty was it?" Tendell asked. He had remained in his car throughout the entire episode.

"No, it wasn't," Brad agreed. "The reasons were about what we expected. How soon will it be before some sort of proclamation about Keith can be forthcoming?"

Tendell shrugged. "Hard to tell. Depends on who the old man gets for a lawyer. If he doesn't fight things, we could probably have something in the news within a week. Of course Rawson's arrest will make the papers right away. This town's not going to like it!"

"To hell with the town!" Brad spat the words.

Tendell grinned. "You're sounding like Keith now." He looked sideways at Evans and added, "You two fought, didn't you? Not that it's any of my business."

Brad shrugged. "He misunderstood why I was on duty during that demonstration a few weeks ago."

"Is there any reason for keeping him in the dark now?" Tendell asked. "He'd rather hear the news from you, I think."

"I want to be sure he's going to be cleared without more difficulties," Brad offered as an excuse. "I'm beginning to see how biased everything is when a case involves homosexuals. You'd think simple justice would mean *something*."

Tendell hooted. "You expect too much. This time, however, I don't see anyway they can railroad Keith. Rawson's confession is definitive. There is the escape business, but I expect to be able to work around that. Under the circumstances, they'd be fools to press the matter."

"They've been fools before," Brad commented darkly.

But not this time. The good folks of Tilton appeared to have had enough of their infamous case. There were mutterings amongst the citizens, but there were no incidents. The judiciary, too, seemed eager to rectify previous errors—probably in the hope that past mistakes would be quickly forgotten. A week after Jeb Rawson's arrest, the murder warrant against Keith was withdrawn. The Judge went on record stating that all charges would be dropped as soon as Keith appeared before the court. Brad traveled back to Atlanta, hoping to convince Keith that the time was at hand for him to do just that.

31

Keith had been furious when Brad left him. As soon as the door closed behind the cop, Keith was ready to write the guy off as a bad experience. He managed to retain that attitude for all of a day or two. But as the pain in his arm and disgust in his mind subsided, Keith regretted his hasty words to Brad. Still, thinking about the ramifications of the affair made Keith's head ache. He pushed thoughts of the cop aside for a couple of days. As much as he could. His attitude alternated between righteous anger and repentance. After all, it had been he, not Seth, who argued they should live separately in Tilton—to appease the community's "sensibilities." Was his attitude *then*, any different than Brad's *now?* Keith had to admit that being open about his sexual orientation was never farther advanced than the next declaration. And each declaration was almost as hard as the first. Keith, recognizing his own ambivalance in the matter, admitted to himself that Brad was no doubt doing the best he could. It couldn't be easy, being queer and working around cops. A week after the demonstration, Keith broke down and dialed the number Brad had given him. There was no answer.

His arm healed. Keith returned to the eatery. The cops, distressed by the publicity which surrounded the riot ceased overt harrassment of the gay community. Keith's life settled into the peaceful routine he appreciated. Work at the diner, workouts with his weights. Reading in his apartment. In the back of his mind was the hope that Brad might drop in again.

Keith was finishing his workout one afternoon when the knock came on the door. He wiped sweat from his eyes and opened the panel, expecting his talkative landlady. On seeing Brad he almost grimaced.

"You do manage to pick the worst times, don't you?" he said.

"I . . . could come back later."

"No. I . . . was just doing the last set. I—it's okay. Come in."

Brad entered the room tentatively, unsure how to approach the man he'd come to care for.

"Let me get cleaned up. I'll be back in a minute," Keith said as he stepped into his tiny bathroom. As the water ran in the shower, Brad waited, surprising even himself by his nervousness.

Keith emerged from the bathroom wearing only a pair of gym shorts. He sat down on the bed across from Brad. "What's on your mind?"

"Don't you listen to the news or read the paper?" Brad asked, returning question for question.

"It's too depressing since the fascists took over," Keith stated. "I keep the radio on the classical music station."

Brad nodded. "I ought to have thought of that." He stared intently at Keith, then added in a low voice, "it's all over."

Keith misunderstood. "Huh? What's all over? You're talking in riddles today."

"Jeb Rawson confessed to Seth's murder a week or so ago. The warrant against you has been dropped—or will be as soon as you appear in court. All that's needed is your appearance—" Brad broke off, seeing his news was more of a shock to Keith than he'd expected. Rising from the chair Brad stepped across the distance separating him from Keith and knelt by the bed. Keith automatically reached out for Brad's strong arms and looked into Brad's face, trying to decide if truth was there.

"Will I be appointed Seth's executor?" Keith whispered at last. "Can I finally have his wishes carried out?"

"Wade says yes. That may take some time, but he says it can be done. Seth's lawyer, Thompson, phoned Wade before I left."

"You were down there?"

"Yes."

"You found where he bought the gun, didn't you?"

"Yes." Brad told Keith the story, omitting only the fact he was leaving the force as a result of the methods he'd used to gain control of the case. As they talked, Brad found himself on the bed with Keith touching him, clinging to him. Their proximity comforted both. It was a position Brad had longed for; to Keith it was like coming home.

At last the tale was told. A long silence ensued. Keith finally broke it.

"I can't believe it's all over. I think . . . I'm still scared. What do I do now? How do I know they'll keep their word? I can't stand the idea of being back in that filthy jail, with those cruddy guards—"

"You won't be," Brad interrupted. "All you have to do is show up. In court. If you'll come to the station, you'll be put in my custody for the trip down there and we can go to Tilton together." He hesitated, adding, "But I don't want to impose. You don't need me; you could hop a bus and go back yourself."

Keith looked at Brad, aware that they were lying in each other's arms and that the cop by his side wasn't even sure he was gay. Keith backed away.

"I'm sorry. I wasn't thinking. I don't mind your going alone."

Had Brad looked disappointed when Keith moved away?

Keith couldn't be sure. And suddenly, he needed to be sure. He sat up on the bed and moved away from Brad. They stared across the expanse of bedspread.

The cop's name came hard to Keith's lips. "Brad . . . I appreciate everything you've done . . . but . . . well, if I'm speaking out of turn, I'm sorry. But I have to know. Why are you doing all this? Why have you done all this?"

Brad looked at Keith. Then, sighing audibly, he answered, low, but distinctly. "Because I love you."

"I . . . " Keith could not go on.

Brad continued. Soft, quietly. "I know it's too early to say that. If you hadn't asked me, I wouldn't have said those words to you. Not now, not at this time. But that is why I've worked on this case." He swallowed, then spoke again with a visible effort. "Ever since I saw you sleeping in that house, I've felt love for you. All I want is a chance, once all this is behind you. I don't expect anything from you, Keith. I'll never make demands of you. Hell, I don't even know if we'd be compatible. Once things are straightened out, if we could just have a couple of weeks to get to know one another . . . " His voice trailed off, but his eyes pleaded.

"Brad . . . " The name sounded sweet to Keith's ears. "If you'll give me time . . . now . . . I promise we'll have that chance. At this moment, however, Seth is with me. He's been with me ever since this nightmare began. Comforting me, pushing me when I needed to be pushed. Trying, as only a precious memory can, to help me. He'd never want me to be alone. I accept that. I accepted that long ago. He'd approve of you. I feel he does approve of you." Keith looked away. He couldn't continue gazing into Brad's dark, beautiful eyes. "God knows, you're all I've ever dreamed of in a man. I need a guy like you; there's nothing I'd not do to make you happy." Keith looked back at Brad, a smile playing at the corners of his mouth. Just for a moment he wondered if Brad could visualize what was meant by those words. But the burden of his promise to Seth settled on his shoulders, conditioning desire with fateful obligation. "But first I have to keep my promise to Seth . . . scatter his ashes to the wind . . . regain all the material things he's given me . . . after months of running, of fears, learning to cope . . . the idea it's all over takes some getting used to."

Brad moved across the bed and reached for Keith. He held the man's face between two strong, work-calloused hands and stared deep into troubled eyes.

"That's what I mean. I . . . I'm uneasy too. I've never been in love with a guy before, only with the idea. We both need to grow to know one another." Without thinking about it, Brad assertively pulled Keith's head down to his chest. Suddenly he was holding a sobbing man. His strong arms encircled Keith, his strength offering protection, his love a haven against the coming storm.

At last, with their hearts aligned, they discussed the practical side of the days ahead.

"I can't simply walk out on Fatman," Keith protested. "He's been too good to me."

"Of course you can," Brad countered. "We'll talk to him. He'll understand. Come on, we can go over there now. Then hit the station house, get you placed in my custody and drive to Tilton. Don't sit around thinking about it, let's do it! We can take your things to my place. Wade's willing to put us up at his place in Tilton until your house is open again. Come on!"

Action seemed the best way of convincing Keith the case was, at last, going to be concluded.

Fatman, when he heard what was going on, reluctantly agreed Keith should leave the eatery immediately.

"Gonna miss you, though," he said as they prepared to leave. "Stop in and see me when you're back in Atlanta," he invited. Keith agreed that he would. As they walked out, Fatman reached for his sign, "Dishwasher wanted, inquire within."

At the police station Keith was reintroduced to the real world. The dislike directed towards himself, he could understand; why it extended to Brad, he could not. The Captain was not pleased by Brad's entrance with Keith—but the fact that the sooner the case was out of the way, the sooner Brad would be off the force made the man willing to expedite the matter.

Sitting in the small waiting room, Keith heard phones ringing . . . the bustle of the station . . . and conversation not meant for his ears.

"Did you see that fucking Evans coming in with his queer? I can't believe he's still on the force."

"He won't be long. He made a deal with the Captain— gonna resign once his pet case is out of the way."

"Won't be too soon for me. What the hell the department's coming to—a fag on the force."

Keith almost stopped breathing. It seemed an eternity before Brad returned and even longer until the paper work and procedures were over with.

A few minutes at Keith's apartment were sufficient to pick up the items he'd accumulated during his tenure as a fugitive. He gave the keys back to a disappointed landlady and they drove to Brad's condo.

Over a supper carelessly tossed together, Keith probed, seeking an answer to the remarks he'd heard earlier.

"I didn't know you'd resigned already."

"Yes. More or less. You're my last assignment as it were," Brad grinned.

"How come they think you're queer down there?" Keith asked the question bluntly.

Brad laid aside his fork. "What did you hear?"

Keith offered an edited version of the remarks he'd overheard.

Brad sighed. "I told them. Told the Captain, at least. He'd made some politically embarrassing statements about the demonstration. I threatened to go to the press with them. I also told him I was queer and if he didn't want me fighting to stay on the force, he'd go out of his way to make sure I had my way on this case." Brad laughed. "The bastard didn't like it, but he did as he was told."

Keith fidgeted. "I hope you didn't take everything I said the last time we talked too seriously. I'd hate to think I caused you to do something like that."

"Why? You were right. It was time I made up my mind. I would have left the force soon enough in any case." He glanced at Keith, an amused look played about his lips. "I'm a determined guy. I usually get what I want."

Keith, not quite at ease, went back to eating.

"I hope so," was all he said.

They went to bed early that night. Each to his own bed. Daybreak found them on their way to Tilton and what both hoped would be the final act of a long drama.

32

Brad and Keith's drive down the interstate, through the heartland of Georgia, was silent.

Brad's lack of words was due to his own character, which avoided great amounts of verbal contact. He sensed Keith must be suffering, but having no way to ease the distress, opted not to interfere.

Keith's mind was so full of the past that he could divert precious little attention to the future; even a future which contained Brad Evans.

Every mile which fled beneath the wheels of the car carried Keith back. Back in distance as well as back in time—to an uncertain situation in terms of his legal predicament, to total remembrance of Seth, to the hideous pain of his loss. Keith knew his return to the community would not be welcomed. He'd grown up in and around Tilton, lived there almost all his life. He was not, however, a part of the community. He'd always felt like an outsider. All his days in the region had been focused on one object: Seth. Keith's abandonment by everyone who knew him never had surprised him. He'd have been astonished had things turned out otherwise. Now, he wanted to end it all. Pack up those things he wished to take with him and abandon the seedy town and wild countryside for some sanctuary where his memories of Seth could mellow and his love for Brad grow.

They pulled into Tilton close to noon. Their first stop was Tendell's office. The lawyer's wife, Joanne, who ran the office, was gracious in her welcome. When Tendell himself showed up, the gestures of pleasure were repeated. Keith tried entering into the spirit of things, but he found their friendliness oppressive. Tendell, heedless to the atmosphere, chattered on about how much money they would be obtaining from the insurance company and Seth's lawyer, Thompson. It was at lunchtime, at a local restaurant, that they ran into their first taste of what the town thought of Keith's return.

They found a table and seated themselves. The place was crowded, but conversation ceased the minute the four of them entered the door. Half an hour passed without a waitress approaching their location. At last Tendell went and spoke to one of the women. She glared at him with glinty eyes, her roughed, wrinkled face taking on the glare of righteous indignation. "You might as well go somewheres else," she told Tendell. "I'm not a'gonna serve one of those kind. You and your wife oughtta be ashamed of what you've done, the harm you've caused the Rawsons. Nobody's gonna wait on you in here. I'd sooner serve the devil!"

"So much for lunch," Tendell said ruefully as he rejoined the others.

"Has this happened often?" Brad asked as they rose to leave.

Tendell glanced at his wife who responded to the question.

"We've been snubbed a bit since they arrested Jeb Rawson. Before that, nobody cared. They believed Keith guilty and the case settled. This newest development has upset the town. When papers for exhumation are filed, there's going to be hell to pay."

Keith's lips tightened but he said nothing.

Brad asked, "You don't expect violence, do you?"

"Let's hope not," Tendell said, always the optimist. "As

for us, my practice is finished here. I've been accepted by a large firm in Atlanta. Joanne is going up there shortly, apartment hunting." He grinned briefly at Keith. "With what we're going to make on this case, moving will be a snap. I'm not billing Keith too much, but I'm sure going to soak the insurance Joes and Thompson. I'm negotiating with them already. As soon as Rawson admitted he was guilty, they lost their case. If I were you, Keith, I'd sell the garage, your house and the farm as soon as you can—without taking an undue loss. I don't like being an alarmist, but things could get sticky."

"Sounds fine with me," Keith replied. "What do I need to do to get things going? I'd like to pack up the stuff at my place and send it to Atlanta. Have I got to wait until I'm cleared? *If* I'm cleared," he added.

"You will be," Tendell stated automatically. "With the power of attorney you gave me earlier, we can start getting things done right away. Want me to see to it?"

"Yes," Keith answered with a glance at Brad.

They dropped Joanne off at the law office and drove to the police station. News of their arrival had preceded them. Links came out of his office as soon as they entered the station and ushered them into the privacy of his small cubicle.

"Calls coming in already," he told them. "I've spoken with the Judge and he's going to expedite the hearing." The Chief turned to Keith. "You should be a completely free man by tomorrow evening."

"It won't be too soon for me," Keith said, feeling some response was called for. The Chief and Tendell arranged what details were necessary. Tendell signed a paper or two and inside half an hour, Keith was back outside.

"So much for the bureaucracy," Tendell said brightly. "Where to now? Should we go see if the bars will serve us?"

Keith shook his head. "I'd like to go to my house for awhile, if you don't mind. If it's going on the market right away, I need to decide what stuff I want to keep and what I want to get rid of."

Tendell stared at him for a moment. "Okay," he agreed after a second's hesitation. "But for God's sake don't get lost. You're my responsibility until that hearing tomorrow. They'd like nothing better than tossing me in the can." He said the words with a cheerful smile, but Keith could sense uneasiness behind the statement.

The lawyer rummaged around in his pockets until he came up with the key. "Electricity is still on; never shut off, just disconnected the phone."

Keith took the keys and looked questioningly at Brad. The policeman shook his head. "I'll take up Wade's offer of a drink; the drive down here this morning was tiring. We'll pick you up later. Need a ride?"

"No. It's only a few blocks. I'll walk."

Keith turned in the direction of the house he had left so long ago. The long months which had passed since then melted into a dismal fog of memory. It could be any day before Seth's death, with Keith coming home from the office to fix their dinner. In spite of the fact they had not lived in the same house, they'd been together most of the time, usually at Keith's place. Seth, more and more of late, had threatened to move in.

I never made it, did I? Told you we shouldn't wait.

Seth! Seth! If only I'd listened to you!

Think that would have stopped the old man? He always was crazy as a loon. He'd just have gotten both of us. I'm glad that didn't happen.

Keith turned the corner of the street and saw the house. The yard was overgrown, but otherwise looked much as it should. He opened the front gate and walked up the steps, noticing how the trees and shrubs had grown. They'd always made the house cool in summer. He fumbled with the key before unlocking the door and entering the house.

Nothing had changed. Tendell never had rented the place, having used the money from Keith's farm to keep up the house payments. Everything was dusty, but relatively neat and in place. Keith's hands went out to the books he'd been forced to leave behind. Old friends, missed more than any of his other possessions. And his records. How the ghostly presence of Seth haunted every inch of space, every doorway where he had lounged waiting for Keith to finish some chore. His half-naked body gleaming as he laughed over some silly incident which was always happening at the garage. Keith half-stumbled to a chair and collapsed into it, overcome with remembering. At no time since Seth's death had he been allowed the luxury of having the physical mementos of their life together around him. Now, it was almost too much. The very chair he sat in was one where Seth had sat and held him. Keith's hand touched the fabric of the furniture, trembling with a longing which would never again be fulfilled.

Play a record. Put on the one I want, a reminder to you that you've still got to get me outta this damned dirt.

Keith moved hesitantly from the chair to the record cabinet and found the disc. One of their favorite Joan Baez albums. Almost every time they'd gotten a bit drunk, they'd pull it out. Now Keith's fingers trembled as he activated the controls of the stereo; the singer's pure, perfect voice floated forth and his mind rose and fell in rhythms of recollection as precious as pain could ever be:

. . . YOU SUFFERED SWEETER FOR ME,

THAN ANYONE I'VE EVER KNOWN . . .

The words rang so true. They had suffered for each other, but it had been the melancholy sweetness of love, a love so beyond compare it inspired death!

. . . JUST ONE FAVOR OF YOU MY LOVE,

IF I SHOULD DIE TODAY,

TAKE ME DOWN TO WHERE THE HILLS

MEET THE SEA ON A STORMY DAY.

RIDE THE RIDGE ON A SNOW WHITE HORSE,

AND THROW MY ASHES AWAY

TO THE WIND AND THE SAND WHERE MY SONG BEGAN . . .

I will, Seth, I will!

I know babe. You always kept your word to me. You were the perfect lover, exciting and new every time we touched. All I ever wanted . . .

Seth's presence faded as Keith experienced pain and remembrance almost beyond endurance.

33

To Keith's amazement, the following day brought an end to his status as a fugitive. The charges stemming from the murder accusation had been dropped earlier. This time, the business of his escape was dismissed with an admonition from the Judge that Keith should have had more faith in the system. Wisely, Keith kept silent and in less than an hour found himself a free man.

Following the anticlimatic session in the Judge's chambers, Tendell and Keith retired to the lawyer's office to go over the rest of Keith's affairs. Thompson and the insurance company were prepared to go a long way towards settling the matter of Seth's estate without recourse to a lawsuit. Tendell was pleased.

"You're going to end up with a great deal of money," the lawyer told Keith. "I'm not going to be charging you *too* much for defending you—that all started out in the public defender's office anyway, and God knows I've gotten a reputation out of the publicity surrounding your case—but I'm going to take Thompson and the insurance company for all I can get."

"That's fine with me," Keith said. "I'm ready for it all to be over with. How hard is it going to be getting an exhumation order?"

Tendell sighed. He didn't relish that part of the job.

"I'm working on it. I can't answer you. If, and it's a big

if, Alma Rawson and the family don't oppose you, we can have everything wrapped up in a couple of weeks; if they fight, God only knows."

The meeting over, each went his own way. Now that Keith was cleared, Brad was driving back to Atlanta, taking Joanne Tendell with him so she could look for an apartment in the city.

"I wish you weren't staying down here," Brad told Keith as they said their good-byes. "This community isn't sane; you could be in danger, you know."

Keith shrugged. "I've survived everything thus far, what's a bit more? I . . . couldn't control myself if I were around you up there. Whenever I'm near you now, it's harder and harder not to go ahead and make excuses. There isn't any reason to wait, except in my head—and half the time I'm finding my head's fucked up. You've been so patient . . . "

Brad reached out and pulled Keith to him, cutting off the flow of embarrassing words.

"Enough of that. We are men. We ought to be able to endure a little self-control. When we decided to wait, I approved the decision. I still do. Until you've carried out Seth's wishes, it won't kill us to wait. I don't think." He added the last doubtfully. "Pack up whatever you want to keep and have it shipped to my place. I'll stack it in the guest room." They kissed and Brad drove off.

The following days found Keith settling into a dull, uncomplicated routine. The sale of his property occupied a lot of time. The garage went fast, as did the old Wilson place. His house in Tilton took longer but finally a buyer was found for that, too. The lawyers met off and on, and at the end of his second week in Tilton, everyone had agreed upon a settlement which left Keith with an astonishing amount of money. The movers arrived and packed up the things Keith wanted shipped to Atlanta. He held out several books and spent much of his time in Tilton reading. He'd always been buying books and setting them on his shelves.

Seth had laughed at the habit.

"You'll never read all those damned things," he'd say, then sit down and read them himself. Keith sensed Seth had read so much because he'd always felt keenly the difference in their educational levels, considering himself dull and uninteresting. "I'm just a grease monkey," Seth had said on more than one occasion. Nothing Keith could do ever dispelled Seth's dissatisfaction with his mental abilities.

Keith had only one visitor during the period he was in Tilton.

He was sitting in the swing on the porch—almost the only furniture left in the house, the rest having either been moved or sold—when the creaking gate alerted him to the arrival of company. Keith looked up to see the shabby, stooped form of Alma Rawson coming up the walk.

Seth's mother had aged greatly since Keith had seen her last, when he had been on trial for the murder of her son.

"Come in Mrs. Rawson. Won't you sit down?"

He moved to the steps, letting the old woman have the swing. Her eyes gave no indication of her feelings. She sat down heavily and the chains squeaked in protest under her weight.

A moment of silence resulted while she caught her breath. Then she spoke: "Mr. Thompson's tol' me you want to have Seth dug up and cremated?"

"That's right. It was what he wanted done."

"What *he* wanted done!" The force in her words startled Keith.

"All this trouble's because he, and you, *always* did what you wanted. Never a consideration for anybody else, never a care of how much the rest of us were hurt. All those years you and he was making a spectacle of yourselves, and me and Jeb and the girls had to put up with the gossip. Never any feelings on his part over what his sinnin' was doin' to *our* lives, our reputations. I don't excuse Mr. Rawson—punishment is the

Lord's business, not our'n, but he was driven to it."

Her voice ceased. She reached into a pocket and pulled out a much-crumpled handkerchief. With this she wiped her brow and looked out across the ill-kept lawn.

"My family's had enough of Seth," she resumed. "Alive, he disgraced us; dead, he ain't allowin' us no peace either. Mr. Thompson says I can fight you; that I might win." She looked directly at Keith for the first time since her arrival. "I talked it over with the girls, with their husbands. We decided it ain't worth it. Seth thought so little of us, he placed *you* in charge of his affairs. We'd rather you let him be—we're sick and tired of the shame and embarrassment. But I reckon you'll do what you want anyways, won't you?"

"Yes, Mrs. Rawson, I will. I'll do my best to carry out Seth's wishes." Keith's words were softly spoken, but firm.

"In that case, I'm gonna instruct Mr. Thompson to coop-erate about it, sign whatever's necessary so's you can have your way. There's just one thing we ask of you." She hurried on, not waiting for any comment from Keith, embarrassed at asking anything of him. "Git through with it!" she exclaimed. "We want it over—as soon as possible. We want to forget it all."

Forget? It was a typical remark from a family such as Seth's. Let them forget. In at least one heart Seth would dwell forever, a memory more precious than life itself. A monument which would strengthen Keith; a presence which already had made him more of a man, more of a human being.

"About that," Keith assured her, "you have my promise. I want it over with as much as you. Seth should never have been buried against his wishes."

The superficial politeness was over. They stared at one another—all the animosity each possessed for the other's way of life glowed and flared in hostile eyes.

Alma Rawson stood up. "I'll call Mr. Thompson today," she stated. Without another word she turned, moved slowly

down the steps, crossed the walkway and passed out of the
gate. A car driven by one of the Rawson daughters pulled up
and Alma got in. It was to be the last time Keith ever saw any of
Seth's family.

Alma kept her word. After her visit, Keith walked down to
Tendell's office where he relayed the news. The lawyer was
pleased—and relieved.

"That saves so damned much trouble. I'm surprised, but
thankful. Find an undertaker who'll do the job. I'll get the
legal complications out of the way."

Finding an undertaker was the last obstacle in Keith's
path. No one in Tilton or the surrounding communities would
touch the business. Their objections ranged from a dislike of
queers to the more polite fear of losing business from disgrun-
tled citizens of the region. After a day and a half of fruitless
journeys from one local establishment to another, Keith hired a
firm from Atlanta to do the job.

Late afternoon, four-thirty, with sweat dripping from his
face, Keith stood off at a distance while men he'd hired removed the remains of his lover from an unquiet grave. The
scene was surreal. Alma's pastor, Reverend Hendly, accompanied by deacons of the church, gathered at the front of the
cemetery. They watched the proceedings with rapturous disapproval. Their spirits, goaded as much by what they hated in the
world as by the few things in it they professed to love, were
seldom given an opportunity to express their hatred so right-
eously as during the present goings-on.

The operation was quickly over. The casket was loaded
onto a hearse and the grave refilled. The undertaker approached Keith.

"We're finished here, Mr. Wilson. We'll have the remains urned and ready for you day after tomorrow. Will that be
satisfactory?"

"Yes. Thank you."

34

K eith was tired. The drive from Atlanta to the coast had
been exhausting. As was the reason for the trip to Brad's
cottage. Keith unlocked the door and switched on a light. Then
he went back to the car and unloaded the urn containing Seth's
ashes. Ever since he'd accepted the jar, Seth's presence had
grown, flooding Keith's consciousness.

And Brad! Keith was almost ashamed of himself, knowing
that by this act he was freeing himself to be with Brad. Last
night at the condo was almost more than he could bear. Seth's
ashes upstairs and Brad across from him—so strong, so desirable, so alive.

There was no phone in the cottage. Keith could count on a
night without interruptions. Brad assured Keith privacy was a
special feature of the place. Privacy and the sea. Like everything else involving Keith and Seth, the final act of scattering
Seth's ashes was probably as illegal as their lives together had
been; Keith hadn't bothered to check. In the distance he
heard breakers rolling in, crashing onto the shore. The smell of
salt hung in the air, unfamiliar yet distinct.

. . . TO THE WIND AND THE SAND WHERE MY SONG BEGAN . . .

Keith had come to the right place.

Another trip to the car to carry in the beer Keith had purchased. Brad had said there were a few cans left in the fridge,

but Keith wasn't taking any chances. He found, however, that Brad was right—Brad always was. Keith opened a can then went around raising windows in the cottage. The back door opened onto a patio. After removing all his clothes except a pair of shorts, Keith settled himself on the patio and watched the darkening sky produce a deep purple which precedes night's total darkness. Stars blazed overhead with a brilliance Keith had never noticed before. A slight chill crept into the air, announcing the fact winter was not far down the road.

It was late October. So long from that night in March when Keith and Seth had been together for the last time. Keith shivered, and it was not from the breeze which stirred and brushed his naked flesh.

He could almost feel the hand on his shoulder.

It's almost over, man. Bear with me just a little longer. You've kept your promise, better'n even I expected. Over these past months, all the hell you've been through—they've made a man outta you.

Oh Seth! Seth! *You* did that! I could never have endured all I went through without your memory, the example you set for me. I can't let you go, I can't . . .

Keith found himself clutching the beer can in his hand in a deathgrip. He shook himself, frightened by the emotions he felt raging through his body.

You overestimate my influence. You were always strong. That was why you so willingly submitted to me. I wasn't smart like you, but I picked up stuff outta those books you always bought. I loved lovin' you. Your strength, your willingness in offerin' yourself to me, built me up, carried me over the fears of what we was doin'. I was scared, lots'a times, but you wouldn't let me stay afraid. You got that inner strength people talk about. I reckon you've needed it, these past months, me buttin' in with everything else—

Seth! Don't abandon me! *You* were what kept me going—
*Don't keep interruptin'. You got Brad now. He'll take
care of you.*

Sitting still as stone, his eyes half-closed, Keith could see
Seth grinning at him, familiar, near, yet so very, very distant.

*You and he'll get on real good together. Wish I was gonna
be there; I'd like makin' it with him, too. 'Cepting we're too
much alike, him 'n me. We'd fight over who'd git which position.
He won't have that problem with you. I'm happy for you,
Keith. Maybe he won't cause you all the trouble I have . . .*

One day with you was worth all the trouble, all the pain.
Oh God, Seth, you must know that.

*I do. I did. Always. From the time we was kids messin'
'round, to that time by the river, through our last night . . .
when you wanted so bad for me to shut up so you could go home
and sleep. But I wouldn't and you didn't. You stayed with me,
let me have you. I died loving you, with your smell on my flesh,
your warmth not yet dissipated. Jeb woulda hated knowing I
died at peace, content to be loved by you . . . Ah, don't cry no
more Keith. You got the future ahead of you; go to it with my
blessings . . .*

Keith leaned back against the deck chair, his tears
streamed from open eyes, silently, unstoppable. Every star
which shone appeared to be a candle lit in celebration of their
love. If a God existed, if *anything* existed, their love would always be rewarded, never chastised. And the laws, the reli-
gions, the societies which persecuted them would one day
themselves be held up to scorn. Suddenly he got up and rushed
inside to get the urn. Emotionally drained, he sat it down by his
chair, close enough for his hand to touch the brim.

Time slipped away but Keith was no longer aware of it. He
remained by the urn, quiet now, calm, accepting those things
he could not change. He felt Seth by him. Keith believed in no
religion, caring little for thoughts of life after death. Yet in his
sorrow, and out of his love for Seth, grew a certainty, that on

this night at least, he was not alone. Questions he could not frame, answers he would never accept fled before the knowledge that Seth was with him, satisfied with Keith's accomplishments, trying as best he could, to prepare the living man for the final scene. Keith, opening his soul, allowed his consciousness to flee into the unknown, and, finally, slept by the urn filled with Seth's remains.

He awoke at peace. After a light breakfast, Keith walked outside and surveyed the landscape. The area was isolated, windswept, with scrubby pines clinging to rocky soil well back past the cottage. In the distance, Keith could hear the eternal sea. He left the cottage, and took a worn path leading to the edge of the cliff.

After his walk, Keith drove to the riding stables. Brad had phoned the owner to prepare him for Keith's request. The stable had no solid white horses, but there was one which was close enough.

Late afternoon. Dark clouds billowed up on the horizon, rusts of wind broke the stillness of the evening. Keith sighed. The time had come. His heart contracted. He looked at the urn, suddenly unwilling to toss aside the last remains of love. He sought some sign from Seth that he might be spared this last wrenching pain, but his mind remained silent and empty, carrying just below the surface of his consciousness, the refrain:

. . . JUST ONE FAVOR OF YOU MY LOVE,

JUST ONE FAVOR OF YOU MY LOVE . . .

Keith rode the animal down the lane and onto the road.

The urn was awkward and difficult to handle. The horse found it disturbing but quieted down under Keith's calming voice. Keith led the horse along the pathway towards the sea.

Heavy clouds boiled across the sky. In the far distance thunder rumbled. Keith stared out across the tumultuous water, knowing he could not go through with the ritual. He clutched the urn, all the pain of his loss filled him.

You must!

I can't! Please, Seth. I can't do it!

He mumbled the words to the horse, to the wind, to the earth; to whatever god had brought him to this time and place.

Keith! Alive, I asked so little of you. Set me free. Allow me all the peace I've ever dreamed of. I've blessed your union with Brad; I've tried to show you I approve. These past months my love for you expanded in my pride of you. Now end this. Death is nothing to fear; we all come to it. What matters is how we survive life. Put me away, let me drift back into an eternal nothingness of slumber and forgetfulness. Let me go—and run to him. He'll make you remember all the joy we experienced. He'll ease the awkward times. Let me go, Keith. Let me go!

. . . RIDE THE RIDGE ON A SNOW WHITE HORSE

AND THROW MY ASHES AWAY

TO THE WIND AND THE SAND WHERE MY SONG BEGAN . . .

Slowly Keith guided the horse down the path. Then, with the sea on his right, he headed the beast up the ridge. His hands dropped the reigns loosely across the animal's neck and reached into the urn. His eyes sought the sea, the sky; with the wind in his face, he slowly drew forth his hand and raised it towards the ocean. Using his knees, he urged the horse up the trail. In motions slow and deliberate the beast picked its way up the cliff. With each step Keith released Seth's ashes. The wind picked them up, wafted them away from horse and rider, carrying them out towards the sea. By the time he reached the uppermost part of the path, it was done.

Keith was crying, without having realized his tears were falling. They fell on his hand, rinsing away the remainder of ash. He turned the horse around, urging it back down the path they'd just climbed. When they reached the bottom, Keith dismounted and walked onto the sand, close by the water's edge. A little distance in the water stood a clump of rocks. He waded a few steps into the sea, lifted the urn high above his head and dashed it against the stones. All his anger at the world which had forced this necessity upon him went into the destruction of the urn. A piece of it fell near him. He picked it up and hurled it back at the rock. Every piece which he could see in the water, he retrieved and smashed, until the fragments were too tiny to be reduced further. Washing his hands, he waded back to the shore and sat down on the sand.

His mind was numb.

It was over. And he felt so empty.

Until suddenly, warmth flowed all around him. A gentle breeze touched him; he could feel the breath of love.

I thank you. Now it is truly finished. He's waiting for you; go to him, my love. We part in peace.

Keith shook himself and with an urgency he could not comprehend, got to his feet and stumbled towards the waiting horse.

Silhouetted at the top of the cliff, against the dark, forboding sky was the form of another horse and another rider.

Brad!

Keith mounted the horse and rode towards the other figure.

All uncertainties dissolved in the anticipation of their love. An end and beginning, all becoming one in the circle of eternity. Pain and suffering giving way to joy and fulfillment. It would all be his and Brad's. As they neared and Keith saw Brad's face clearly, his heart swelled.

They met.

Brad dismounted and pulled Keith from the white stallion. With Brad's strong arms around him, their lips touching, Keith was at last home, his future, born of love, at last secure.